DREAMWOOD

HEATHER MACKEY

G. P. Putnam's Sons

An Imprint of Penguin Group (USA)

G. P. Putnam's Sons
Published by the Penguin Group
Penguin Group (USA) LLC
375 Hudson Street
New York, NY 10014

USA | Canada | UK | Ireland | Australia
New Zealand | India | South Africa | China
penguin.com
A Penguin Random House Company

Library of Congress Cataloging-in-Publication Data
Mackey, Heather.
Dreamwood / Heather Mackey.
pages cm
Summary: "12-year-old Lucy Darrington goes on a quest to find her missing father in a remote, magical territory in the Pacific Northwest"—Provided by publisher.
[1. Supernatural—Fiction. 2. Adventure and adventurers—Fiction. 3. Missing persons—Fiction. 4. Forests and forestry—Fiction. 5. Runaways—Fiction. 6. Northwest, Pacific—History—19th century—Fiction.] I. Title.
PZ7.M198636Dre 2014
[Fic]—dc23
2013039402

Printed in the United States of America.
ISBN 978-0-399-25067-5
1 3 5 7 9 10 8 6 4 2

Design by Annie Ericsson.
Text set in Adobe Jenson Pro.

*For my mother
and father*

Ever since the lumberjacks boarded the train, Lucy Darrington had been watching them, wondering when they'd make trouble.

It was late afternoon, and she was sweaty in her blue wool school dress. Crabby, too. Her fingers itched inside her gloves, her petticoat was heavy as a wet mattress, and her toes were falling asleep inside her stiff lace-up boots. Since running away from the Miss Bentley's School for Young Ladies in San Francisco, she'd spent four days on this train and felt like she couldn't take another minute. She'd been staring out the window at the endless northern forests when the lumberjacks boarded—three men in shirtsleeves and suspenders—stomping in like elephants and taking up about as much space. Their legs splayed into the aisle amid a growing cluster of empty amber bottles. Right away they started drinking and farting and telling one another stories that made her shudder even as she crept two rows closer to hear them better.

Now one was telling the others about a friend who'd been

awakened one night by strange noises. "He gets up and looks out his door. In front of his barn he sees a terrible shadow. A monster."

"What did it look like, Bert?" one asked. He was younger than the other two, with thick blond hair and a simple face.

Bert, the biggest of the three, peered slyly at the other two and dropped his voice. "Big. Ragged and feathery. Like a wolf crow."

A *wolf crow*. They were silent, the better to think about such a beast. "So what happened?" asked the third man, sour faced under a wiry black beard.

"He goes outside. Suddenly behind him he hears the monster's terrible screams and snorts. He turns, and there's the wolf crow coming straight for him. And right before it reaches him . . ."

Bert took a deep breath. His chin quivered as if he were trying to hold in some terrible truth. Lucy leaned forward, listening hard. And then it came: a belch so loud her ears rang.

The other two groaned.

"Come on, Bert, what happened?"

"Was it the wolf crow, Bert?"

Bert leaned back, pleased. "Naw. He fainted is all. When he wakes up there's his pig standing over him—with a chicken on its head. Dang thing had gotten out of the barn."

A chicken riding a pig!

They pounded on the seats, this was so good. Lucy thought the wooden slats of the benches might break.

More burps, farts. Bert stroked his beard—his was the sort that shot out in all directions: a frozen explosion of hair. The train shuddered and clacked; outside the forest went by unendingly.

Lucy fell back in her seat—she'd have to remember that one. Imagine being scared of a chicken riding a pig.

Pity she had no one to tell the story *to*. She had no friends from her time at Miss Bentley's; she was poor, and her father was eccentric. The girls had been a bunch of sheep who cared only about stockings and hair ribbons. No one had been interested in science, and certainly not in ghostology, which is where she intended to make her name one day—even if her father thought she should enter a field with a more promising future.

Ghost clearers were a dying breed, the profession grown disreputable, even mocked. In their heyday, they'd helped the country heal after the bloody North-South War, when whole pockets of land were overrun by angry spirits. But that was forty years ago; the country had been consumed by grief, giving ghosts the energy they liked to attach themselves to. It was a new century now, and ghosts, which were sensitive to electricity, were disappearing as more places used electrical lights. Ghosts had become an unfashionable problem most people would not admit to having.

Her old friends—a gang of ragtag children she'd played pirates and forts with—were thousands of miles away in Wickham, Massachusetts, the little town outside of Boston where she'd grown up. Her father hadn't said it at the time, but from the way they'd left—quick in the dead of night, barely ahead of the debt collectors—she doubted she'd ever see the place again.

She missed their comfortable house in Wickham, the basement laboratory where her father conducted his research into the unseen world of spirits, she sitting at his elbow, jumping up to assist when needed. The scandal that cost him his job destroyed their old life permanently.

But, there was no sense regretting the past. "Onward, eh, Lucy?" he would say, readying his ghost-clearing bag. She could picture him fastening his high collar and ascot—he always looked proper, no matter how low their fortunes sank—his blue eyes twinkling in a conspiracy he shared only with her.

Onward, she thought dully, pressing her nose against the window.

Was the train *slowing*? The scenery outside hadn't changed; there was the thick, unvarying forest and a distant band of blue on the horizon that marked the Pacific Ocean. Still no signs of any town or settlement. But maybe they were coming up on Pentland. Lucy unlatched the window and stuck her head out, risking cinders from the whirling smoke. She squinted up at the steam engine, puffing along. They were definitely losing speed.

She sat back down and brought out her map. Everything a hundred miles north of San Francisco was green, First Peoples's Federation territory. Here and there were small orange blobs, marking outposts of the American States. Saarthe, a mitten-shaped peninsula that stuck out from the coast like a hand grabbing at the ocean, was one of these. Pentland, its capital, was where her father had gone nearly six months ago, and where the train was due to arrive that evening.

If she survived that long without exploding from impatience. From the small black case on the seat beside her came the low ticking of mechanical workings. But none of the instruments inside it was a watch. She debated whether to ask the lumberjacks for the time. Bert had just started a new story. This one was about a man who'd gone into his shed to get what he thought was an empty sack.

"Only he picks it up, and it's *really heavy*. So he thinks, I'm just gonna put my hand in there . . ."

He went silent, and Lucy readied herself for another operatic belch. But the burp she expected didn't come. With a squeal of brakes and a puff of steam, the train stopped.

Quiet descended on the railcar, the three lumberjacks staring gloomily at something on their side of the train. The only sound was the vibration of the devices in her black case.

That was odd. They never reacted unless there was a strong energy source around.

She couldn't see anything from her window, so Lucy crossed the aisle to look out on the other side of the train.

Now she understood why the lumberjacks were quiet.

Just outside the train a cluster of thick wooden poles rose into the sky, standing like guardians of the dark and brooding forest behind them. They were carved and painted with faces—unsettling combinations of animal and human—and their eyes stared fiercely ahead.

Why are you here? the poles seemed to ask. *Explain yourself.*

The door to the car opened, the young red-haired porter holding it solemnly as if attending someone of great importance. A girl walked in, the cape of gray fur about her shoulders not quite concealing the quiver and bow on her back.

Lucy had seen First Peoples before, of course. Back in Wickham she'd seen Wampanoag along the deer path in the woods behind their house, collecting chestnuts in the autumn or at the market, selling deerskin shirts and gloves. Several of them would come and talk to her father, staying late into the night. They'd been kind and joking; some who visited year after year were like family.

This girl was different.

She held herself like a queen, not deigning to look at either the lumberjacks or Lucy. The ruddy, freckle-faced porter bowed his head as she stepped past him.

Her shiny black hair was woven with beads and charms and something soft and glowing: gold. She had gold, too, in her ears, around her neck, and around her wrists.

One of the lumberjacks muttered something under his breath. On their way west, Lucy and her father had landed in a few places where there was prejudice, hatred even, between First Peoples and settlers. And she knew that decades ago, parts of the northwest had been consumed in bloody fights for territory. The Lupines, the most powerful people in the region, had managed to hold vast tracts of forest . . . maybe to the resentment of the surviving settlers. She'd heard something in one of the stations they'd stopped at yesterday about a problem with Saarthe's timber and settlers being out of work.

The door closed, and with a whine of relief, the train began to move again.

To get to the empty seats at the back, the girl would have to walk by the lumberjacks at the front. Bottles and other trash were littered about the aisle by their feet—an obstacle course. The men watched silently, sullenly as the girl balanced herself while the train swayed and shook.

She took light, graceful steps, avoiding the mess.

And then there was a jolt.

A foot came down wrong, and a beer bottle went fizzing on the floor. One of the men cursed. "Look at that!"

Bert, closest to the girl, stood up and reached out a powerful arm. He towered over her, and as the train shuddered it looked like he pushed her.

"Don't do that!" Lucy said, rising from her seat and bursting into the aisle, black case in hand. It had sharp corners, and she could bring it down on someone's knee if she had to.

The lumberjacks turned to her in surprise, and Lucy realized they'd forgotten she was even there. In their beer-soaked brains they were probably struggling to account for this small, fierce creature who'd come out of nowhere to challenge them. She was halfway past twelve and any day would have a growth spurt. But for now, people—especially dim-witted ones—looked at Lucy and saw only a child.

A sweet, milk-faced child, with unruly curls of hair like a cherub's. Lucy watched as they registered her appearance. The teachers at Miss Bentley's always complained that she was desperate for attention—they couldn't understand it. Why wouldn't she simply be quiet and do as told, especially when she *looked* (well, except for that hair) like a nice, docile girl: cornflower-blue eyes, a small chin, and delicate blond eyebrows arched like a china doll's. But Lucy didn't want the attention such girls got—pats on the head and an opportunity to bring chalk to the teachers. She wanted to make a mark on the world—and you couldn't do that by fading into the background.

"What? Bother her? No! I was trying to help her was all." Bert's blocky face fell. Rather unnecessarily (for the First Peoples girl had regained her balance) he still held out one meaty forearm to her. "I didn't mean anything. Honest."

"My friend's got terrible manners," the blond one said, bowing his head as the girl looked down on him. "We're sorry this mess got on your boots."

It took Lucy a moment to catch up. They hadn't meant to bother her; instead, they were frightened they'd offended her.

Embarrassed, Lucy slunk back into her seat. "My boots have seen worse than your beer, settlers," the First Peoples girl said in a raspy, accented voice. "No harm is done."

Then she made her way down the aisle and slid into the seat facing Lucy's.

An awkward silence ensued; at least it was awkward for Lucy, who tried not to stare at her new companion. The girl had a finely sculpted face, delicate ears, and lovely dark eyes. She was sleek and composed and taut as a bowstring even when sitting. The fur she wore was a black-tipped gray, rough and bristly. It occurred to Lucy that it wasn't rabbit or anything soft, but the fur of a predator . . . a wolf, perhaps.

"Is that a weapon?" the girl asked, eyeing Lucy's black instrument case. It had been vibrating ever since they'd seen those frightening poles. But in the excitement of the last few minutes Lucy had forgotten all about it.

"*This?* No. I just thought I could wallop somebody with it." Lucy watched it shake. "I've never seen it act like this, though." Frowning, she unlatched the case and opened the lid. A brass disc flipped out of its position in the velvet drawer, like a fish. Lucy forced it back into place and shut the lid.

"What is it?" The girl leaned back, her glossy black brows drawn together in suspicion. "Does it explode?"

"No!" Lucy thought this was funny. "It's just a vitometer. It won't hurt you. In fact, it almost never moves. My father invented it. He's invented a lot of things." She couldn't seem to stop herself from running on—it had been days since she'd seen a girl close to her own age—and only now did Lucy realize how lonely she'd been. "He's been living in Pentland and I'm going up to live with him." She had his letter, thinned from the many times she'd unfolded and folded it again, safely in her pocket even though by this point she knew it by heart:

9

I'm on the verge of a breakthrough. Though I don't know how I'll manage without my trusted assistant.

"Oh." The girl received this information coolly; she was busy rearranging her fur. "Is he a tree cutter?"

"No, he's a . . ." And here was where Lucy ran into difficulty. Not long ago, she would have proudly called her father a ghostologist. But the girls at Miss Bentley's had made it clear this was a ridiculous profession. Even now with the school hundreds of miles behind her, Lucy still felt hurt: They'd wanted to hear her stories, and then they'd acted as if her father was no better than a rat catcher.

"He's a scientist," Lucy said, lifting her chin. He was! You had to know an awful lot about energy and physics—psychology, too—if you were going to hope to understand ghosts. And there was more to their study than just knowing how to clear them. One day Lucy could see herself touring the country giving ghostology demonstrations, rather like her idol, the glamorous paleontologist Irene Zerinka, who packed lecture halls and was rumored to require ten railcars just to transport her dinosaur skeletons.

The girl smiled and Lucy gathered she liked this answer better than tree cutter.

"I am Niwa Sillamook," she said. Her eyes flickered with defiance, as if she expected Lucy to react to her name—and not in a good way.

But to Lucy the name meant nothing, and she already

admired the girl's poise and self-possession. "Lucy Darrington," she replied eagerly, reaching out a hand to shake. But the girl raised her palm up, fingers spread. And after a moment, Lucy stripped off one glove and did the same. Their palms touched. Niwa's hand was warm, with a ridge of callus.

The touch seemed to melt any remaining awkwardness between them. Niwa leaned forward and confided, "I am meeting my father, too. I would travel on foot, but he is impatient."

"You'd travel by yourself on foot? Through the forest?" The girl was maybe sixteen, but Lucy thought even an adult might not want to travel in such a wild, untamed place. Her father had never been much of an outdoorsman. And although they'd traveled many places it had usually been by train. They'd never camped.

Niwa seemed amused to be the object of so much awe and admiration. "You travel by yourself," she pointed out. "On a train."

Lucy regarded the jostling, jerking railcar. At the front, the lumberjacks had begun to smoke, and a noxious, gray, tobacco-scented cloud rose in the stale air.

She'd been on many trains since leaving Wickham. Her sojourn at Miss Bentley's had been the first time she'd been in one place more than three months at a time. Before that had been New Orleans, where the local voodoo doctors hadn't been very happy to have a ghost clearer from Massachusetts horn in on their business. And before that they'd been in Nebraska, her father somehow running afoul of the snake-handling tent preachers that crisscrossed the prairie.

Her father had gone up the coast to make a new start. Lucy hoped that meant clearing a few ghosts and putting down roots in a town where they could stay awhile. He'd promised to send for her when he had a place for them to live. But she hadn't been able to take Miss Bentley's any longer—they were always rapping her knuckles or making her stand in the corner for speaking out of turn or correcting the teachers when they were wrong. And when he'd written that he was on the brink of uncovering something important, she couldn't stand to be left out.

"I'm running away from school," Lucy confessed to Niwa. She remembered the morning her father had left her in Miss Bentley's office, while the prim, impeccable headmistress looked on disapprovingly. Even the objects on her desk were arranged in a grid. "We'll do something about her hair," Miss Bentley had assured him, "and"—she had tapped a ruler ominously on her desk—"her fidgets."

"I don't care about that," her father said, winking at Lucy. "Lucy has always been high-spirited. What I *do* want is for Lucy to be safe." *Safe from what?* Lucy should have inquired. Only she'd been too delighted at the moment by the look of shock on Miss Bentley's porcelain face to ask.

Niwa liked this. "Good!" she said and clapped her hands. "Were you made to go and stay there and wear different clothes? Did the teachers not understand the things of importance?"

"Yes," Lucy said in wonder. She pointed at the blue dress she hated. "This is my uniform. They wanted us all to act alike and look alike." Think alike, too. Whereas she had always intended to be extraordinary. "How did you know?"

Niwa nodded sagely. "My father put me in school. He cares that I should know many languages so I can speak to people of different countries and nations and I will sit at dinners and understand what may go into a treaty. It is so one day I will be on our council." Her mouth tightened for just one moment. "But on council it is about business and do we have jobs for settlers. Why does that concern me?"

"Oh . . ." Lucy's school had focused on rote memorization, the object being to parrot back exactly what the teacher had just said. She knew her father didn't think that was true learning; she suspected her two fearsome aunts back in Boston were the real reason she'd been put in Miss Bentley's. Her father's sisters, both extremely well-to-do, never took much interest in Lucy unless it was to suggest she be sent somewhere correctional.

Niwa tossed her head, and the gold in her ears flashed. "I told him I would live my own way. So I left. And I have lived these two months in the grove of the wolf woman."

The train careened around a steep curve, revealing for a moment a steep slash of rock with a waterfall hanging down from it like an icicle.

"*Oh.*" Lucy's jaw dropped open as she swayed with the train. She didn't even know what Niwa's "own way" meant, really—or what the grove of the wolf woman was—but it sounded daring. At the mere thought of such an adventure she felt herself enlarge and grow, like a balloon filling with air.

She looked out the window at the mysterious forest, rimmed with a gray fog. "I'd like to see that for myself," she said.

"It is my favorite place in the forest," Niwa replied, although there was a note of sadness in her voice.

Lucy leaned forward so they were both looking out the window now, resting elbow to elbow. She shot a glance at the Lupine girl. Niwa was exactly the type of girl she intended to be: independent and self-assured. She had done the right thing by leaving Miss Bentley's.

She was still thinking on this when the train began to slow in little hiccupping jerks.

"Is this Pentland?" Lucy asked, searching the trees for signs of civilization.

"No," said Niwa, gathering up her quiver and cloak. "This is still Lupine."

"The town?"

"The Lupine Nation," Niwa said, sounding almost as if she'd like to add "silly." She tilted her head in a way that reminded Lucy of how her father would look when she asked to hear another ghost story.

Lucy pointed out the window. "But there isn't a station here."

The train had nearly stopped and still it was nothing but trees, oppressively thick and tall. Suddenly another carved pole loomed outside the window.

"They will stop the train for me." Niwa looked out at the forest, surveying her domain.

At that moment, the train shuddered to a halt.

"You're going already?" Lucy slumped down, suddenly aware again of her sweaty dress and uncomfortable boots.

"I have to." For a second Lucy thought she saw a flicker of reluctance cross Niwa's face. She adjusted her fur and her weapons, then stopped and considered Lucy. "You are different."

"Different from what?" Lucy loved to be told she was different.

Niwa laughed. "From the settler girls I meet. Many are afraid of Lupines." Almost as an afterthought she added, "They think we are witches." Her expression was unreadable, but she watched Lucy, waiting for her reaction.

"Oh, witches," Lucy said, with a lighthearted shrug. For she had been brought up not to believe in magic or witchcraft—they weren't scientifically proven, after all. And although she felt bad about what it said of her character, she *did* look down on superstitious types. "Of course you aren't witches."

"No." Niwa's eyes clouded over as she fingered the grip of her bow. "If we were, the trees would not die."

What was that supposed to mean? Lucy stood up, but the Lupine girl was already walking down the aisle. The porter appeared again and bowed as he ushered her off the train. Lucy flopped down in her seat. Had she said something wrong?

Niwa's departure lifted the lumberjacks' self-imposed silence. Now they made up for their earlier quiet.

While the train idled, they leaned to the window, their hulking shoulders crammed together, and watched as Niwa stepped off the train.

"Look out, Bert," said the blond one. "She sees you staring at her and you'll be hexed."

Bert, having recovered his bravado, thrust a leg into the aisle. "I'm not afraid of a Lupine witch."

"You were plenty scared earlier, when you thought you'd tripped her on accident. Never seen your face so white!"

"Naw, the only thing that scares me is an empty stomach."

"It's the same thing," the third man muttered sourly.

"What do you mean?" asked Bert.

"They've cursed the trees, haven't they?" said the third man. "There's your empty stomach for you. No trees, no work."

But no one could "curse" the trees, Lucy thought. And whatever was happening, Niwa was upset by it, too. She put her chin in her hands. Already Saarthe struck her as someplace where it was hard to see the truth straight on. Like Bert's wolf crow.

The train began slowly to move, and Lucy hurried across the aisle once more, opening the window and leaning her head outside. Lucy could see Niwa some distance down the track, already receding, a small figure dwarfed by the crumbling poles. And then the train curved and she was gone.

2

At last the train slowed with a finality that suggested it had reached the end of the line. A wooden station came into view.

Lucy watched the lumberjacks rise, noticing how their faces set into hard defeated lines as they made their way off. Now that they'd arrived, the three men became grim and somber. They left the train as if their joints ached and they were looking to punch someone because of it. Lucy waited awhile before climbing down after them.

She stepped off the train and into the cool air of a late June evening in Outer Saarthe. The station was no more than a few rough-hewn structures still sporting bark on one side. Behind it rose the tallest trees she'd ever seen. There was a station house, and a few people milling about. She looked at all of them expectantly, but there was no one with her father's neat beard, jaunty walk, or winking smile. She walked farther into the station, lugging the instrument case along with her.

Perhaps he'd gotten delayed or caught up in conversation.

There was no one for talking like her father. She was always having to remind him of the time.

"Don't run off yet, miss," the porter from the train said, jogging up to her. "You need your luggage."

She'd forgotten her trunk. It was there alone on the platform, looking as battered as it had in all the previous moves.

"Anything else?" he asked, checking the platform diligently, as if he worried she might still be too preoccupied to remember the rest of her belongings.

"No, just the trunk." It wasn't like her to forget things, but she was busy keeping an eye out for her father. Lucy scanned the station again.

"First time in Outer Saarthe?" the porter asked. He wasn't going away, so she turned her attention to him. He had a friendly, open face and an easy way of holding himself. The deep brownish red of his hair seemed somehow familiar. When she looked over his shoulder, she realized it was the same color as the bark on the gigantic trees. Hundreds of feet tall, they towered over everything around them. She looked up and it gave her a funny feeling, a bit like vertigo in reverse.

"First time anywhere in the Northwest Regions," she admitted. Though she had read plenty of adventure novels set here, full of brawny woodsmen, sharpshooting women, and wolves.

"Well, trees are what we're famous for," he said. "Though the way things are going, who knows how long we'll even have them. The trees are coming down sick. More people are leaving

Saarthe these days than coming. He cocked his head round at the sleepy station. "The eight o'clock train used to draw a crowd." A thought occurred to him. "Say, is anyone meeting you?"

"My father." She squeezed her shoulders together. She'd written to tell him the date and time of her arrival. He was absent-minded, but surely he wouldn't forget about *her*.

The train's whistle sounded.

The porter hiked up his shoulders in apology. "Sorry, miss. That's the signal."

As soon as he said that she realized the sun was going down. In the time they'd been talking the station had cleared out.

"Don't worry now," the porter reassured her. "He'll be along. There's delays on the road all the time on account of the logging wagons. You'll be fine here. And if you do get worried, tell Old Wundt, the stationmaster—he'll take you inside until your pa can collect you."

The train began to move slowly, and he jumped onto the step. "Make sure you don't leave the station alone," he called. "Not with evening coming." He tipped his cap to her and stepped inside. Lucy watched the train go. Then with a sinking feeling, she turned back to the platform.

She wandered to the stationmaster's office. An old man lay asleep there. He wore a threadbare striped cardigan sweater, and his outstretched arm, which trembled slightly from the rhythmic force of his snores, held a pipe. She gathered this was Old Wundt. He did not look helpful.

Pinned up on the wall behind him were row after row of

Wanted posters. She hadn't imagined one little settlement could produce so many outlaws. If she encountered one, she supposed she'd have to outsmart him . . . which she could probably do. Outlaws weren't smart, were they?

She peered at the woods outside the station. They were dark and concealing, as if within their depths all manner of evil lurked. The evening was growing cooler, and she shivered. Where was her father? Could her letter have gone astray? It hadn't worried her that he'd never replied—until now.

Panic flared. *Stop it,* Lucy told herself sternly. She'd figure something out. There was still some light. She would manage. Didn't her father always say she had a cool head? She'd saved them both the time they'd gotten locked in the Wickham churchyard while trying to take a spirit photograph of the old priest's ghost. She'd remembered there were candles kept in one of the crypts, and with the light steadying her she'd been able to manage the lock.

Lucy went back to the platform and tugged at the handle of her trunk; she could carry it, but awkwardly, and she let it fall back down again with a thud. The air felt still and quiet, so that she almost disbelieved there was anyone else within miles. But she was wrong about that. For there, at the end of the station, emerging from the shadows, was an enormous man in a dark coat with a huge shaggy head of hair, as if he were built on the same scale as the giant trees, moving toward her with the slow, purposeful stride of an undertaker.

The huge man was definitely coming for her.

Lucy's heart hammered in her chest, and she thought of the many Wanted posters papered over the station walls. It seemed unfair to have just arrived and already have to face an outlaw.

She abandoned her trunk and took a few steps backward. "What do you want?" she called out.

There was no answer as he bore down on her, closing the space between them in a few giant strides. Lucy got ready to swing her case. She'd hit him in the shins, and that would hurt, then she would run.

But the man stopped before it came to that. She looked up and he looked down. He must have been close to seven feet tall, with a long mane of dark brown hair that came over his rough collar. He wore a weathered black coat and black clothes under that. One of his eyes was dead; milky white, it drooped, as if trying to see the wrinkled scar on his cheek below.

"Able Dodd," the man said, and pointed to himself. "You're to follow me."

Not without an explanation she wasn't.

"Who sent you?" she demanded, stiffening inside her rumpled dress. Behind him she could see the station exit and beyond that the mysterious forest.

"Knightly," he replied, before turning his back on her and picking up her trunk. He lifted it as if it weighed no more than an empty box.

Lucy swallowed, still gripping her case. "Who's that?"

"Lawyer," he said over his shoulder.

Lucy watched him retreat across the platform. She didn't

know any lawyers. And he couldn't just take her things. She ran after him, the black case banging against her leg.

Able Dodd walked through the station and outside to where a buckboard wagon was waiting with two horses in harness. Lucy followed, out of breath, and watched as he tossed her trunk into the wagon bed.

Was her father in trouble with the law?

"Did he borrow money?" she asked. "He's good for it if he did. You don't have to take me to a lawyer. Just take me to my father and I'll get this sorted out." She pulled up her gloves and straightened her hat. People often looked kindly on a pretty, well-mannered girl.

"Can't," the man said with strange finality, as if her father were beyond his—or anyone's—reach.

"What do you mean?" Lucy dropped her case on the ground. A thousand fearful thoughts flew through her head: Perhaps he was in jail. Or maybe he was sick or ill. She pressed a hand against her mouth.

"I'll let Knightly say." Able Dodd gave her a dark glance and made to tie her trunk fast with ropes, leaving her to fret in silence.

When he was satisfied with his knots, he faced her. For one irrational moment Lucy was afraid he was going to throw her into the back of the wagon and tie her down, too. Instead he turned to the horses.

"This is Whitsun," he said, pointing to a white horse. "And this is Snickers." Snickers was roan. They both looked at her intelligently; they seemed to understand Able Dodd's words.

Their wise, kind faces seemed to see right into her. Strangely, she was reassured. A person who cared enough about his horses to make sure she knew their names could not be all bad.

"Lucy Darrington," she found herself saying to them, as if she were introduced to horses all the time.

Able Dodd nodded to say she'd done well. Then, with an air of getting on with his work, he simply picked her up and sat her down on the rough plank seat of the wagon.

"But where are we *going*?" Lucy squirmed on the seat.

"The Knightlys' place," Able Dodd said as if they'd already been over this. He walked around to his side of the wagon, and she watched him. Lucy couldn't see any luxuries to him: no rings or watches or belt buckles or anything fine. His austerity was so complete it had the air of a philosophy, and she sensed that such a person wouldn't give in to pleas or pestering. Which meant she was stuck with him . . . for the moment.

He climbed up beside her and flicked the reins lightly.

"Gee up."

Whitsun and Snickers took off in a slow clip-clop down a narrow road that plunged immediately into the shade and still-ness of the forest. For a while Lucy tried to pretend Able Dodd wasn't so terribly strange or that this journey was something she'd laugh about soon with her father. But it was hard to keep her spirits up with such a dour companion. To all her questions Able Dodd replied only with a "hm"—or sometimes, more el-oquently, with a "hmpf"—and at last she gave up and turned dully to study the forest.

The forest.

Never had she been in woods so thick and pressing. It was as if they were traveling through a mountain of living wood.

The trees were everywhere: huge ones that must have been thousands of years old, and frail seedlings poking up from the mulch on the ground. The hollow trunks of dead trees stood secretive as caves, and fallen logs were covered with thick green moss and the shoots of new trees. Soft needles and smoky red bark covered the forest floor like a carpet. Only the treetops were invisible, veiled by a still and blanketing mist that gave everything a suspended feeling, like the forest itself might be a dream.

Lucy hugged herself and peered into the gloom, unable to shake the feeling that this forest was hiding her father—had swallowed him up, and would swallow her, too.

It was dark by the time they reached their destination.

Even before Lucy saw the house, she smelled roses. A rambling garden was spread before them, full of rosebushes. Behind the roses, coming into view in the gray twilight, was a large Victorian house, leaning a bit tipsily under its spiky decorations, quite like one of Lucy's fearsome dowager aunts back in Boston.

Able Dodd helped her down and began to untie her trunk from the back of the wagon. Lucy stood, squinting up at what must be the home of the mysterious Knightly.

The front door opened and a man and a woman came out standing rather protectively like a barrier at the top of the steps.

"Hello," the man said down to her. He was stout, with round pink cheeks and shiny flaxen hair, which was arranged in timid wavelets. His soberly cut dark suit gave the impression of dull respectability. "You made it here, at least. The roads aren't safe at night. We've had some troubles."

"Thieving and banditry," the woman clarified. She was tall and pinched, with hair a fading flame color and slightly protuberant blue-gray eyes. She had the startled, nervous look of an exotic bird. One hand clutched compulsively at the neckline of her dress, as if she were constantly recovering from a state of shock.

He inclined his head to her, perhaps hoping that between the two of them they would eventually arrive at an accurate statement. "Many of the men are unemployed, and—"

"They turn to crime," she broke in.

"Yes." The man nodded. He appeared quite used to this funny way of speaking and turned to his wife, waiting for her next interruption.

"It's getting harder and harder for decent folks," she pronounced. Her eyes widened even more, sweeping around the porch to make clear who the decent folks were.

Lucy stood on the bottom step and looked between the two in confusion. It was almost as if they blamed *her* for the thievery and unsafe roads. "Excuse me, I'm Lucy Darrington and I'm looking for my father, William." She bit her lip. "I thought he'd be at the station to meet me."

"I am Gordon Knightly," the man said, with obvious fondness for his own name.

"And I'm Dorothea. Though you may call me Dot. Everyone does," the woman added quickly, making it clear this was not a special invitation to friendship. "Welcome," she said, pursing her mouth in a way that wasn't welcoming at all.

Lucy was beginning to feel that something was terribly wrong. "And my father, is he here?"

Gordon rocked on his toes. "Well now, this, you see . . ." He looked at his wife for help.

"He's gone," she said starkly, her fingers clutching at her chest.

"But . . ." Lucy blinked, trying to make sense of this. "I wrote him I was coming."

"And that's the only reason I knew to send Able Dodd to pick you up," Gordon said, as if he deserved congratulations for sending a terrifying giant to kidnap her. "I've been collecting his mail. I don't know what else to do with it. He left some papers here as well."

"Piles of notebooks," Dot sniffed. "They make an unsightly clutter."

This was too much to take in. Lucy grasped the banister. Her father had left?

"He must have been working a job," she said, half to herself. "Someone must have hired him to investigate a haunting, clear a ghost. Did you?"

"What?" Gordon looked affronted. "Me? No. Certainly not. Nobody hired him, not that I know. He just appeared in town one day. I rented a room to him. He said he would be working on something in the woods, away from people."

"Odd," Dot said with a worried look at her husband. "A bit suspicious if you ask me."

"But he would have to have a clearing job here." Lucy twisted her gloves into tourniquets around her fingers. If he stayed in Outer Saarthe there had to have been a reason. And his last letter hinted at something extraordinary.

"Clearing? I don't know." Gordon puffed out his chest, as if needing a bulwark against her questions.

"How long has he been away?" Lucy asked. She looked at Able Dodd, who was standing motionless in the darkness, his mouth a grim arch of disapproval.

Dot's large eyes blinked rapidly. "Perhaps three weeks. Maybe more."

So long? Lucy looked from Gordon to Dot with a sudden feeling that she could not get enough air. "And when did you expect him back?"

"Well, that's what makes this so, erm, awkward," Gordon said, and Lucy realized that the terrible expression on his face was pity. "He didn't say he was coming back."

Lucy sat on the lumpy mattress in the tiny third-story bedroom, crammed with three-legged chairs, a collection of moth-eaten taxidermy, chipped crockery—and now, her.

A half-full teacup sat precariously near the edge of the bed, sloshing when she brought her boots up to sit cross-legged. Already a good deal of weak tea had splashed out of the saucer and onto the ugly, itchy blanket.

Earlier, Dot had brought up the tea and a few pieces of cake, and Lucy had been too miserable to mumble more than a few words of thanks.

But now, wiping crumbs of spice cake from her mouth, Lucy realized she needed to make arrangements. She couldn't stay here, in this stuffy room, with its sloping floor, peeling wallpaper, and spare furniture draped in dust cloths. She had already seen the room her father had rented: slightly larger, equally depressing. But very few of his personal items remained. He'd left behind the notebooks Dot had complained about (full of numbers and random notes in her father's cramped script—Lucy had flipped through them quickly), a pair of slippers, and the old plaid shirt she was wearing now. Apparently he'd sold or given away everything else.

She needed to go into town, she had to make an investigation, get people involved. Should she go to the police? No . . . not yet. But a man couldn't simply disappear.

Lucy drank the rest of her tea and with her skirt blotted dry a few of the drops she'd scattered over the bedspread. On the pillow, gazing at her blankly, was a chipped and ragged doll, too stupid to know it had been abandoned. She picked the horrid thing up and shoved it into the depths of a gloomy armoire that hulked against the wall.

Then she went downstairs in search of Gordon or Dot. Or (she hoped it wouldn't come to this) Able Dodd.

The stairway was steep and dark. A grandfather clock the size of a coffin was at the bottom. Lucy stepped quietly down the hall.

There was light coming from the room on her left, and she opened the door onto a high-ceilinged parlor. A boy sat in one of the dainty chairs, whittling, his feet up on a table. A pile of wood shavings had fallen on the ground around him. He was tall, perhaps a year older than she was, solid looking. His hair flew about in auburn jags and his gray-green eyes were narrowed, all the fury of his being concentrated in his carving knife. Mounted on the wall behind him was a gloomy crowd of antlered animal heads; they looked as if long ago they'd resigned themselves to watching the boy whittle as their only entertainment.

He didn't look up as she came in, so she coughed and planted herself in front of him. "Hello," she said, leaning forward.

"Ah," he cried in frustration as his knife slipped, "you made me nick it!" He cast the piece of wood to the floor.

Lucy didn't think this was her fault. Any number of things could have startled him. That old grandfather clock could have chimed or a spider fallen from one of the stuffed heads above him. "I was just looking for Dot or Gordon."

"They've gone to bed." He twisted in his chair, grinding the pile of wood shavings into the carpet as he did so.

He was careless and coddled and full of himself, she concluded, and Lucy saw no need to be polite. "Who are you?"

"Me?" The boy put his knife down. He had straight, dark brows, and his snub nose was absolutely covered with freckles. He wasn't bad-looking, she supposed. "I'm Pete Knightly. Who are *you*?"

"Lucy Darrington." Because Pete showed no reaction—and

because she was proud of her escape from school—she added, for his benefit, "I came up by myself on the train."

But Pete had retrieved the piece of wood he'd been working on and was now studying it, frowning.

"It was very dangerous," she added, pulling awkwardly at her father's old shirt as she stepped closer. "Some of the men could have been outlaws."

"Uh-huh." Pete gathered up his knife and carving wood. "I guess some of the lumberjacks up here must look pretty frightening to a schoolgirl."

Lucy was aware of her Miss Bentley's School uniform, her untidy hair, and her round face with the disappointing eyebrows (no character whatsoever). Her father's oversize shirt didn't help—it probably made her look even more like a little girl. "I don't frighten easily." She thrust her shoulders back and faced him. She was not going to have him get the wrong idea about her.

Pete nodded gravely, as if *he* would be the judge of that. "You're not afraid of the dark, are you?"

"No."

Pete grinned. It wasn't a mean grin—she'd seen plenty of those. In Wickham, there'd been boys who followed her home from school and called her "ghost girl" before pulling her braids. Pete's grin transformed his face and made him appear . . . well, not so bad.

"Good. I'm going up. If you're not afraid of the dark I'll let you turn off the light. That's the switch there." He pointed carefully to a switch on the lamp, as if still a bit amazed by it. "It's electric, you know," he said with pride.

"I know all about electricity," she said at once, for when it came to science and technology she had a bit of a competitive streak. "I came from San Francisco, where my school had electricity, and I've ridden on trolley cars and automobiles and spoken on the telephone."

She was bragging, and she hated people who did that, especially about city things. Her awful Boston cousins did that all the time. Abruptly she stopped.

"Well, good for you," Pete said. He wasn't grinning anymore. He brushed past her, taking up space and standing very straight. Second to braggers she hated people who deliberately made it obvious they were much taller than she was. "Good night."

"Night," she said sullenly.

And then he was gone.

She flipped the switch with a sigh. It wasn't all that dark, not with the moonlight coming in. And not scary at all. If anything, she thought with a sigh, the dead deer on the wall seemed to regard her with sympathy.

Lucy changed into her nightclothes and sat in bed hugging her knees. She would just have to find her father, that was it. There was no other thing she could do.

Her mother had died before Lucy could remember her. And her mother's family—the thin, elvish Stepwaiths—had died out as well, like an ancient race that had found itself too fragile for the modern world.

Her father's family, back in Boston, was robust and well-to-do. She thought of her formidable grandmother, dressed in black and reigning in her mansion filled with Chinese porcelain, gloomy antiques, and tiny lapdogs. There was her spinster great-aunt who lived alone, except for servants, surrounded by the portraits that had been painted of her seventy years ago when she had been a renowned beauty. She had two uncles, one in steel and one in railroads, and their children were insufferable brats.

At one time, her father had been a promising young man. He'd gone to the best schools, been taken up by a community of respected scientists, and published several articles about energy fields. But gradually he'd turned his back on all of it to pursue ever more eccentric research into the spirit world. And the world of science, publications, and universities had turned its back on him.

"Ghostology is important, even if it's not well respected," her father told her one evening after she came home complaining that her cousins had teased her for wearing old shoes. "We may not have fine things, but what we do we do for the glory of science." Yet another reason Miss Bentley's was all wrong for her—the only glory they cared about there was the glory of obedience.

Lucy shifted on the uncomfortable bed. The little room, with its odd assortment of broken and unwanted things, was the perfect place for a ghost. And the third floor hadn't been wired: The only light came from a hurricane lamp filled with a viscous oil that made the room smell like fish. If the Knightlys' house had a ghost, Lucy bet it would show up here.

Lucy slid off her bed onto the cold bare floor and went to where she'd propped her instrument case on a broken cane chair. The case opened up into three tiered drawers—each holding a collection of mechanical devices her father had made.

She dug past the od-oculars, the energy dowsers, the vitometer (which had gone completely quiet after its fit of shaking on the train), and the archevisual spectrometer. These were all things her father had built in his pursuit of ghosts and spirits, and as such always gave Lucy an ache in her heart. He poured himself into his work, but with little result. Even his inventions hadn't brought him the fame he deserved. He had labored on them many hours in his laboratory in Wickham, but he hadn't the commercial knack to make a success of selling them, and so they remained personal tools—the only ones of their kind in the world.

In the bottom drawer was a brass egg about six inches high. She lifted it out and placed it on the floor near her bed.

It promptly fell over on its side.

"Oh, come on!" she said.

Lucy picked up the egg and shook it. Then she tapped it with her fingernail until with a slight whir, two spindly legs with broad flat feet extended from it. From its sides emerged two tubular arms with small hooks at each end. She set it on the floor again. Even though she'd outgrown her fear of ghosts, she still sometimes set the ghost sweeper out at night, like an old lovey she couldn't part with.

She'd climbed onto her bed again when the egg wobbled slightly and took a few steps.

Lucy blinked. It hadn't done that in ages.

She waited, hardly daring to breathe in case it kept walking. But it stopped.

Disappointed, Lucy turned her back on it and pulled up the covers.

She'd been six years old when her father made it.

"This, my dear, is a genuine ghost sweeper," he'd told her that first night as he tucked her under her quilt. "Specially constructed—just for you—to rid the immediate premises of ghosts, haunts, and emanations." His blue eyes twinkled as he said this. And on that first night, the little brass egg marched around the room like a busy soldier. It twittered and huffed, stopping occasionally to blast out a whistle of air.

"Is it really sweeping them away?" she asked, shivering happily. It was the last evening in October, and a trickster wind made the skeletal branches scritch like fingernails against the window of her bedroom in Wickham.

"Yes indeed," her father replied, watching the sweeper go about its work. "My, my, this room needed a good sweeping out."

Inside the little sweeper was a miniature engine that shot out jets of ionized silver. This slight electrostatic charge dispersed ghosts—their subtle frequencies were sensitive to electricity and energy currents.

Her father had discovered that emotions created energy fields, and even emotions of many years ago would leave a residue, an echo that the ghost could attach to. But this nearly imperceptible energy could be disrupted. Her father's ghost-clearing bag was full of tools that scrambled these fields: electrostatic engines, voltaic batteries, even strong magnets.

William Darrington used *science* to clear ghosts, unlike healers or folk doctors, who used remedies like herbs or protection stones. Her father always said there might be something to the stones—any dark stone was supposed to absorb negative energy, and in laboratory tests obsidian had shown weak powers of disrupting etheric bodies—but he wasn't willing to bet his life on them.

So he made Lucy her very own ghost sweeper, and soon afterward he announced that she could go to work with him. For the next few years she followed along, going from gloomy mansion to sinister farmhouse, playing in poltergeist-guarded parlors or suicide-haunted broom closets, her ghost sweeper marching along at her side, like a friendly dog, chuffing and whistling if any spirits made the mistake of getting too close. And she helped her father clear lots of ghosts simply by holding magnets in just the right place or managing the battery rigs. He always said she was the best assistant anyone could hope for.

Those had been good days. But it had been ages since he'd taken her along on one of his clearing jobs. And now the ghost sweeper was winding down, as if it, too, was leaving her behind.

Lucy sighed and blew out the lamp. The light from the moon turned the floor to pale silver. The ghost sweeper stood guard, motionless but alert, its stubby body casting a long shadow across the floor. Within minutes she was asleep.

3

Lucy awoke with a single-minded determination. She would go into town and ask everyone she encountered if they had seen her father.

Last night Dot said he wanted a room, but his work was in the forest. That could be anywhere. So Lucy's first task was to figure out who'd hired him.

There was the question of how to get to Pentland—for she remembered traveling awhile by wagon with Able Dodd last night. But she was used to finding her way around places. She'd gotten lost in several cities, for her father often sent her on errands, typically mistaking one critical detail, such as turn *left* at the tomb of the pirate Jean Lafitte, not right, or knock twice at the shop with the dragon painting in the window (not the phoenix). She believed she could handle one tiny logging town.

The more pressing matter was breakfast.

Lucy put on her other scratchy blue wool Miss Bentley's dress (she had two; they were identically awful), shimmied into her petticoat and pinafore, and passed a brush in the direction of her hair. Without the threat of Miss Bentley's morning inspection, she saw no need to waste time on hair brushing.

Then she made her way downstairs.

The three Knightlys were at the dining room table. The morning light revealed wallpaper that was faded and peeling in places and a threadbare carpet. The general air of shabbiness was relieved only by a nosegay of freshly cut flowers on the table.

"Good morning," Lucy said brightly, "I'd like to go into town today to conduct an investigation. Could I have a ride, please?"

She caught a quick glimpse of Gordon's grimace before he flung the newspaper up in front of him like a shield.

Dot looked even more startled and nervous than she had last night. Her bulging eyes darted this way and that before settling on the jam jar. She began to spoon jam onto her bread with utmost concentration.

Lucy's shoulders slumped and she looked at Pete.

"I'm going fishing with Nibs," he protested, caught in mid-chew. There were crumbs on his chin, and a half-eaten slice of toast in his hand.

Gordon flicked down the edge of his paper. "I can't take her. I'm riding out with the tree doctor to take a look at the, erm, *problem*."

Dot's eyes widened in alarm. "My nerves are far too frayed already. I can't take the bustle of town."

"All right." Lucy crossed her arms. "I'll walk then."

"No, no," Gordon huffed. He seemed to realize they needed

to show some decency. "Dodd is running an errand. Pete can take you."

"But I'm going fishing!" Pete said again—again with his mouth full of toast.

Gordon waved his hand as if shooing away an insect. "You'll take her and that's that." The newspaper sprang up a final time.

After that warm reception, Lucy hardly felt like eating with them. She wandered down the hall in search of the kitchen.

She found a cozy, stone-floored room at the east end of the house. There was a large fire warming the hearth and a long plank-wood table on which were laid out a loaf of bread and creamy pats of butter in a bowl, along with a jar of jam. It looked like blueberry.

That would do nicely. Lucy took up a knife and sawed herself a chunk of bread.

From the pantry, just out of sight, came a noise of great clatterings and cursings. Then a woman's voice erupted.

"That pie tin was just here! Where has it run off to?"

A large woman came through the door. She was tan, muscled, and apple-cheeked, with a long brown braid of hair wound in a circle around her head. She looked strong and fierce minded, and Lucy took a quick step toward the door, hiding her stolen breakfast behind her back.

The woman's sharp eyes darted to the mangled loaf of bread; they narrowed. Lucy stiffened. There was a large crock of wooden spoons nearby, and Lucy's knuckles ached reflexively at the sight of it; they'd been rapped several times in the last year by the Miss Bentley's School cook, a creature who was possibly part ogre.

"Don't worry, child, I'm not in the habit of starving the hungry." The woman clanked two enormous roasting pans into a large stone sink and sat down heavily on one of the wooden benches. "I like to know where my handiwork is going, is all. You must be Lucy."

Lucy relaxed slightly. "Did you make the spice cake I ate last night?"

The woman smiled slyly as if quite aware of the quality of her spice cake. "I did indeed. Now, what will you be having with that lump of bread you're hiding: tea, coffee, or chocolate?"

"Chocolate, please," Lucy said eagerly. Miss Bentley girls were never allowed sweets except on holidays.

"You sit down." The woman gestured. "I may as well toast it for you, so hand it over."

Lucy did, and the cook popped it onto a metal rack that was suspended above the fire. "My name's Anya. Ask Missus Dot—I've never bitten anyone yet." She reached into the fireplace and turned the bread just as it turned golden brown. A toasty, vanilla smell spread through the kitchen. "Course I've heard a lot about you already."

"You have?"

Anya deftly picked up the toast and slid it onto a plate. She stirred a saucepan of milk and chocolate while Lucy applied heaps of butter to her bread and spooned gobs of blueberry jam onto it.

"I knew your father. He used to come here. Sit right where you are now."

Lucy put down her toast. "He's missing."

"So I heard." Something on Anya's face told Lucy the cook had her own opinion about the matter. She poured Lucy a cup of steaming hot chocolate, but Lucy's appetite had disappeared.

"Anya, did he say anything to you? About leaving?"

The cook gave her a thoughtful glance. She floured part of the table and brought out a bread bowl. Lucy watched as she punched into the pillow of risen dough; with quick and practiced movements Anya began to knead.

"I think he may have gone off chasing after something that he shouldn't have."

"Well. He's always chasing after something." Lucy tried to sound light.

Anya sighed as if wanting to get something off her chest. "You know your pa was interested in all the old tales. Used to come sit with me to hear my stories." Anya kneaded and the table creaked. "I told him all my good ones. All about shifters and magic trees. The black boats and the Devil's Thumb."

Lucy felt the back of her neck tickle pleasantly. She could just imagine her father at the table, his eyes shining with excitement. How many times had she seen him with First Peoples or theosophists, inventors, Chinese doctors, peddlers, and wanderers? Her father wanted to talk to them all. If any had a story he thought would further his research, he pursued it single-mindedly. He'd encountered such a story here, Lucy guessed.

"Anya, in any of your stories is there an uncanny place? Are there graveyards where people see ghosts, hollows where people hear voices even when no one's around?"

"Oh ho." Anya chuckled. "There's stories like that a penny a pound in Saarthe." And Lucy's face fell.

The cook continued. "But the stories he most wanted to hear were all about the Thumb."

Lucy frowned at this. "What's that?" How could there be any good stories about a place named after a finger?

Anya pressed her floury hand onto the table. "This here's Saarthe. She pointed to her palm and fingers. "And this is Devil's Thumb."

The cook's broad brown knuckle jutted out into the snowy white flour. A memory stirred in Lucy: the peninsula she'd seen from the train when it stopped to let Niwa on.

"Why is it the Devil's?" Lucy asked. She remembered the fierce guardian poles at that place and the way the lumberjacks grew quiet and uneasy.

Anya wiped her hands. Her eyes held Lucy's. "Because it's cursed."

Lucy swallowed. In the course of her short, strange life she met plenty of grown-ups who liked to scare children. Her father had given her good advice: Get scared on your own evidence.

They'd been in Nebraska, when she was frightened of a man with pale eyes who spoke about voices in the cornfields. She had nightmares about it.

Her father took her with him into the cornfields at night—a

night of the full moon, no less—and she listened to the vast rustling earth. But the corn didn't speak, she was pleased to tell the pale-eyed man next time she saw him. There were no voices in its green world. And she had the evidence: a wax cylinder recording she'd made. Her father was proud of her, if a little disappointed there was no message from the cornstalks.

So now Lucy asked the obvious question: "Cursed how?"

Anya looked at her pityingly. "No one's ever come back from it to say."

"Oh," Lucy said quietly. She took a small bite of toast. Just because he wanted to hear stories about it didn't mean he went there, she told herself.

"But he wouldn't have gone there," Anya said, "not for all that he was fascinated with it."

"Why not?" She looked up hopefully at the cook's broad, friendly face.

"Well, he wouldn't have left you, would he?" Anya said. Then, distractedly, she clapped the flour off her hands and poured more chocolate into Lucy's cup, though Lucy had only taken a few sips.

The door opened and Pete came in, his hair brushed and sleek, looking like a young master. He leaned casually against the table, crossing his arms. He was a boy beginning to get broad and take up space. Trying on gestures too big for him, Lucy thought.

"There you are." Pete glanced only briefly at Lucy. "I'm ready if you are."

"Ready? Aren't you going fishing?" Anya asked. She leaned against the kitchen sink. "I packed a lunch for you and made a lemon custard."

"Can't," Pete replied with a heavy sigh. "We're going into town instead."

"Well, take some pie with you," Anya said, bustling again.

"Oh, that reminds me, I used one of your pie plates," Pete said. "Nibs and me were panning for gold. Hope you didn't miss it."

Lucy wanted to see Anya scold Pete for using one of her tins. Instead the cook smiled at him fondly.

"That old thing?" Anya went to the counter and gave him a few slices of pie on an enameled tin plate that she wrapped with a dishcloth. "Don't you worry about it. Now, what's keeping you from the river on such a gorgeous day?"

"I've got to help Lucy." His shoulders fell at this heinous chore.

"I'll try not to take too much of your valuable time," Lucy told him coolly, and slid off the bench. "Thank you for breakfast, Anya."

She came from a family of great ladies, and though they'd tried—and failed—to make a lady of her at Miss Bentley's, she could imitate one in a pinch. With her head held high she left the kitchen: the picture of dignity.

She was on the other side of the door when she heard Pete say to Anya, "You'll have to put more protection charms around the house to make sure she doesn't bring in a bunch of bad luck like her dad."

The hurt was swift and pointed. It was always the most superstitious, small-minded people who blamed her father when things went wrong, not realizing he was trying to help them.

She stayed a moment, hoping to hear more about this "bad luck" her father brought. But all she heard was Anya urging Pete to take more pie, followed by the sounds of loud, appreciative chewing—which did nothing to improve her mood.

Pentland was a tough and charmless town. Lucy felt sorry for the buildings, which all looked like they'd been slapped together in whatever way was fastest and cheapest. Most of them were unpainted: dreary, weathered, and gray. A few of the enormous, red-barked trees loomed over them, making the town feel small and flimsy—a toy town that might get kicked or stepped on at any moment.

Pete drove the Knightlys' two-seat buggy through the crowded streets, dodging wagons and street urchins and even the odd chicken, while Lucy peered skeptically at the rough saloons and lumberyards. There might be ghosts here. Mining towns, settlements, outposts were all good places for them, attracting gamblers and strivers: people who might die young and leave behind dashed hopes. But ghosts like that were often the easiest to clear. Her father had written he was on the verge of a breakthrough, his biggest discovery ever.

Lucy stared at all the activity around her. Men stomped down the wooden sidewalks, barking out orders to tradespeople. Wagons trundled by, swaybacked under loads of timber. She saw women in simple cotton dresses trailed by freshly scrubbed children, and others carrying brown paper packages from the butcher's or the mercantile. The people looked plain, but proud.

Then they were at the town square, where there was a small park and bandstand. Pete tied up the horses at a hitching post amid smells of lumber and dust.

Lucy readied herself to jump down, but her way was blocked by Pete, who held out his hands like a boy forced into a dancing lesson. She jumped and came to an ungraceful landing, clipping his shoulder as he tried to catch hold of her.

They disentangled themselves without looking at each other.

"We should start at the mill," he said, moving forward without enthusiasm. "Everyone looking for work ends up there."

Her father wasn't everyone. And if he needed money (which he always did) he'd look for someone who needed a ghost cleared. At least that's what she hoped he had done. Anya's words—*the stories he most wanted to hear were all about the Thumb*—echoed uneasily in her mind.

"We should start with the saloons," she said, straightening her skirt. There was one facing the square that looked promising. It had a near life-size carved wooden bear out front, and a sign over the door read ONE DEAD MULE SALOON. ESTABLISHED 1862 FOR THE REFRESHMENT OF REPROBATES, INCORRIGIBLES, AND HOLY TERRORS. Her father always said there was nothing like a good, persistent haunting to drive men to drink. He'd found lots of his clients in bars.

From the saloon came the sound of a bar fight—bottles

crashing and chairs smashing—and then a man came flying out the doors to land in the dust.

Pete looked doubtfully at the man, whose struggle to rise was hampered by the fact that he was also trying to throw a bottle at whoever had thrown him out. "Maybe we shouldn't."

Lucy put her hands on her hips and turned. "Well, which way's the cemetery?" This was another of her father's first stops in a new place.

Pete's forehead crinkled in alarm. "Why'd you want to go *there?*"

"To find out if there are any ghosts here, of course." You could sometimes tell who was a ghost from the condition of their grave: The soil around it tended to oxidize and turn red. Lucy's nose tickled from the dust and she coughed as another buggy tore by. "If there are ghosts here, someone might have hired him."

"You're wasting your time," Pete said. He plunged his hand into his pocket and brought out a shiny black stone. "See this?" From the appraising way he held it up, Lucy supposed she was meant to be impressed.

"Yes," she said, fussing with her gloves.

"This is my ghost stone," Pete said, with unmistakable pride. "So, you see, we don't need ghost clearers around here. We know how to protect ourselves."

The remark she'd heard Pete make to Anya about her father and "bad luck" still rankled. Lucy took hold of the stone and examined it critically. "I've seen loads of these protection stones," she said, which was perhaps a slight exaggeration. "But real ghost clearers don't use this kind of thing. Even if this is obsidian"—she rubbed the stone as if she doubted its qualities—"it's unreliable at best. Keep it if you think it works for you, though," she said, handing it back to him.

Pete stared at her with an open mouth. Then, with a rather wounded look, he took the stone back and returned it to his pocket.

"I think I'll start *there*," Lucy said, pointing up to a grand mansion on a hill.

She wanted to let Pete know her father was used to dealing with the highest society. And besides, behind a large fortune often lay the crimes and hurt feelings that let a ghost fester.

She started walking, making her way past a group of men in shirtsleeves who were unloading a wagon.

Pete bustled a few steps in front of her, as if she couldn't be trusted to find the way on her own. "That's Angus Murrain's place. He's the richest man in the territory." From the reverential way Pete spoke the man's name, you'd have thought he could make coins fall from the sky. "And he's probably down at the mill. See, I told you we should start there."

Pete's eyes were a bright green in the sun. Maybe he was sore at her for dismissing his stone—she had been a bit harsh. Whatever the reason, he insisted on taking charge and leading the way.

They walked down to a large, flat-fronted building with the words PENTLAND TIMBER COMPANY painted on it. But the man in the front office told them Angus Murrain was out and didn't know when he'd be back. They walked outside again, passing by the lumberyard. A huge shed was open to the front, revealing a steel blade as tall as a two-story house. Ten men wrangled a giant red tree trunk into position and the saw began to roar.

Lucy stopped to watch.

"Those are kodok trees," Pete shouted above the noise of the mill.

"What?" she shouted back.

"The red trees are kodoks. They've had to invent special saw blades big enough to cut them. They're the biggest trees in the world!"

Pete looked as proud as if he'd grown the trees himself.

The great saw spun through the log, casting off a red haze of sawdust and wood chips.

She stood watching the saw; she loved to see mechanical things at work.

The mill workers brought in another log. The saw spun like flashing silver. But after a moment, it slowed, chugging through the wood as if moving through a sticky cake. When the wood fell apart, Lucy could see congealed red veins lacing its interior. And she could smell the rot.

The mill workers looked at one another and began to clear away the pulpy mass. One man threw a piece of the rotten wood, and it splatted against the ground like a soggy pumpkin.

The trees are coming down sick, Lucy remembered the porter saying. She stepped closer, and was surprised to feel Pete's hand on her shoulder.

He was trying to pull her back just as things were getting interesting. She shrugged out from under his hand and stepped away.

"Hey! We should get out of here." Pete jogged to catch up to her again.

Men were streaming by them now, going to look at the rotten wood. Some were shouting. This felt like a protest or a march. Lucy pressed closer to the mill.

"I want to see what's going on." She shouldered her way through the crowd.

"I'll tell you what's going on," Pete said in frustration. "It's Rust, and it'll get this bunch riled up. Do you want to get caught in something?"

If it was interesting, yes, she did. And there was no Miss Bentley around to rap her knuckles for demonstrating "excessive curiosity."

"What's Rust?" she asked.

"That mess. It's putting people out of business," Pete said, raising his voice above the men, who were shouting now. Lucy resisted for a few more moments, but she was getting jostled. Someone stepped on her foot and she felt suddenly small next to all the angry men. She was carried several feet, just as if she'd been caught by a wave in the ocean. She'd lost sight of Pete's russet hair. Where was he?

And then he was there, grabbing her hand. This time, she held on tight and followed him away from the mill.

✦　✦　✦

Pete thought they could get a root beer at Dawson's general store and ask Mr. Dawson if he'd had any dealings with Lucy's father.

"I'll bet you fifty cents he knows something about your dad," Pete said. They'd both been a bit shaken by the mob at the lumberyard. But Lucy's confidence returned once they were seated at the soda fountain in Dawson's store.

It turned out that Mr. Dawson *had* seen her father. Three weeks ago William Darrington sold him his horse and saddle, bought jerky, salt pork, and hardtack, and cleaned him out of his stock of writing paper.

"Didn't care about the price he got for his horse," said Mr. Dawson, looking down his long, thin nose. "Didn't want to catch his own food. He was particular on that account. Excitable fellow."

The storekeeper licked his pencil and made a tiny, precise notation in his account ledger. Lucy figured most of the world appeared excitable to Mr. Dawson—he was as slow and dry as a tortoise. But he did tell them that her father also spoke of needing to pick up supplies from the apothecary.

Their next stop was a crowded little shop stuffed with jars and bottles of all kinds of medicines and miracle cures: Dr. Lloyd's Toothache Drops, Stickney & Poor's Female Tonic, Dr. Kilmer's Swamproot Kidney Cleanser, and many others. The proprietor of this medical wonderland was an Arthur Lyman: a man in his early fifties with a twitchy nose, untamed eyebrows, and an air of nervous energy that made Lucy think of a high-strung rodent.

William Darrington had come here with an unusual request. He asked the apothecary to make up a tincture to stop dreams.

"And it used some very expensive ingredients," Mr. Lyman said petulantly. He clearly felt he'd not been well compensated for his potion.

But he didn't know why Lucy's father didn't want to dream. Nor where the ghost clearer had gone once he received his dreaming cure.

They asked a few more questions. But the druggist made it clear that if they weren't in the market for vitamin drops or a baldness tonic they were wasting his time. He turned his back on them and began unpacking a box of skin creams.

"You might try the Climbing Rose," he told them, seeing they were still there. "A drinking establishment of the lowest sort." He picked up a feather duster and applied it to one of his shelves.

But as they turned to leave, one last thought occurred to Mr. Lyman. He stopped, poised with his feather duster in the air. "He is not *the* William Darrington, is he? Of Boston?"

With a twist in her insides Lucy nodded. "Yes," she said, feeling nothing good could follow this. "That's him."

The druggist's eyes turned bright with malice. "I *thought* so. Yes. Your father acted as if he were doing important research. But the William Darrington I'd heard of was famous for trying to save a rock because he claimed it housed a local deity." He clucked his tongue. "I knew that man was a crackpot as soon as I set eyes on him."

"What's he talking about?" Pete asked. "What rock?" He

looked at her in confusion. But Lucy, too humiliated to answer, pushed through the door, Mr. Lyman's laughter ringing in her ears.

Once they were outside, Pete ran to catch up with her.

"What was that about?" he asked. "Your father thought a rock was a god?"

This made it sound even more ridiculous than it was. Pete had a smirk on his face, which she supposed she deserved after the way she'd treated his precious stone. If he wanted to get her back for it, he couldn't have done any better, for the story was the most humiliating thing that had happened to her.

"No!" She crossed her arms. "Well, not exactly."

"What was it, then?" Pete shrugged as if he were simply curious. Maybe he didn't want to make fun of her after all.

Lucy went to the edge of the wooden sidewalk and leaned her elbows against the railing. She might as well tell him.

"Living things are alive, right?" she asked Pete. She didn't expect him to understand what she was about to explain.

Pete's face contracted as he thought this over. "Er, yes."

"How do you know?" She tilted her chin at him.

"You just know?" He sounded as if he knew this wasn't the right answer.

She shook her head. "There's something that shows they're alive. It's an energy called the Od. Life energy. And you can measure it with a vitometer, which my father invented. People have more Odic force than, say, chipmunks. Ghosts are part of the Od, too. But they're fainter."

So faint, her father had to create special oculars to see them.

"Okay," Pete said. "I *better* have more Od than a chipmunk." He flexed his arm muscles to reassure himself.

"But then my father started thinking that he could detect the Od in things that weren't alive. Rocks, rivers, caves . . ." Lucy frowned. This was where everything had started to go wrong.

"There was a big rock near where we lived, the Maran Boulder. It was famous for being haunted. People would hear noises, they'd get lost. Old folks would say, 'Don't wander there by yourself, you might not come back.' But they also said the First Peoples would go there and ask for a vision, if hunting was bad or people were sick. Some folks from our town would leave little bits of things there for good luck: bread, bones, flowers . . ."

Lucy paused, remembering the strange lichen-encrusted rocks poking up like teeth, the little piles of offerings, and emerging at the center of the rock field, the great black boulder itself.

Pete settled against the railing next to her. She liked telling stories, but this wasn't one of them.

"The railroad was coming and they were going to lay track right where the boulder was—so they planned to dynamite it. But men started getting sick, and the dogs kept running off. The mules were spooked and wouldn't pull. So the railroad hired my father to fix it. We went out to the Maran Boulder thinking it was no more than a bad ghost."

The morning they set out was the most exciting of her life. She got up before dawn to help her father pack the equipment and make sure the instruments were in working order. For the first time, she would have her own vitometer to help her search out places where the Odic force indicated spirit activity. She was to take the south side of the rock field and her father the north, which, being colder and darker, was more likely to be the ghost's terrain.

"The first clue that anything was wrong was the vitometer— that's the instrument he invented to measure Odic force. The reading was higher than for anything he'd ever recorded. So if this was a ghost it was a humdinger."

"And was it?" Pete's eyes were wide now.

"No." Lucy still felt the confusion of that day. "We tried clearing it. My father's the best ghost clearer *in the world* and nothing worked."

She looked out onto the town square with its cheerful bandstand and shivered. "It was getting late, and I wandered off. I remember I felt kind of sleepy. I must have stumbled, and then . . . somehow, I fell into a crack in the rock and got myself stuck."

She still felt chills when she thought of it, recalling how she tried to call out, how faint her voice was, almost as if she'd fallen into a lake. The world felt like it was rising away from her, while she fell, pulled deep by something ancient and hungry.

"I was wedged in tight and couldn't move. Then I saw my father. He looked like he was shouting. He was pulling me, but I was stuck tight."

"So what happened?" Pete asked.

Lucy bent over the wooden railing and stared at a police wagon coming up the dusty street. "I don't know. It loosened up a bit. I popped out."

Pete leaned an elbow on the railing beside her. His eyes were thoughtful. "And you were okay?"

"Sure. All I did was get my leg stuck. Only after that my father said it wasn't a ghost after all, but something else, something he'd suspected but no one had ever proven the existence of. A nature spirit."

That night her father was more distracted than she'd ever seen him. Muttering to himself, marching up and down.

"Then after that he didn't want the railroad to dynamite anything. He called the newspapers and said there was a spirit in the rock and he'd prove it to everyone. He went out there with his thought interferometer—"

Pete's forehead wrinkled. "What's *that*?" He had some sunflower seeds in his pocket, which he now began to eat, cracking and spitting them over the edge of the sidewalk into the street.

"It's like a colander with wires. You wear it on your head. And his od-oculars." She heaved a big sigh. "They're like goggles. But the newspapers just took photos of him." Her father, wearing a colander and goggles, pointing to a rock. Headline: *Ghost Clearer Gone Mad*.

The next day the railroad went in with dynamite and blew the Maran Boulder to smithereens.

Lucy sucked her lip. People in Wickham believed in ghosts, but not *rock spirits*. She was a laughingstock among her friends.

"My father lost his teaching job. No one would hire him, not even for ghost work. Then we lost our house and . . . just moved on." She stared out at Pentland's modest, weathered storefronts—their displays of burl art and saw blades—suddenly pierced with homesickness. It wasn't even Wickham that she missed so much, just the way things used to be.

Pete thrust his hands in his pockets, perhaps hoping to find something useful there to say to her. "That's rough," he said, not quite meeting her eyes.

She shrugged. "It's all right."

A few doors down, there was bang of doors and another man was thrown out of a saloon. Lucy watched him roll like a tumbleweed into the street.

She hadn't told Pete the worst of it: her secret. Sometimes she wondered if her father had gone crazy; she wasn't sure she believed his obsession with nature spirits and the Maran Boulder. Maybe he was wrong. And maybe he suspected her of thinking that. Since that day he hadn't taken her on any more clearing jobs. The day she slipped into the crevice did more than ruin her father's reputation; it changed something between them.

But what was the Darrington motto? Onward.

She straightened her shoulders. All her posture lessons at Miss Bentley's hadn't been completely wasted. "Come on," she said. "Let's find that Climbing Rose."

4

The Climbing Rose was a saloon on the far end of town set away from the other buildings. Its outside was painted with eyes and a mouth, like the faces she'd seen on the Lupine poles. Ancient rose vines climbed up its sides, and beyond stretched a muddy flat grown thick with blackberry brambles. Beyond that was a gray and tumbling river. A pack of skinny dogs trotted by, following a trail of scent along the mucky ground.

Inside, the place was dark, with a hammered tin ceiling reflecting the glints of hurricane lamps. An elk's head hung on one wall, the antlers so large across that a grown man could lie down inside them. A motley assortment of drinkers were gathered about the bar, seated at tables, or in the back, throwing darts. The men looked to be mainly of two kinds: big and mean or scrawny and trigger-happy.

The bartender had two long braids and a scar across one cheek. He was polishing a glass and put it down when Lucy and Pete came in.

"This isn't a place for children," he said. "Get on with you."

Children? Her eyes narrowed. If he thought that was going to get them out his door, he was sorely mistaken.

"We're looking for my father, William Darrington," Lucy said in as loud a voice as she could manage.

Pete, who'd also bristled at "children," stepped forward, blocking her way. "Lucy, I can handle this."

One of the men drinking at the bar sniggered at Pete's bravado, and Pete shot him an angry look.

"I can handle this myself," she told Pete. She clambered onto a bar stool to get everyone's attention. "We heard some of you here knew William Darrington."

Pete looked up at her in embarrassment. "What are you doing?" he hissed.

At her father's name, a few men had looked up from the table where they sat. Dark-eyed, with their black hair worn long, they were First Peoples in settler dress, wearing dungarees and flannel. One had a string of bear claws on a leather thong around his neck. She thought of Niwa and wondered whether these Lupines lived in Pentland among settlers.

At the far end of the bar, a man in a worn deerskin jacket inched his hat down lower on his face.

Nobody was going to talk.

After a moment the men turned to one another and resumed their conversation, their solitary drinking, their dice games and dart games. The bartender went back to polishing glasses.

"Come on, Lucy," Pete said in defeat. He held out a hand to help her down.

But she couldn't leave without an answer. She climbed from the stool to the top of the bar and stamped her foot—hard. Whisky jumped in glasses the bartender had set out. All eyes turned to her and the room was so still, she could hear the quiver of a dart still shaking in the board.

Pete crossed his arms nervously.

"Now see here." She mimicked the stance of her most intimidating Miss Bentley's teachers: arms crossed, beetled brows. "I *know* he talked to you. And he wanted to hear your stories. He was looking for something. A ghost or a spirit. So what I want to know is, what's the biggest haunt you've got?"

She held her breath and crossed her fingers.

"Your father came in here, sweetie," said an old man with a great white mustache that curved out on either side of his jowls. "And he did ask questions. But that's where you should leave it."

At that moment, the doors to the Climbing Rose banged opened and a man walked in. Lucy's first glimpse was of someone tall and broad—a general impression of power—caught in silhouette against the light.

The drinkers in the Climbing Rose sat up, as if a current ran through them.

Once the doors had shut behind him, Lucy could see the newcomer more clearly. He had gleaming dark hair, swept back from a strong, handsome face: square-jawed under a black beard, with deep, commanding eyes.

He raised one eyebrow as he saw Lucy.

"What's this?" he said to the bartender. "You're letting girls run all over your place now?"

"Ha-ha." The bartender laughed with no sign of humor.

The big man settled himself in, as others made way for him. Lucy could see at once the fine cut of his clothes and the gold watch chain peeking from the folds of his morning coat. He was the only person she'd seen so far in Pentland who appeared to be prospering.

"I'll warn you, Shatterhand," he said to the barkeep, "you're about to have a thirsty crowd in here. There's been more Rust at the mill. Logs from Billups's place. Who knows how many of them."

There was a general intake of breath as the men in the Climbing Rose took in the bad news.

A scrawny, toothless drinker sidled up to the big man's side. "Mr. Murrain," he said fawningly, "how is Billups? He gives me work now and then and I fear to see him ruined."

The big man frowned. "I haven't talked to him yet. But the infection is far gone and spreading." He took a drink from the bartender and emptied it in a swallow. Then, seeing the plaintive look on the toothless man's face, he put a coin on the bar in front of him and gestured at the barkeep to pour for the little man as well.

Murrain? Lucy tried to catch Pete's eye. Was this the man they'd been looking for earlier?

"Pete," she whispered.

But for some reason Pete was too deep in his own thoughts

to hear her. His forehead was knit with worry as he stared into a middle distance.

"Pete!" she said more loudly.

Hearing her, the big man looked up. "You're still here?" he asked Lucy. "What are you now, a bar ornament?" He produced a handsome calfskin case from his pocket and took out a cigar.

The men around him laughed; his toothless friend laughed loudest.

"No." She'd been stuck up there thinking how she would gather her skirts to climb down with dignity. "I came to ask after William Darrington. I was hoping someone here would tell me how to find him."

"Darrington." Mr. Murrain cocked his head and put his cigar down, unlit.

Lucy settled for scooting down on her backside. The stranger had taken the stool she used to climb up on, so she had to turn around and dangle for a second before jumping to the floor.

"Yes," she said once she'd landed. "He's my father."

He swiveled on his stool to face her, his handsome face animated, eyebrows arched in surprise.

"Then you must be Lucy. But you're supposed to be in San Francisco."

Now it was Lucy's turn to be surprised. "Yes! How did you know? Have you seen him? Where is he?"

"Whoa there." He rested an elbow on the bar as his dark eyes swept over her. "I do know your father. I met him here, in fact. I'm Angus Murrain."

"The head of Pentland Timber," the toothless drinker told her, adding in an awed whisper, "A *very important* man."

Angus smiled tolerantly. "It's my mill, so that means a great deal around here," he said, as if amused by how much importance people gave to this little detail. "But your father was doing significant work. He told me he could find a cure for Rust." He leaned back, smoothing his luxurious silk tie. "I told him I'd give a thousand dollars to any man who could deliver the cure."

It went silent inside the Climbing Rose as everyone contemplated this sum, something so vast it was like trying to grasp the size of the universe.

Even Pete was jarred out of his thoughts. "Jiminy," he said and whistled quietly.

Lucy couldn't speak. Was this the breakthrough her father had written her about? William Darrington had always been careless of money. Had he finally grown tired of being poor, stopped looking to understand spirits, and simply decided to use his scientific abilities for personal gain? It didn't sound like him.

"A pity," Angus said, stroking his chin. "I thought he was the first person who stood a chance. Your father's a very convincing man, Miss Darrington."

She couldn't have stood on a bar stool now; her confidence was too shaken by the timber baron's casual attitude—about all that money, about her father's disappearance. "Wha-what did he say about the cure?" she asked. "Did he tell you what he thought it was?"

"He told me he believed it could be found on Devil's Thumb."

It was as if a wild animal had come into the room. Eyes went wide, chairs scraped.

A man in a chalk-stripe suit with a handlebar mustache slammed his glass on the bar. "If it's on the Thumb, it may as well be in hell."

The men around him muttered agreement.

Lucy had an image of Anya's brown thumb sticking out into the white of her bread dough. Her stomach sank. From the moment she heard of Devil's Thumb she'd been carrying a fateful dread that that's where he had gone. And now it was confirmed.

Another man spoke up. "No one's come back from the Thumb in a hundred years."

"You forget," said a giant lumberjack. "Brocius Pile went in five years ago and *he* lived."

"But not to tell," said the gentleman in the striped suit, his eyes blazing. He raised his voice, his mustache quivering with emotion. "Whatever he saw in that forest stole his wits. His brain's a mass of jelly now."

"Brocius Pile was a strong man, but no one would ever call him an intellect," Angus countered. "Who's to say the Thumb had anything to do with the state of his brains?"

The man in the deerskin jacket had been watching all this from under his battered hat; now he spoke up, revealing a thin, sallow face. "I do." He set his glass quietly on the bar. "There's something there that wishes humankind ill."

"Scare stories," Angus said with a shake of his head. "Superstition."

At their table, the group of Lupine men were silent. Watchful.

"If something's haunting the place it can be cleared away," Lucy said, pitching her voice to the room. "Hasn't anyone thought to try that?"

An uncomfortable silence fell.

"Everyone's too afraid." Angus planted a broad fist on the bar. "Why, this slip of a girl has more sense than you."

A few of the men hung their heads. Lucy loved to be held up as an example—it happened far too infrequently since she had left her home in Wickham. But she tried to keep her tone modest as she added, "You just need to take a scientific approach."

"Exactly, exactly what I always say." Angus turned to her. His eyes were the deep brown of expensive leather, and Lucy found herself nodding to his words. "Don't fall prey to every spooky story you hear. Approach it rationally, with logic."

Lucy stood up taller. She'd hardly expected to agree so much with the head of Pentland Timber, but it was as if they were two minds with the same thought. Pete was looking at her with an awed expression.

"A sarsaparilla for the young lady, Shatterhand," Angus ordered. Then, catching sight of the openmouthed Pete, he frowned slightly. "Make that two."

He indicated two seats beside him where he wanted Lucy and Pete to sit. Obediently they climbed up on the stools.

The sallow-faced man in the deerskin jacket had had enough.

He slammed down his empty glass and stalked past them on his way out. "I respect what's in that forest. You'd do well to do the same." The doors banged closed behind him.

Angus made a face of mock fear. "Oh no. Beware the curse. I'm terrified."

Lucy giggled. She glanced at Pete, who appeared shocked, as if Angus had just blasphemed. Then he gave a tentative laugh, looking like he expected any moment to be struck by lightning.

"You see what people are like here," the timber baron said to her. His eyes, rich and sharp as coffee, gleamed under thunderous brows. "They don't test things. They're not open to new ideas. Your father thought something very valuable was hidden in that forest. I've been thinking of sending my own men to the Thumb to explore."

"Don't do that, boss." The Lupine man with the bear claw necklace spoke up. His companions looked away, seemingly annoyed he'd decided to break their silence. "You'll make it worse."

"Make what worse? What do the Lupines know of this?" Angus demanded sharply. He turned on them. "Are you suggesting there *is* a connection between that place and Rust?"

The Lupines were now muttering among themselves in their language.

Lucy leaned forward even though she couldn't understand what they were saying.

"We don't know about Rust," said the man with the bear claws. He gave an apologetic look to Lucy. "But the forest there . . . it's not good. If that man went to the Thumb, he's dead."

Lucy couldn't breathe. This was her fear, coiling inside her like a snake, all along. Now it had struck and she felt the shock, just as if a real viper had bitten her.

Dead.

She turned to Pete, her eyes brimming. "He's not," she said. "He's not!"

Pete's mouth twisted and for a moment he looked stunned. "Naw. Course he isn't," he managed at last. But he sounded uncertain and Lucy was not reassured.

Angus was off his stool and standing. "Shame on you, scaring a lady like that," he said, scolding the Lupine man.

Now the air was tense. And Lucy waited to see what the Lupines would do. But they were silent, making no apology. The staring contest stretched on.

Angus shook his head as if washing his hands of the lot of them. Then he turned and offered Lucy his hand. Oh, the power in his hand! She took it gratefully, feeling somehow unable to move on her own, and he helped her down off the stool.

"Take her home," he told Pete, speaking in a low voice, man to man. He thrust something into Pete's hand and clapped him once on the shoulder. "And buy yourselves some candy or something." He glanced once at Lucy. "It'll make her feel better. Scare stories," he muttered, shaking his head again. Then he turned back to the bar.

5

I'm sorry about your pa," Pete said on the ride back from Pentland.

Lucy sat beside him, sucking on a horehound drop, a bag of hard candies on the seat between them.

"Oh, he's not dead," she told him in a sticky voice. "No, sir." Not William Darrington. She looked off to the side of the road: the sickening, stupid endless forest. The giant trees dripped cold drops of condensed mist onto her head (for of course she'd forgotten to bring a hat), making her even more miserable. He wouldn't have come all the way up here and written her a letter saying he didn't know how he would manage *without his trusted assistant* if he was only going to go off and die.

And then she was crumpling: forehead, mouth, eyes, all folding like a bent accordion. But she wasn't going to cry. She rubbed her nose so hard her nostrils stung.

The candy shattered into bittersweet shards, which she crunched angrily before reaching for another.

Life without her father. This was a cliff's edge that she

approached full of dread, peering over it for a hasty, sickening glimpse of the abyss beyond. What would she do?

"Well," Pete said and flicked the reins unhappily. Something was eating him, too. "Guess I got to tell Pa there's Rust on the land next to ours. Billups is our neighbor. What do you bet we'll be next?"

She didn't know what to say. The Knightlys had seemed strained and worried when she'd arrived. She realized they could face disaster.

Lucy rubbed her sticky fingers on her dress. She'd lost a glove somewhere in the wagon. She'd have been punished for such carelessness at Miss Bentley's. Now she rather hoped it never turned up—in the current darkness of her mood, she felt like tossing the other glove, too. "Does it spread that fast?"

Pete looked down at the reins in his hands. "Faster and faster. Like it's speeding up."

It was strange to think the massive kodok trees were vulnerable. They rose like towers over the fern-filled glens.

"But your father's a lawyer," she said, remembering what Able Dodd had said about Gordon at the train station. "You don't depend on the forest, do you?"

Pete's cheeks were sucked in as if the air had been let out of him. "Pa made some bad investments." He looked worriedly over at her. "I think they were counting on selling the land to pay their debts."

Then the Knightlys were in trouble. Lucy picked awkwardly at the buttons on her blue wool dress. "There's bound to be a way to fix it," she said. "You heard them back there—my father said he'd found a cure."

"Uh-huh," Pete replied. He took a candy from the bag but crunched it without much energy. "Too bad he didn't get a chance to tell anyone what it was." He gave a heavy sigh.

Whitsun and Snickers made their steady way down the road. Lucy took another candy and hunched her shoulders against the drippy mist. If her father had said there was a cure, then a cure most certainly existed.

As it turned out, Pete needn't have worried about telling his parents they might have Rust on their land.

In the time they'd been in Pentland, Rust had already been discovered in the Knightlys' trees.

Lucy and Pete walked in the front door to find a scene of chaos. Able Dodd thrust past them carrying a yoke and two large oilskins, which gave off a strong stink of fish.

"Back to snake oil," he muttered darkly. "Never should have changed to electricity in the first place."

Lucy and Pete shrank back against the wall, giving him a wide berth.

"What was that about?" Lucy asked. "What's snake oil?"

"For the lamps," Pete said. "It's cheaper than electric. I guess we're turning off the power." He was about to say more when Anya came bustling by with a tray of coffee and sandwiches.

"Thank goodness you're back," she said breathlessly. "They're in a state."

"Anya!" called Gordon from his study.

"Coming!" the cook replied and hurried off.

Lucy and Pete followed after her.

The door to the study was open, and Lucy could hear Dot's agitated voice as well as Gordon's defeated replies. They were standing in a small room decorated rather severely with gloomy landscape paintings and dark wood furnishings.

"He was growing it, Gordon. Right here. On our land!" Dot was standing over a desk, rifling through an explosion of papers. Two livid spots stood out on her thin cheeks.

"Let's be calm," Gordon said, pacing behind her. "I'm sure he wouldn't do any such thing."

Dot's voice got high and shrill as she bent down to read. "It's all here. Written down. Pages and pages of notes about how it grows. Look, it says here, *Rust is a fungus. I've managed to grow it and study it in a controlled environment.*"

Lucy stepped closer. Pages and pages of notes—that had to be her father's research.

Gordon coughed. "He does say *controlled.*"

"It doesn't matter!" Dot, her head down, hadn't noticed Lucy's approach. "He brought this on us," she said despairingly. "We should never have let him anywhere near us. And to think—we took in his *child.*"

Lucy's stomach churned as she realized Dot was talking about her.

Dot looked up and at that moment saw Lucy. But she didn't

apologize. Instead the sight of Lucy seemed to push her past some final barrier of rage. "Your father has ruined us!"

It was as though she'd been slapped. For a moment Lucy was numb, unable to speak. She put a hand on one of the room's high-backed chairs. "What do you mean?"

"His experiments." Dot thrust out a notebook in front of her.

Gordon looked at Lucy unhappily. "I was searching for some papers relating to our land deeds and I happened to look through your father's notebooks. He grew Rust on our land and now it's spread to our neighbors' as well."

Lucy felt as if a block of ice had settled in her chest. Her father never would have done anything to hurt someone. And people were always grateful for his work. Sometimes they might pooh-pooh his ideas or methods. But he'd never been accused of anything like this.

"Those notes are his research for a cure," Lucy said. She looked at Pete—who'd come to stand beside her—hoping for corroboration. But he was stock-still, a look of anguish on his face.

"We're lucky he's disappeared then," Dot said in fury. "Any more of his cure and the whole forest would be gone."

"Dorothea," Gordon said, reaching for his wife. "She's just a child. She had nothing to do with this."

But Lucy had heard enough. Anything said against her father was as good as said against her.

"He was trying to help!" she cried. She knocked into Pete as she turned, storming from the room. She slammed the front door behind her and had the satisfaction of hearing the windows rattle.

And then she was running, running with such fury she didn't know where she was going, just away.

For some time Lucy simply crashed and ran, pell-mell, into the woods. There'd been a path, of sorts, and she'd followed it—or thought she had. Eventually, exhaustion overtook her and she stopped to catch her breath. Her side ached. Sweat soaked the heavy fabric of her dress. Her lungs felt raked with fire.

So . . . the path.

She put her hands on her hips and walked a circle, gasping for breath. It had to be here somewhere. But then even the starting point of her circle had disappeared, swallowed up in ferns. The trees all looked the same. The filtered light gave no hint of the location of the sun.

Lucy tried to quiet the pounding of her heart. She had an excellent sense of direction, she reminded herself. The path was just over to her right. It had to be. She plunged ahead, the moments going by in hot, sweaty distress.

Or maybe it was to her left?

She stopped, knowing it was no use. She was lost.

Lost in the woods of Saarthe!

As soon as she thought this she felt the immensity of the forest, its wild and hidden life. Somewhere above her a bird gave a sinister croaking call. Ahead, the underbrush rustled, waving as some invisible animal slunk through it . . . toward her.

Wolves. In her adventure novels, the forests were always full of wolves.

She ran again, panic racing along her nerves. But before she had gone very far her foot snagged on a root and she went sprawling on the soft humus of the ground. She lay there, heart pounding, and spat dirt out of her mouth. Then she sniffed the air.

Was that wood smoke?

Cautiously she got to her feet, brushing off kodok needles and dirt from her dress. Ahead of her she saw a small peaked-roof cottage, so decorated it might have been made of gingerbread. Every surface was covered with wooden cutouts of animals, flowers, hearts, and stars—everything whimsical and charming.

Lucy went toward it, pulling kodok needles out of her hair. The smoke she'd scented was streaming merrily out the house's chimney. Someone was at home.

Slowly she climbed the cottage's wooden steps and stood before its door. An ingenious design of different colored woods made a scene on it as fine as any painting: a river valley cutting through forested hillsides.

For just one moment she hesitated. In fairy tales, this was exactly the sort of place where witches lived, hiding their wickedness behind an enchanting exterior. But she was not the sort of girl to put stock in fairy tales.

She swung the knocker three times and waited.

The door opened, revealing a short, round little man about

her own size. He had bandy legs, a full beard, and long white hair tied in braids on either side of his head. Slung around his waist was a leather belt bristling with tools. He had wire-rimmed glasses and on top of his head was a jaunty striped stocking cap.

"My goodness!" he exclaimed. "A child." He peered up at her with bright blue eyes under bushy eyebrows. "And you've been crying."

Behind him, coming from the interior of the cabin, Lucy heard a strange click and clack; she had the strongest impression of something moving within.

"No," she said, though perhaps a few tears had fallen during her flight. She wiped her eyes to get rid of them. "I'm lost."

"Oh no," the little man said, his eyes widening. "But come in, come in. I'll make us some tea."

There was that odd noise again, almost like hundreds of dominoes softly falling against one another.

Lucy hesitated. "Please, could you just point me in the direction of the road . . . ?"

"Certainly. But have some tea first." He waved her inside. "Come in, come in . . ."

He was so small—and jolly as an elf—that Lucy gave in to his insistence and stepped over the threshold. When her eyes adjusted she found herself in a room filled to bursting with carved wooden toys: animals of all kinds real and unreal, dolls that had such lifelike faces they might have been real people, an army of wooden soldiers. They hung from the carved rafters or sat on shelves or nested in the branches of the great carved wooden tree that took up the far corner of the room.

"What you need is some tea," the little man said, bustling in his kitchen.

"I guess I am a little thirsty." She tugged her hair back into a semblance of a braid and smoothed her skirt nervously. Something felt strange about the place, but she couldn't say what, exactly. It wasn't the toys, although they were remarkable. She stopped to run her fingers over a lion's polished wooden mane.

They were beautiful—pity she was far too old for them. She put the lion back down and turned to join the little man in the kitchen.

That's when it happened. She had just turned her back when out of the corner of her eye . . . the toys *moved*.

She drew in a sharp breath and whirled around.

Everything was still. Her eyes darted about suspiciously. But under her scrutiny, one tiny hedgehog curled into a prickled wooden ball.

"Aha!" she exclaimed, running over to it. "I wasn't imagining it. They did move." And then they all did.

With a soft clatter of wood on wood, a miniature toy horse cantered around the room, an alligator snapped its jaws. An angry rhino came charging out and bowled over a squadron of soldiers who fell down like ninepins. At once the other toys began to march and dance and run and scurry.

Lucy turned to see the little man standing in the doorway, a pleased look on his merry face.

"They're alive," she said in wonder.

He shook his head. "No, my dear, it is merely the appearance of life. But I'm forgetting my manners. My name is Ulfric Amadeus Svendegard. And this"—he gestured round at his creations—"is my workshop. I am a toymaker. Retired, mostly."

As he spoke, a tiny brown monkey, no bigger than a parakeet, clambered out of his shirtfront pocket and begun to swing from braid to braid.

"Ooh, stop that," Ulfric said. "He is the naughtiest of all." As Lucy watched, Ulfric made a futile attempt to catch the monkey, slapping himself like a man beset by mosquitoes. The monkey was always too fast, however, and Lucy found herself hugging her knees with laughter.

"I give up," he exclaimed and turned back to his tea preparations, the monkey perched on the top of his cap.

She scrambled to her feet and followed him to the next room, where a cheerful fire lay burning in the stone hearth.

Soon the kettle was whistling. Ulfric put a china teapot and cups onto a tray, which he carried to a low table set in front of the fire.

"Come now," he said, indicating a carved wooden chair with a pretty embroidered cushion for her to sit on.

He poured a small amount of tea into a china cup and watched until she'd taken a sip of it.

As soon as she did she understood why the toymaker had

insisted she have some. The tea was extraordinary. It had no taste exactly, unless you could say it tasted of sunlight and air and the broad green strength of earth. With each sip, hope and determination came flooding back. Her anguish about her father, the Knightlys' accusations, and her fearful journey through the forest felt as distant as if they had happened to another person.

Ulfric's kindly face crinkled into a smile. "Better now?" he asked. He pushed his glasses higher on his nose and distractedly patted his pockets.

"Much better." Lucy settled deeper into her cushion and swung her feet. Miss Bentley had frowned on fidgeting. But here in Ulfric's cottage Lucy felt safe, as if she were small again and all her childish manners and fidgets were loved. "But what is this? It makes me feel like . . . like I'm at home."

"Ah." The toymaker nodded with satisfaction. "You are drinking a dreamwood infusion. It takes only a small amount, but the effects can be transformative."

"I've never heard of dreamwood." Lucy swirled the golden liquid in her cup. "Though it's a pretty name."

"Hm?" Ulfric asked absently, still searching his pockets. "Oh yes. A very unusual tree, known by many names. Golden wood, ghost wood, and in the native tongue *His-sey-ak*. The Lupines hold it sacred for its healing powers."

At the mention of Lupines, Lucy sat up straighter, thinking of Niwa. Maybe dreamwood was the reason the girl was so confident and strong. "So it grows around here?"

Ulfric shook his head sadly. His search had produced a pipe, but he seemed to have forgotten to light it. "No longer. The last one was cut down more than a hundred years ago. In my youth I did a service for the Lupines and was given some as a gift. But I don't believe they'd be as generous now. They say they have little of it left for themselves, and the wood that remains to them is guarded as carefully as gold."

While Ulfric had been talking, some of his toys crept closer, like children drawn to a story. A family of mice ventured out from a hole in the wainscoting and sat attentively with their neat little paws folded under their chins.

She turned in her chair and studied them. "How do you get your toys to move? Is it a secret?"

"That it is, but one I'm happy to share." His eyes sparkled merrily and he held out both hands to her so she could see the translucent web that crisscrossed his palms. "All I need is this. Go on. Touch it."

Experimentally she ran a finger over the webbing. It felt more substantial than she expected. Ulfric made a gesture and immediately the animals sprang into motion. A bear stood on its hind legs and reached for a beehive; a swarm of bees flew out like an angry cloud.

As they passed by, Lucy reached out and caught one. The tiny wooden insect struggled in her hand for a moment, then went still. She turned it over, searching for puppet strings or gears, some mechanism. She found nothing, just the smooth grain of wood.

She opened her palm and the bee took to the air again,

buzzing furiously. She'd been brought up to believe in science, not magic, but this seemed as close to magic as anything she'd ever seen.

"Dreamwood again," Ulfric said, twisting proudly in his seat to watch his bees swarm back to their hive. "This web is made of spider silk soaked a hundred times in dreamwood sap. As near as I can explain, dreamwood connects with living things and with things that once lived. That is why I don't need wires or strings; dreamwood carries spirit. The web is sensitive to my thoughts and intentions—sometimes I don't even know what they are myself until they're expressed in the wood."

Lucy sat up in astonishment. This sounded like Odic force, like the web itself was a conductor for the Od. But how? With a pang she thought of her father. How amazed he would be to see Ulfric's web!

"And the trees are really all chopped down?" she asked. But the remarkable tea made her feel anything was possible. They might not be. If she found a dreamwood, perhaps she could measure its Odic force with her vitometer. Already she was imagining the attention she might get if she could prove that a tree had such a high concentration of the Od. She could redeem her father's reputation, finish the work he'd begun at the Maran Boulder.

"Yes," said Ulfric frowning. "The only place they grew was Devil's Thumb. But there are no more dreamwoods now."

Devil's Thumb again. Lucy drew in a breath. This felt like more than coincidence. She took another sip of dreamwood tea and by the time she put her cup and saucer down she'd made a decision.

She'd go there herself.

At the mention of Devil's Thumb the family of mice had put their little paws over their eyes in fright.

Lucy looked at the mice sternly. "It can't be that awful," Lucy said. "Can it?"

Ulfric poured a few teaspoonfuls of dreamwood tea into a saucer and drank them in a quick swallow. "Yes, I'm afraid. You see, the forest on the Thumb turned years ago." He pushed his glasses up on his nose and settled deeper into his armchair. At last he completed his thought of lighting his pipe, and the spicy-sweet smell of smoke filled the room.

"There used to be a settlement there, founded by Denis Saarthe, a sailor who was the only one to have survived the wreck of his ship by sea serpents. Lupines and settlers lived there together, felling dreamwood as they needed. Back then Pentland was little more than a trading post. According to local legend a party from the settlement came into town with dreamwood to sell. They told everyone this was the last of it; they had cut the last tree they could. Soon after, they returned home and were never heard from again. Those who ventured to the Thumb to look for them didn't return." Ulfric's voice quavered. "Without dreamwood's protection the Thumb became an evil place."

It was as if a shadow had fallen across the workshop. The toys were stilled. Nothing moved from fear. The great tree in the corner creaked ominously as its branches swayed on an invisible breeze.

But Lucy, cradling her cup of dreamwood tea, had never felt more hopeful. She thought her father would do all right in that forest. He was the smartest person she knew, and he didn't frighten easily.

"But couldn't someone survive there?" she asked, leaning forward in her chair.

The monkey made a leap from the table to her lap and stood on the blue wool promontory of her knee, looking up at her.

Ulfric stroked his chin. "Perhaps it's possible . . ." He got up and banked the fire with a poker.

"How?" Lucy asked eagerly.

The toymaker poked the fire again, staring into the coals. "The forest—from what I have heard—is . . ." He paused, spreading his fingers, and the great tree in the corner stretched its branches out toward him in answer. "Connected, like the web connects my toys. A cut, a blaze in one part is felt in another. If I were going there myself, I would make sure not to disturb it. Cut nothing, hunt nothing. I wouldn't light a fire. I wouldn't even pick a berry."

Lucy thought this over. This would explain why her father had gone to Pentland and bought food for a long journey. But why had he visited the apothecary for an anti-dreaming remedy?

"Do you know why it's important not to dream in the forest?" she asked. She cupped the monkey in her hand, letting it scamper across her fingers.

"Ah." Ulfric frowned. "That is one of the many strange stories about dreamwood. They say the trees had the power to get into your dreams. An herb called dreamer's broom is the traditional remedy. A tincture of that could be made up, I suppose, and if the drops were taken at moonrise, that might stop the dreams."

"What do the dreams do?" she asked, for it didn't seem all that bad just to dream. She *liked* her dreams.

Perhaps the toymaker's somber expression inspired the monkey to mischief, for now he leapt from Lucy's hand, clambering rapidly up Ulfric's shoulders, pulling and tickling along the way.

"Well . . ." Ulfric adjusted his striped cap, which the monkey had tried to pull down over his eyes. As soon as he got one eye free, the monkey pulled the cap over the other. "So . . . it's not exactly clear . . . hard to say . . . Oh bother."

"Are they nightmares?" She had the funniest feeling Ulfric wasn't telling her all he knew—almost as if he didn't want to frighten her. "I suppose I'll have to get some of that potion made." She scrunched her face at the thought of going back to Mr. Lyman's shop.

Ulfric froze. The monkey, too, went still in surprise. "What did you say?"

"I'll make sure to get a tincture of dreamer's broom made up." Lucy resettled herself in her chair, already making lists in her head for what she would need. "What else would I have to bring?"

The little toymaker reached out a hand to steady himself on his stuffed armchair. "But you can't go there, child. Why on earth would you want to?"

Lucy put her teacup down. "That's where my father's gone."

Ulfric's bushy eyebrows arched like frightened cats, hair standing on end. "Oh my. Your father's gone to the Thumb?"

Lucy swung her legs for emphasis. "Yes, and I'm going there to find him."

The monkey stood bolt upright in shock before pulling the toymaker's hat over both Ulfric's eyes. "Now hold on . . . just a moment," the toymaker sputtered blindly. But then an ornate cuckoo clock began to chirp and gong, bringing forth bird after bird from a series of hidden doors. It was seventeen after the hour, an unusual time for a clock to chime, and Lucy was pretty sure Ulfric had crooked his finger at it.

He'd finally succeeded in getting his hat out of his eyes. "My goodness," the toymaker said, gazing at the clock, "look at the time. We should be getting you back to your people."

That evening Lucy sat on a bench in the Knightlys' rose garden. The northern sky was a filtered dove gray. The treetops feathered into dusk. She had her vitometer next to her; for the last fifteen minutes she'd been using it to take readings in different directions.

She heard footsteps crunching down the path toward her, and then Pete's voice. "There you are," he said. His hair was brushed back—orderly once more—and the white cotton of his shirt shone against the garden's dusky blooms.

She'd avoided the Knightlys since Ulfric had brought her within sight of their house, especially not wanting to see Dot.

And now Pete almost certainly blamed William Darrington for their misfortune.

"She's sorry, you know," Pete said, looking awkwardly at his feet. "She didn't mean to say those things. It's just hard for her is all."

Lucy swallowed. She was hurt, but some part of her had already forgiven Dot, for she knew how frightening it could be to have one's life turned upside down. "It doesn't matter," she said. "I'm leaving soon, and I won't be a trouble to your folks any longer."

"Oh," Pete said. The stripe of freckles across his nose flexed in surprise. He put his hands in his pockets and kicked the ground. "Back to San Francisco, or . . . ?"

"No." She couldn't keep the bubbling pride out of her voice. "I'm going to find my father." She pulled her knees up on the bench. Above her a wooden arbor billowed with pink climbing roses.

Pete squinted in disbelief. He put a hand on the arbor, then quickly yanked it away from the thorns. "But he went to—"

"Devil's Thumb, I know." With the rising moon and the scent of roses heavy in the air, the haunted forest sounded more exciting than frightening.

"Wait a minute," Pete said, hands on his hips. "You can't go there."

She turned to him, frowning. "Why not?" Pete couldn't tell her what she could and couldn't do.

"Well, you're just a bitty girl for one thing."

"Take that back." She jumped up.

"Hold on before you hit me," Pete said, backing away behind the safety of the arbor. "What I meant was that Brocius Pile was six foot two and could split three feet of wood in one stroke. He came back scrambled like an egg. You heard them in the Climbing Rose."

"Nobody's going to scramble *me*." She thrust her hair back angrily.

They stood facing each other. Twilight was falling. The almost-full moon hung in the sky, looking too heavy to rise. It rested on the treetops, like a fat man pausing to gather his strength before climbing the next flight of stairs. "That's what you think," Pete said, breaking the stare first. "But people around here are scared of the Thumb for a reason."

"I'll bet you I've been in worse places." She tilted her head up at him.

"The Thumb might be the worst of the bunch. A whole settlement disappeared," he said. "You're the one interested in ghosts. If there are any around here, that's where they are."

"I'm not scared of ghosts," she snorted. "I know how to handle them. The main thing is I know what my father discovered about the place. I know what the cure is."

Pete's brows were straight as arrows across his forehead. "What is it?"

Lucy made a decision. She was going to trust Pete. She leaned toward him and lowered her voice.

"He went there for dreamwood," she said, eyes widening.

For a long moment Pete didn't say anything. His mouth twitched. He couldn't be about to laugh. This was much too important. She flew in front of him, fists at her sides. "You *do* know about dreamwood, don't you?" A rose petal fluttered down onto her shoulder and she brushed it off impatiently.

"Of course." Pete threw up his hands. Then he shook his head as if he had the regrettable duty of informing her of basic facts. "But that's like asking if I know about dinosaurs. Yes. And they don't exist. At least not anymore."

"This isn't *dinosaurs*," she said in withering tones. "Dreamwood used to grow on the Thumb." She gestured toward the forest, an inky black mass stamped against the indigo sky. "What if it's still out there?"

A tiny shiver of excitement ran down her spine. Maybe Pete felt it, too. He came around the bench to stand next to her, facing the rustling nighttime forest.

"People around here do tell stories about it," he admitted. "Old-timers especially. The people who used to live on the Thumb had plenty. But no one I know's ever seen any. Pancake Walapush—you don't know him but he's an old rascal—liked to say his granddaddy had some. But if he did, they'd be rich and he was as poor as dirt. So it can't have been true."

His forehead creased as he thought about it. This was all the encouragement she needed.

"My father told Angus Murrain the cure for Rust was on the Thumb, right?" She was pacing now. Her thoughts made her feel that she could fly. Like a kite catching the air.

"Ye-esss." Pete crossed his arms and sat back on one of the bench's arms.

"And Devil's Thumb is the only place where dreamwood grew." She was sketching it with her hands—the Thumb, the tree, the points that—*boom, boom, boom*—all fell into place and made it have to be true. "This wood with incredible healing power." She stopped in front of Pete. He had to see how this fit together. She took in a deep breath. "*That's* the cure my father went to the Thumb to get."

Silence.

Then Pete hiked his shoulders in apology. "I don't know, Lucy. It seems pretty far-fetched."

He didn't believe her. For a moment she was crushed. The air went out of her and she was falling back to earth. Pete *would* go and poke holes in everything.

But it was only for a moment. What did Pete know, anyway? *She* was the scientist in the making, the one who could read a vitometer, the one who had experienced firsthand the power of a few sips of dreamwood tea. Whereas all Pete had were a few stories from a person named Pancake. She was right, he was wrong. Realizing this made her feel better immediately.

"I'll just have to bring some back to prove it," she said, clicking her heels together. "*When* I bring my father back." She picked up her vitometer from the bench and headed inside.

6

It didn't matter that Pete didn't believe her. Now she could simply go about her preparations without having him as a distraction. Her biggest problem was that she had no money—and anti-dreaming drops (as she discovered when she went back to Mr. Lyman's shop) were outrageously expensive.

She couldn't ask the Knightlys for help. They were going to have to sell their house and move to a smaller place in town. In fact, Angus Murrain was coming that very day to sign the papers; he was the new owner. Anya had told her so that morning, blowing her nose behind a great lace handkerchief and pretending her tears were from cutting onions.

Of course Lucy felt terrible about what was happening. But Anya had given her an idea.

Lucy waited in the parlor for what seemed like hours, watching the door of Gordon's study while he met with Angus. Some men came by and carried out the old grandfather clock on a hand truck. They removed most of the furniture from the parlor but told Lucy she could stay in the chair she was sitting in. By the time they were done it was the only chair left in the room.

"I suppose no one's bought *you*," she told the deer heads on the wall. Presiding over the empty room they looked gloomier than ever.

At last the door to the study opened, and Gordon came out, pale and sweating. He leaned against the doorway as if he needed the support.

"Thank you, Angus, you've been more than decent," he said faintly. He wiped his forehead with a handkerchief and went away with a heavy tread, his shoulders slumped in defeat.

Lucy waited for him to go, then slipped through the door.

Angus Murrain was gathering up papers spread on the desk in front of him. Against his powerful frame the graceful rosewood desk and chairs appeared as flimsy as the furnishings in a dollhouse. He wore rich clothes, beautifully cut; everything about him spoke of his success.

"Mr. Murrain." She used her strongest voice, already knowing that he was someone who valued strength.

He looked up in irritation, not expecting the interruption. "Yes," he said sharply. Then his posture relaxed as he recognized her. "I remember you, you're Shatterhand's bar ornament. I didn't expect to find you here."

"I've been living here while I continue my father's research," she said.

"Really?" He gave her a winning, sidelong smile. "And have you discovered anything of interest?"

He continued to shuffle papers as he asked this. But Lucy wanted his full attention.

She put her hands on the desk in front of him. "Do you still say you'll pay a reward to anyone who can find a cure for Rust?"

He looked up, surprised. "I do."

Lucy pulsed with excitement. She sat down in the chair opposite him as if they were having a proper business meeting.

"I know how to earn that reward. All I need to bring you the cure is an advance on that money."

The timber baron laughed, not maliciously, but with a note of admiration. And Lucy took heart things would go her way.

"All right," he said, "I have to confess I'm interested. I'd like to hear more, Miss Darrington."

Lucy lifted her chin and tried to look as relaxed and confident as Angus. "My father is a great scientist, and he was doing experiments on Rust. What do you think he found?"

He adjusted a golden cuff link. "I don't know."

"The cure for Rust is . . . *dreamwood*." There. She'd said it.

Angus didn't react. Instead he went almost frighteningly still. Finally, after a few long moments he tented his broad fingers under his blocky chin. "So, the one thing that can cure it is the one thing we don't have. How does that help me?"

"Well, it does, see." She couldn't sit still. She jumped up and now she was telling the story. "Everyone believes dreamwood is gone. But what if *they're* wrong?"

His deep brown eyes followed her as she stalked about the room. Maybe she wasn't being businesslike, but he was really listening—and it gave her hope. "What if dreamwood still exists? And what if someone has secret knowledge, secret information that would let them go after it?"

Angus leaned forward, intent. His fine wool morning coat couldn't conceal his broad lumberjack's shoulders. "What kind of secret information?"

Her hair had come loose again and she brushed it impatiently out of her eyes. "How to find it. How to survive in the forest without going crazy or getting killed. If you lend me that money, I'll go get some for you."

The timber baron settled back into the chair, which looked too small to bear his weight. His eyes glinted with interior thought.

"Well, that's an interesting idea," he said, playing with a handsome gold-plated fountain pen. "The truth is, I have heard rumors about dreamwood surviving in that forest. And if tales are true of the golden wood's powers, perhaps it could save our trees. But I'd like to hear why you think you're able to find it, when so many other men have gone to the Thumb and failed. Men who were bigger than you and stronger than you. Although"—he smiled again—"maybe not smarter than you."

Lucy tingled at the compliment. She sat back down in her chair and leaned forward. "That's just it. Being big and strong doesn't matter. You just need to know enough science to be able to find dreamwood. Plus, I've spent my childhood in haunted places, so I don't plan on getting spooked." She lifted her chin. "In fact I'd say I'm better qualified than anyone."

His handsome face grew serious. "That may be, but I'm loath to send a child into the haunted forest. What if by giving you this money I'm signing your death warrant?"

"You're not," she said quickly. She didn't think that way, why should he?

"You're new to Saarthe, Miss Darrington. You don't know our forests. It was perhaps that same misplaced confidence that led your father to Devil's Thumb. And now he's lost. Whatever he met there waits for you as well."

Lucy snorted. "If I'm going to let *you* scare me I might as well give up right now."

He chuckled. "Very amusing." He stretched his arms behind his head, thinking, while Lucy prickled with nervous energy. At last he spoke. "It's true that we tend toward superstition in Outer Saarthe. But I'm a man who likes to think for himself. I'm a rational man . . . A fair one, too . . ." He gave an apologetic look at the Knightlys' study as if regretting that he now owned it.

"I liked your father a great deal," he said. "We came from different backgrounds, but I thought we understood each other." He paused, and when he continued there was a slight catch in his voice. "I was orphaned at an early age, so I know what it is to make your own way. To break free of the constraints others want to put on you."

Yes, thought Lucy, *that's it*, feeling somehow that Angus was speaking not only about his childhood, but about her own secret thoughts and hopes.

"Which is exactly why you should invest in my expedition," she concluded for him. "My father always said it was important to make his own way, and he passed that on to me. He trained me on his tools and methods and his way of thinking." Her voice trembled; she *hoped* she was convincing. "If you want that cure, I'm your only chance."

"I see." He drummed his fingers on the desk. "I suppose I'd be foolish to pass up this opportunity."

Lucy held her breath.

The timber baron clapped his hands together. He was decided. "All right then, I'll give you fifty dollars. You could buy a horse with that. It should be enough for . . . What kind of supplies did you say you needed?"

"Food," she said eagerly, and now sensing that she'd won, she couldn't contain herself. "You can't eat anything that's there or make a fire. And you can't dream while you're there, either—it's too dangerous—so you need a potion to stop yourself."

"And you've figured all this out?" Angus said, sounding impressed. "You're a remarkable young lady."

Lucy swelled with pride. She wished Miss Bentley—who always threatened that Lucy would not amount to anything if she would not behave—could hear this.

"If you do find dreamwood—and of course I hope you do—you'll be a very rich young lady, too."

She hadn't thought of that. The idea came at her as a shock, for of course she had only thought to find her father. Though she supposed—after seeing how the Knightlys were suffering—that she did want to cure Rust. Without her even realizing it, a pleasant picture had formed in the back of her mind of her return: She and her father had restored the forests, they were celebrated in Pentland. Maybe a band would play in their honor—a brief image came vividly to life of the Pentland bandstand, people clapping, her father making a speech, free lemonade for everyone. But money . . . riches? She swallowed on a suddenly dry mouth.

"I'll get the reward," she said tentatively, "won't I?"

"Of course. But that's nothing compared to how much you would have if you brought any dreamwood back."

More than a thousand dollars? Lucy reeled at this thought. This went beyond her experience at bluffing and into a realm of pure fantasy. In fact it frightened her, and she didn't know what to say.

Angus was watching her closely. "Some of that would be mine, of course." He smiled gently. "Let's say I'd take half. As a return on my investment."

Lucy took a deep breath, feeling something momentous was occurring. The head of Pentland Timber Company trusted her enough to treat her as a business partner. But after all, she thought, why shouldn't he? In the end it was a simple thing. She had no doubt her father would find dreamwood on the Thumb. By finding her father, she'd find the golden wood. She'd already said as much to Pete. But Angus actually believed her.

"Of course," she said, still feeling a bit dazed.

"I think it's customary at this point to shake hands," he said, rising from his seat.

"Oh . . . right." She was too excited to think straight.

Her hand looked very small in comparison to his. Feeling the great strength in his grip, she had a moment where she feared he would crush her. But he shook once and then released her.

Now she could not wait to go.

She nearly ran to the door. There was so much to do. And she wanted to get started immediately.

"Miss Darrington," he called after her. The timber baron had a rather bemused smile.

"What?" she asked, turning around.

Angus held up his wallet. "You forgot your money."

Lucy was in her room, packing her rucksack, when she heard a knock on her door.

When she opened it she was surprised to find Pete on the other side. His auburn hair was mussed, and there were circles under his eyes.

"What were you talking about with Angus Murrain?" he said, striding into the room. There wasn't much space for the two of them, and Lucy found herself backing up, almost knocking over the mangy remains of a stuffed otter. One benefit of leaving the Knightlys was the certainty that wherever she went would have less taxidermy.

"Nothing," she said. It wasn't that her deal with Angus was

secret. She just felt it was private—just as her packing was private, too. And here was Pete stomping around and peering inquisitively at everything. She tried to block his view.

"And what's that you're doing?" He gestured at her rucksack.

"Packing."

To her surprise, he blew out a deep breath and flopped down on the bed. "I thought about what you said. About dreamwood still being on the Thumb." He stared at the ceiling and Lucy looked around the room helplessly.

"You know, I *was* in the middle of something." She tugged on the shawl he'd half sat on.

Still looking at the ceiling, Pete announced, "I'm coming with you."

This was the last thing she'd expected. For a moment she was too shocked to respond.

"You don't need to chew it over so much." He sat up violently. "Now you're making me feel low."

Lucy blinked. "Just hold on . . ." She paced about the small rectangle of floor. "Of course I have to think it over. It's dangerous."

"See, that's why I *should* come." He leaned back on his elbows and dug into his pocket. Out came the black protection stone he'd shown her in Pentland. "I know you don't think it's worth anything, but I do have *this*."

Her father always reminded her to be polite, even when she disagreed with other people's ideas. But it was so hard. She tugged on her dress—that lump of rock just reminded her how different she was from Pete. She didn't feel like having someone around who was going to insist his superstitions were just as valid as her science.

"You need more than some folk cure for haunts," she said, looking down at him. "And going to the Thumb requires special supplies."

"Like these?" He'd taken the word *supplies* as an invitation to poke around her things. "So . . . what's all this gimcrack?"

Pete pulled a worn velvet bag out of her rucksack and squinted doubtfully at the tarnished metal tube it contained. "A hollow rod. Definitely need that in the woods."

"For your information, that's an archevisual spectrometer." She bit her lip in irritation.

He rummaged some more, producing her ghost sweeper. "A metal egg, that's useful." He examined it quizzically before tossing it onto the bed. "What's this?" His slate-green eyes narrowed as he pulled out a small brass disc.

"Don't touch that!" Lucy rushed forward and grabbed his arm before he could damage her vitometer. "It's for research," she said, holding out her hand. With a shrug he gave the disc back to her.

"Research." He rolled his eyes. "That'll keep you warm and dry. Have you ever camped before?"

Lucy busied herself with putting her things back. She pursed her lips.

"Just as I thought," Pete said, correctly interpreting her silence. "All right, let's see your provisions."

Here at least Lucy felt prepared. She had bought buns and sweet bread at a bakery. To this she'd added some soft cheese, plums, and a few hard-boiled eggs. It was more than she'd taken from the Miss Bentley School kitchens when she'd run away—her train ride up to Saarthe being her only gauge of how much she needed to eat.

"There," she said, indicating a bundle she'd laid out on the bed.

Pete bent to investigate. "This?" He clucked his tongue. "This won't last you three days and it will go bad in less."

Really? It looked like a lot of food to her. She supposed he ate a lot—another reason he shouldn't come. "Well, I won't be there long, and I won't eat much."

Pete shook his head pityingly. "What else do you have?"

"I'm picking up anti-dreaming drops from Mr. Lyman in town." It had rankled her to go back to the apothecary and beg him to make her the special formula to stop dreams. But if Ulfric was right, she would need it to keep her sanity on the Thumb.

The importance of the drops was lost on Pete. He was searching her rucksack for one last item.

"Where's your knife?"

In answer she dug in her pinafore and brought out a small pocketknife.

This produced a disdainful snort from Pete. "That's not a knife, that's a nail clipper. You need a real knife. I'll lend you one of mine."

"I can get my own knife, thank you very much," she snapped. She flounced away and sat down on a worn velvet settee, producing a choking cloud of dust.

But his dismissal of her knife had introduced a seed of doubt.

"I don't need your help," she told him, coughing slightly. At least she didn't think she did. It was true she didn't know much about camping. But just because Pete knew how to camp didn't mean he knew anything about the supernatural.

"I'm not coming along to help you." Pete's freckles disappeared into his flushed cheeks. "Though you sure could use it. No, if there's dreamwood on the Thumb, I want some, too. If I could bring back the first dreamwood that's been seen in a hundred years, I could pay off my family's debts. Why, I could buy Angus Murrain ten times over." He snapped his fingers. "He'd be working for me. How do you like that?"

Lucy didn't know. She'd told Angus he could have half the dreamwood she brought back. She supposed there'd be enough for her and Pete as well. But in the last few minutes what had Pete done but tell her her knife was useless and she'd packed all wrong?

"Or maybe," Pete said offhandedly, "you just want to keep all the dreamwood for yourself."

"That's not true." She jumped up, horrified he'd think this of her. She wasn't greedy, and she wasn't doing this for money.

"Well then, what's the matter?" Pete took up one of her plums and—in the way that boys always had to throw things and disturb everything—began to toss it in the air.

Lucy sat down on the bed next to him. He was strong, she thought, glancing over at him. She supposed he did know about camping. And grudgingly she admitted she did owe something to the Knightlys. They had fetched her from the train station, and they'd fed her, housed her—even as they themselves were going through a terrible time. She and Pete could come back heroes.

"All right," she said, planting her chin on her palms.

"Really?!" Pete was so excited, he missed catching the plum. It fell on the floor and the skin broke.

A perfectly good plum. And she'd gotten such a nice bunch of food together: all the things she liked.

Pete didn't seem too upset, however. "Don't worry," he said, retrieving the plum from the floor. "I'll eat it."

As if she'd been worried about him *not* eating it. They'd have to buy lots more food, that was certain.

"I'm in charge, though," she told him. Of course now she'd said he could come it was a bit late to be laying down conditions.

"Sure," he said easily, biting into the plum. "Whatever you want."

7

Leaving Pentland was even easier than she had expected, Lucy thought, pressing her nose against the window as the train chugged south. Pete told his parents he would accompany Lucy down the coast partway on her journey back to San Francisco and stop to visit a friend in Crescent City. Gordon and Dot were too preoccupied to ask more than perfunctory questions.

Pete sat in the seat across from her, wearing dungarees and a snap-button cotton shirt, a bandanna loosely knotted around his neck. Lucy turned from the forest outside and watched as he looked into his rucksack and then closed it again, practically hugging himself in satisfaction. Who knew it was possible to find so much happiness in packing?

Lucy wished she could feel so pleased. While Pete made arrangements at the station she had a strange conversation with Able Dodd, and she was still unsettled from it. She'd said goodbye to Whitsun and Snickers and was just gathering her nerve to say the same to the Knightlys' handyman when he cut her off. "Take nothing that is not given," he'd said in his stern, preacher's voice. He glared down at her. Even his milky dead eye seemed to find her at fault. At once she felt so guilty she groped in her pockets. *Had* she taken something? She supposed she had taken sugar cubes for Whitsun and Snickers from the kitchen, but she was fairly certain the Knightlys wouldn't mind.

"What do you mean?" she'd asked in a panic, ready to confess to two sugar cubes. But then Pete came back, and Able Dodd would say no more.

Now she mulled over the warning. Able Dodd couldn't know they were heading to Devil's Thumb—she and Pete had told no one of their plans. Maybe Able Dodd simply meant to give her general words of advice: friendly, life advice . . . which from him sounded absolutely terrifying.

She sighed. Even the new clothes she bought for the journey at Dawson's general store gave her little pleasure: boy's pants in stiff denim, which she had to cuff and belt so they wouldn't fall down, and a shapeless flannel shirt two sizes too big. She changed into them once they were on the train and came back to her seat feeling like she was walking in giant galoshes. When she'd tried finding better-fitting clothes while shopping in Pentland, Mr. Dawson had remarked he had little in stock suitable for girls trying to disguise themselves—and peered at her so suspiciously that she'd rushed her purchase and wound up with the wrong things.

Drat.

The train could not stop on Lupine land without permission, so they were let off near the border. It was only because there were so few passengers—and because Pete had paid some of Angus Murrain's money to the conductor and the porter—that the train stopped at all.

Lucy stepped down from the train, straight-legged in her stiff dungarees. It was a gray, cool day, with a strong breeze that went right to work unraveling her braid.

"Are you sure about this?" the porter asked. Although he'd pocketed the money, he looked as though he was having second thoughts. He sucked his teeth, squinting at the gloom of the forest, which lay brooding a little way beyond the tracks.

"We're just doing some camping," Pete said. He gave a jaunty wave of his hand, indicating the glory of the wilderness.

Lucy breathed in deep; the damp air had the smell of rain-bruised grass. Now that they were off the train she was eager to start walking. "We're sure," she told the porter, nodding briskly.

The porter spat, unconvinced. "If you say so." With one final look of misgiving, he climbed onto the steps, and the train whistle sounded.

They watched the train chug away—each railcar that passed making their decision seem more and more final. At last, it disappeared, like a length of black snake vanishing into a burrow.

Lucy tugged at the straps of her pack. She brought a bedroll, her father's instruments, and the various supplies she'd bought in Pentland, including what Pete deemed a suitable knife. Hidden in an interior pocket was a glass vial of *antimorpheus*—Arthur Lyman's proprietary blend of anti-dreaming drops.

Her pack, however, was depressingly heavy.

Pete watched as she tried to get it on her shoulders but didn't say anything as she heaved and staggered under its weight. His shirtsleeves were rolled up over tan arms, and he hoisted his pack easily as if to make a point about his muscles.

"I'll get the hang of it," she said. At last she managed a somewhat upright position.

Pete had an old pocket compass, which he made a show of consulting, even though they knew where the coast was—the ocean, a wide band of blue on the horizon, was impossible to miss.

"This way," Pete announced officiously, having satisfied himself that, yes, the ocean was right where it should be: in front of them.

"Are you sure? Do you want to check again?" Lucy asked, trying hard to keep a straight face.

Pete ignored her, sniffing once before rather protectively putting his compass away.

They set off, heading away from the railway tracks, crossing a hillocked meadow beyond which stood a line of high, imposing trees. As they stepped under their eaves and into the shadows of the forest, Lucy turned for one last look at the railroad tracks. Even though she was eager for them to be on their way, the tracks were a line back to civilization, whereas they were heading into the wilderness . . . and the unknown.

They walked all day through the dark and whispering woods, a world of shadows and sudden shafts of light. They passed fairy rings: crumbling hollow stumps of trees that made circles of magic, moss, and rot. The giant roots of downed trees. Nurse logs that sprouted with bright green seedlings, tree orchids, and curling ferns. Occasionally a noise would sound in the brush, a fern would wave as something passed beneath it, an antler would spear through the shadows, but nothing showed itself or crossed their path.

In late afternoon they reached the top of a rise and saw below them a large meadow full of high prairie grass.

"We should stop here," Pete said. There were holes in the ground he liked the look of: rabbit burrows. "Wait and see, I'll catch us one."

Lucy dumped her pack on the ground and straightened her shoulders with relief. "You know we can't do that once we're on the Thumb," she reminded him.

"But we're not there yet." Pete grinned, bringing out a slingshot and some metal pellets.

He had taken the rule against catching their own food surprisingly hard, until at last Lucy realized he'd been counting on showing off his wilderness skills.

"Go on, then," she said, waving him away. Then she sat down (difficult in her cardboard-like dungarees) and unlaced her boots.

She'd dozed in the sun by the time he returned, holding a long, limp rabbit by the legs.

"Least you could do is get some wood for a fire," he grumbled.

She hadn't even thought of that. But now she went and poked about in the underbrush, getting her hands dirty and pulling up the biggest logs she could find. She went back teetering under her load, thinking, *Wait till he sees how much I can carry.* She had impressed herself.

Pete was sharpening his knife; he held it up and scrutinized the blade. Only then did he turn and give a quick, dissatisfied glance at the wood she carried. "What, no kindling?"

She dropped the logs in a heap. They'd streaked mud and forest gunk all over the front of her new shirt. "Fine," she snapped.

She'd get the best bunch of kindling ever. After more scrounging, she put together a load of twigs and small branches. These she dropped on top of her log pile. "Where's the tinderbox?" she asked, hands on her hips.

Pete was skinning the rabbit—a quick, efficient bit of work that she knew (but didn't want to admit) took some skill.

He gestured with the gory knife toward where the giant kodoks staggered into the meadow. "Just look under a big toadstool for where the tinderbox fairies leave them."

She sighed. "So I should have brought my own. Can I borrow yours?"

"Sure," he said coolly, "it's in my pack."

But by asking for the tinderbox she'd invited greater scrutiny of her fire-building technique. And, with a knot in his forehead, Pete soon found many flaws.

"You've built the pile all wrong." He bent down, adjusting and fiddling with the arrangement of wood. But then its inadequacy simply became too much to bear; he pulled the whole thing apart, muttering to himself as he did: "You don't put a big log on at the beginning. How's this supposed to catch?" And so on.

"I was going to fix it." Sheepishly, Lucy scuffed the ground with her boot. The truth was, she'd never made a campfire before. She would like to have learned outdoor skills like Pete's, but William Darrington was always too busy. If he wasn't out hunting ghosts, he was home, working on his research or writing what he said would be a history of ghost clearing. Between all that, she sometimes felt she was lucky she was paid any attention at all—asking to go camping would have been an unreasonable demand.

"So how *do* you make a fire?" she asked, admitting defeat. Stiffly she squatted down beside Pete so she could get a closer look at how he arranged the wood.

"I'll show you," Pete said, unable to hide a grin. And he did.

In the twilight the smoke rose into the sky.

A strange type of bird called out mournfully from its roost. Down below their hill, a group of elk emerged from the trees and disappeared into the tall prairie grass. The only sign of them that remained was their antlers, sailing like spiky ships across an inland sea.

The rabbit was delicious, and she was hungrier than she'd thought. She tore into it and licked her fingers.

"So how long do you figure it'll take us to find your pa?" Pete asked, chewing.

"Maybe a day or so once we're on the Thumb," she said confidently. "I'm good at finding things. I once found a two-hundred-year-old key that my father thought he'd lost. He said I saved his life." Lucy knew her father hadn't meant that literally, of course—if she hadn't found the key her father would have merely disappointed the friend who'd lent it to him for study— yet in some mysterious way the incident had made her realize her father did need looking after.

"I never lost anything important," Pete said thoughtfully.

"Really?" Lucy looked into the fire, suddenly thinking of her lost things: mother, home, now her father. She couldn't imagine going through life like Pete, unscathed.

Perhaps Pete realized the conversation had turned more serious than he'd intended. "Well," he said, using a twig as a toothpick, "once I lost my voice."

This sounded like it would be good. "How'd that happen?"

"Curious story," Pete said, getting comfortable on the ground. "We used to have this pig—a sow named Bethany."

Lucy threw a few twigs into the fire and watched them crackle. "That's a good name for a pig."

"It sure was. And she was a good pig. A great big thing." Pete sketched something monstrously large with his arms. His hair shone like bronze in the light of the flames. "One day I was sup- posed to be helping Able Dodd in the barn, but I didn't feel much like working. I wanted to be on the river, fishing."

Lucy tilted her head at him. "What a surprise."

He grinned. "You see, you already got me figured out."

"I'm observant." Lucy hugged the hard denim folds around her knees. It was easy to talk to Pete when he was like this—not so critical.

Pete nodded. "So anyway, I wasn't doing the greatest job with my chores. And Bethany got out. My pa was furious. He said I needed to find Bethany or he was going to break my fishing pole."

"Oh no." She had once jammed her father's microscope in her eagerness to see what butterfly wings looked like, and the repair had taken him weeks. She was banished from his basement laboratory for a month: a punishment that Lucy still believed was unfairly harsh.

"A threat like that, you can believe I paid attention. So I went tracking after Bethany. Took *hours*." Pete sucked on a rabbit bone before throwing it into the brush.

"Did you find her?" Lucy asked. She nibbled her own bone— more gracefully, she hoped, than Pete.

"I did." Pete wiped his fingers on his shirt. "The only problem was someone else had found her first. There was this family that lived out in the woods, the Babkins. The dad had lost his job because of Rust, and now their kids were jumping up and down outside the stall, all excited. And there was Bethany inside. So I just turned around as quiet as I could and came back home."

Lucy thought this was a fine thing Pete had done. It's what she would have done in the circumstances, too. "So that's how you lost your pig. How'd you lose your voice?"

"Then when I got home, I pretended to fall sick and"—his voice got faint and scratchy—"not be able to talk." He coughed and resumed talking in his normal voice. "I didn't want to tell a bunch of lies, so I just said I couldn't find Bethany, and then hoped they'd leave me alone. Now that I think of it, that was a cowardly thing to do. I lost my nerve, playing sick like that. So that's a second thing I lost." He stared into the flames.

Lucy hoped he would keep talking. "Did your father break your fishing pole?"

"Yep." He stretched out his long legs and sighed.

"That's the third thing you lost," Lucy pointed out, not counting the pig, which Pete had found after all.

"Anya says things come in threes," Pete said, throwing another stick into the fire and watching it burn. "Though I don't know how true that is, because if she's right, I've had my three so I shouldn't have to lose my house."

Lucy did not believe in old wives' tales like the law of threes, but Pete had been so nice to give that family his pig, she wanted to reassure him. "And you won't. Because when we return from the Thumb you'll be able to get your house back."

But Pete dropped his chin dolefully to his chest. "I got a new fishing pole later," he said. "I think my pa felt bad. Maybe I still have one loss to go."

Lucy did her own arithmetic of loss. Her mother and her home were two. That meant she still could lose her father. *You don't believe that rubbish*, she told herself. At night, though, it was harder to remember all the things you didn't believe in.

Something rustled close by in the darkness and she shivered. Pete saw her.

"You scared?" Pete asked.

He did not sound as if he would blame her if she was, but Lucy answered right away, "No." She brought out her shawl from her pack and settled it around her shoulders to show she was just cold.

It had gotten dark. They were in the wild land on the edge of the Lupine Nation, and the fear of not finding her father seemed to have stolen in like the smell of campfire smoke.

She no longer felt like talking. Lucy snuggled down into her bedroll and made a lumpy pillow from her shawl. But as she readied herself for sleep, she noticed something flickering out there in the dark.

"Look across there," she whispered to Pete. On the eastern edge of the meadow was a pinprick of orange light. Too sly and small to be a fire. Too large to be the glow of someone's pipe. It twinkled like a misplaced star.

Pete got to his knees, his mouth a thin line.

"Do you think it's an outlaw?" Lucy asked, still keeping her voice low. Their fire had died down and all around them the night was an inky black so solid she thought she could reach out a hand and touch it.

Pete's brows swooped together. "No," he said rather too quickly to assure her. He peered into the darkness and whispered, "Maybe it's a ghost or a haunt, though." His hand went to the ghost stone in his pocket.

Lucy was shocked to realize how little Pete knew about haunts. "It can't be. For one thing, it would be floating around, and it wouldn't have so strong a glow."

Pete said with a grim sort of satisfaction, "Saarthen haunts are probably stronger than what you're used to."

Forgetting to be scared, Lucy got up from her bedroll and went to her pack, dragging out the ghost sweeper. "If it was a ghost my sweeper would react." She held it up by one tubular leg; the egg showed all the animation of a tin can. "My father made this to protect me. There's an actual sweeping engine inside."

Like many boys she'd met, Pete showed an awed respect for the word *engine*. He relaxed his grip on his protection stone and bent to examine the egg. "It isn't moving a lick. That means there's no haunt, right?"

So big, strong Pete, who knew about knives and slingshots, was actually scared.

"You can sleep with it next to you if you want," she said, laying the ghost sweeper on the ground. She settled cross-legged onto her bedroll. The ghost sweeper lay on its back with its legs in the air, a bit like a dead beetle.

"It doesn't look like much," she admitted, "but if anything from the spirit world comes around, it will wake up quick enough."

Pete got down on his hands and knees in front of the sweeper, assuring himself it was completely inert. "Let's put it halfway between us," he said, gingerly positioning the egg and then leaning back to assess whether it was exactly in the middle.

"That's good," Lucy told him, mostly so he would stop fussing. She wished Pete had something similar that would protect them against any humans who might be out in the forest at night—outlaws worried her far more than ghosts did.

"All right, then," Pete said at last. He relaxed enough to lie down and pull a blanket over him. Soon Lucy could hear his breath turn regular and deep.

She spent a long time staring out at the orange light, until it was late and her eyes were bleary with sleep. But the light stayed where it was. Whoever it belonged to was keeping a vigil just like she was.

They walked all the next day, and her feet blistered and hurt. Lucy's skin was chafed from her stiff denim pants, and she felt like her pack straps were gouging into her shoulders. But she wouldn't ask to stop and she didn't say a word about her aching toes.

Every now and then she caught a sound, behind them, that made her turn. And once, when they were going uphill, she'd looked over her shoulder and thought she'd seen something moving through the trees below.

Whatever it was, it kept its distance.

By late afternoon, long streamers of fog unfurled through the trees. They came to a place where the kodoks grew sparse above a pale, spindly grass. Looming just ahead of them were three Lupine poles, crooked and tilted with age. From the distance they looked drunk, like men holding one another up as they stumbled out of a saloon. And as Lucy and Pete approached these three guardians, the thought persisted that they *saw*, were more than wood, even though the faces on them were rubbed out with age and lumpy as candle stubs.

"I suppose we're on Lupine land now," Pete said in a low voice, keeping one eye on the poles as he passed under their watchful gaze.

They crossed the invisible boundary, walking more carefully now, not saying anything to each other. Though the land looked the same, they felt different.

After a while they stopped and Pete again brought out his compass. Not to be outdone, Lucy consulted the map she'd taken with her at the start of her trip. They had veered a little from the west.

Pete glanced uneasily at the sky. While they were stopped a raven flew by, then wheeled around for a second look. It settled into the nearest tree, cocking its head to examine them. Apparently they presented a fascinating sight—two children huddled over a map—for the bird hopped lower, and Lucy had the funniest feeling it was trying to see what they were looking at. Pete noticed and scowled.

"Go on," Pete said to it. "Get out of here!" His voice sounded loud as a thunder crack.

The raven shifted on its sleek black legs, reluctant.

Finally, Pete threw a stone into the tree, careful to get close but not hit the bird. Rather huffily the raven shook out its feathers and then flew off.

"What did you do that for?" Lucy asked, watching the bird circle into the sky.

"They say the Lupines use birds to spy on their land." Pete clutched the shoulder straps of his pack unhappily.

"I met a Lupine girl on the train coming up," Lucy said,

wanting Pete to know *she* wasn't afraid of Lupines. "She was quite nice."

Pete rolled his eyes at her naïveté. "I'll be sure to tell them that before they put a hex on us. Or turn us into rabbits or something."

She thought this was a bit much. "Don't be silly. They're just . . . people." But then she remembered the lumberjacks on the train. *Lupine witch,* they'd called Niwa.

Maybe Pete heard the hesitation in her voice.

He faced her with wide eyes, convinced of what he knew about Lupines. "Oh, they're anything but that. Do you know in the settler wars, when there was fighting all up and down this coast, the Lupines won every time?"

Lucy shrugged.

"They did that through *magic,*" he said, leaning close to tell her this in an awed whisper. "In battle, their men could turn into wolves, the fiercest, cruelest animals ever seen. They'd rip out the throat of any man that stood against them. Well, you can believe faced with that, the settlers turned and ran."

"Good for the Lupines," she said, straightening herself as much as she could under her heavy pack. "Why shouldn't they defend their land?"

Pete was disgusted. "Bah. You don't get it. We've got to be on our guard. They're sorcerers and witches, and that bird was probably a warlock in disguise."

"A waste of its time if it was," Lucy said. "I'm sure *we're* no threat."

Pete readjusted his bandanna so it hung more rakishly around his neck. "Any Lupine we meet is going to have to reckon with me."

"For their sakes, I hope we don't meet any." She leaned forward again, trying in vain to ease the pressure on her shoulders.

"They can't be trusted," he said, shaking his head. Then he stalked off without waiting for her to put away the map. She had to run to catch up.

When at last they reached the coast, they found themselves at a vista high above the beach. There was a notch in the cliff edge and Lucy and Pete squeezed onto it, overlooking the sparkling water below. Laid out in front of them was the Thumb, as formidable as a fortress. A deep, dark green, it was bordered on all sides by iron-gray cliffs and rose high out of the water like a battleship. Above it flew dark birds of enormous size.

"How do we get onto it?" Lucy asked, staring over the cliff with a sick sense of vertigo.

On maps the Thumb was a peninsula. But in reality, a channel of water separated it from the mainland.

A wide channel.

Lucy groaned and pulled on the straps of her pack. She was sweaty and felt the beginnings of a sunburn. She wasn't at all prepared for an obstacle like this.

"Maybe we can swim across?" Pete said, squinting into the sea breeze. He didn't sound happy about the prospect.

Lucy had been studying the water with a sinking feeling.

She did not want to admit to Pete that she was a weak—as in terrible—swimmer.

But maybe they wouldn't have to swim after all. "Look!" she said, pulling him over to her vantage point.

Half uncovered by the waves, a narrow bridge of sea rock stretched like a ribbon from the beach to the Thumb. It was thinnest at the middle, suggesting somehow that the Thumb was breaking away—by inches—making a centuries-long escape.

"The tide's coming in," Pete observed after watching the waves.

Lucy forgot that she was tired and her feet ached. "Then let's hurry."

They scrambled down the slope, slipping and crashing, until they reached the small, curved beach that the Thumb sheltered from the full force of the sea.

All that separated them from their goal were about two hundred feet of ocean-slicked rock and tide pools.

They started across. In the afternoon sunlight, the black rock looked almost beautiful. Sprays of mist wreathed the sea bridge with rainbows. Starfish, anemones, and mussels were bright spots of color at their feet. The weakened tide groaned as it splashed and sucked through the pools. Above them loomed the grim cliffs of the Thumb, but Lucy was too concerned with where she put her feet to notice.

They were not quite halfway across when they reached a sheer expanse of rock, slippery as ice. Ahead, Lucy could see the bridge narrow to a sliver, in some places less than a foot wide.

On either side, the sea chopped eagerly against the rock, breaking over the top and pulling at their feet. Lucy shuddered. She was having trouble in her smooth-soled boots.

"What's the matter?" Pete asked, straddling a gap in the rock. Somehow he was able to keep his balance on the slick, green-black sea algae that covered the bridge.

She pressed her lips together tightly, never taking her eyes off her feet. "I can't swim."

Pete started picking his way back toward her. "That's why I recommend staying on the rock."

"Good advice." She tried to laugh.

A second later she slipped and went down on one knee. One hand splashed into the sea and suddenly her arm was in the water to her elbow. Her heavy pack twisted. She could feel its weight working to topple her sideways into the chilly waves, when Pete grabbed her other arm and pulled her up. Her blood was pounding.

"All right?" he asked. His green-gray eyes stared into hers, but for the moment she couldn't speak; she was too shaken. She stared fixedly at the cliffs ahead and tried to calm her racing heart.

"I'll help you across, okay?" He sounded calm and confident.

She nodded gratefully.

Pete started off.

She had just caught her breath when the arrow hit.

8

The arrow sank deep into Pete's pack. Lucy was absolutely still, every sensation crystallized—her pounding heart, the tension in her legs, the vibration of the shaft.

It was fletched with black feathers.

Pete's face was paper white.

And then time unfroze. "Are you hit?" Lucy reached for him, forgetting about her precarious footing on the sea bridge. She nearly fell again before getting her balance.

Pete shook his head. He was staring over her shoulder. She turned and followed his gaze to the shore.

Three men stood there, capes of black feathers rippling around their shoulders. One man held a raven on his forearm. The air thickened with menace, and Lucy's chest tightened.

"They have guns." She could see the long snouts of their rifles.

"I noticed," Pete said. He brushed his hair back from his eyes and took the deep breaths of someone consciously trying to steady himself.

"Did they shoot an arrow just to get our attention?" She

stared uneasily at the long black shaft. From where she stood, it looked like Pete had been shot in the back.

"I'll take it over a bullet, that's for sure." His jaw hardened as he faced the men.

Lucy didn't believe it was possible for a person to sound so casual after having an arrow shot at him. This was a side of Pete she hadn't seen before. He sniffed and stood straighter, apparently showing the men they'd have to do better than that to ruffle him.

While they'd been talking the men stood waiting, stern and impassive, their capes flapping in the wind. The raven man gestured with his hand.

"They want us back on shore." She squinted over her shoulder at the Thumb. "And we're so close." But not close enough to run for it, nor to jump off the bridge and swim.

The wind tousled Pete's hair, which shone chestnut in the sun.

"I knew that raven was trouble," he muttered. But there was nothing they could do about it now. Holding on to each other, Lucy and Pete made their way back across the slippery tide pools. Her legs were shakier going back, and the return journey was long and slow.

They splashed the final yards of the channel. Lucy's dungarees were wet to the knees, so heavy and stiff she felt as if she were walking through freezing mud. She hadn't even considered the possibility that they'd be stopped from going to the

Thumb—everything they'd heard had been about how people stayed away.

Under their feather capes the men were muscular and compact. They wore dungarees and flannel shirts much like Pentlanders, only their flannels were beaded with designs: wolves, eagles, whales. The man who'd shot the arrow yanked it out of Pete's pack and returned it to his quiver.

She stood shivering as the men examined their things, dumping their packs on the wet sand. At their backs the sea bridge slowly sank under the incoming tide. Pete stood beside her, eyes glittering and jaw clamped, while the Lupines admired his knife. After some argument among them it went to the man with the raven, who appeared to be in charge. The ghost sweeper caused great interest and discussion in Lupine, which of course she couldn't understand. Lucy was afraid they'd take it as a prize, but the men appeared reluctant to handle it. At last one of them replaced it in her pack, holding it out warily, the way one might a snake or other dangerous creature.

"You are in Lupine territory," the raven man said, his voice retaining the harsh accent of the Lupines.

"We're searching for my father," Lucy said, fretting her hands together. She had a foolish hope the men would take pity on them.

The man with the raven examined her while the bird hopped to his shoulder and gave a raucous caw. "You go the wrong way."

"No, actually, we're on the right track. My father—"

They didn't listen. One of the men hiked her hands behind her and tied her wrists with leather straps. Another tried to do the same with Pete, but he resisted.

"What do you think you're doing? We're from Pentland. You can't treat us this way." Pete tried to twist out of their grasp.

Without a thought the man cuffed Pete hard by the ear, sending him staggering to his knees, his skin red with outrage. Behind him the waves crashed, the sea growing bigger on the tide.

Lucy stifled a cry. The men's eyes were hard, merciless. He might be brave, but Pete had been foolish not to see this in their expressions.

We could be killed, she realized. No one knew where they were. Pete's parents thought they were on a train riding south. A sickening sense of vulnerability filled her and she looked over at Pete. But he had a fierce, contained expression, as if it was taking all his strength to deal with the pain in his cheek. This time his wrists were bound without complaint.

Then they were prodded with a rifle butt in their backs and made to walk ahead of the raven men. They marched east, going farther away from the Thumb with each step.

"Where are you taking us?" she got up the nerve to ask. Another prod with the rifle—that was their answer.

At a bright and stony river they crossed a covered wooden bridge, its entrance carved like a wolf's open mouth. She shot a worried look at Pete as they stepped past the wolf's spiked wooden teeth. But he was still closed off, dull.

"Are you all right?" she whispered in the dark of the bridge, their echoing footsteps covering her voice.

He grunted in reply. And then they were across the river and facing a low bank of prairie grass. Over it gray billows of fog caught, carded like wool, on totem pole spikes.

They followed the river's course into a valley. Ranged above them on the hillsides among the giant trunks of trees were the Lupines' massive lodges, frowning down upon them. The buildings were rough hewn and ancient looking, each with a terrible painted face on its front, their eaves dripping with ghostly moss.

As they went on, it became clear they were approaching no mere village, but a large settlement, perhaps the Lupine capital. It wasn't like any town Lucy had been in before—the strange and the familiar so mixed together as to be thoroughly disorienting.

Several times they had to stand aside for great wagons pulling logs or machinery. She hadn't realized that the Lupines would have so much industry. A team of donkeys passed, slowly hauling a saw-toothed wheel as tall as a house. Behind them came a sight that made Lucy stop in surprise: a gleaming automobile, driving slowly on the rutted road. She'd seen horseless carriages before, but only on the streets of San Francisco.

She stared after the automobile, only to turn to see a group of men with wolf headdresses covering their faces and bands of ammunition crisscrossing their chests. Women in elaborate beaded collars hung strips of pink fish on racks to dry in the sun. An old man in a litter of furs was pulled by two wolvish dogs in harness. (Lucy hoped they were dogs.) He cackled at them crazily and waved a long pipe, while beside him in the litter several smaller dogs popped up their heads from their nests in the fur. The litter went over a bump and the old man's head lolled like a rag doll's until he was pulled out of sight. Coming from another direction were a band of children back from foraging, carrying heaps of roots, baskets of berries, and rabbits hanging from leather straps.

The leader of the raven men prodded Lucy to get her moving again. They passed a laundry, smelling of soap and lye. A busy general store had axes in the window and wagons out front. A schoolhouse flew two flags: The topmost was the handprint and thunderbird of the First Peoples's Federation, while the bottom was the howling wolf of the Lupine Nation. She stayed too long looking at what appeared to be a newspaper office, with a printing press and broadsheets hung in the windows, trying to puzzle out the stories from the few English words that appeared among the Lupine.

But then the leader pushed her again, and they went along a dark path to a massive lodge, far grander than any of the others. Three faces were painted on its front in stark white and black and red, and an aura of power came from them, almost as if living spirits were trapped in the painted forms.

Lucy looked at Pete anxiously. She wanted to reach for his hand . . . but to her shame the presence of the raven men cowed her, and instead she put her hands into her pockets.

They passed inside to a vast open space under a roof of giant kodok beams. Along the sides a maze of rooms and hallways were made from hanging animal skins set in wooden frames. Preparations for something important were underway, for there was bustle everywhere. Cooks were working at a stone hearth set at the very end of the lodge; in the central area others were putting out plank tables and piles of furs.

The guards pushed them down one busy passage. Lucy gawked at mysterious glimpses of the rooms hidden behind the leather curtains: children playing, a woman braiding her hair, an old man sleeping under a striped blanket.

From the other end of the passage a girl came toward them. Unlike the other Lupine women who wore long dresses in the settler style, she looked like a huntress, wearing a short tunic over rust-colored leggings, a knife hanging from her belt, a leather bag slung across one shoulder. A very successful huntress—the gold and bright charms she wore caught Lucy's eyes at once. And there was something familiar in the proud tilt of her head. She was walking briskly, just about to turn a corner.

"Niwa!" Lucy cried out before the girl could disappear. For the first time since they'd been captured she felt some hope.

The girl turned, surprise and recognition in her eyes. "Lucy?"

For a split second, Niwa's face lit up in a smile. Then, as she saw the raven men, her expression turned cool and forbidding. Her mouth compressed into a line, eyes like blades. She let loose a string of rapid questions in Lupine.

The raven men answered hesitantly, with uneasy glances at one another. They were nervous, even a little scared of Niwa. And seeing this, Lucy was both proud that she knew the girl, and worried, too, remembering the way the lumberjacks on the train had been afraid they'd offended her.

Niwa had grown impatient with what the men were telling her.

"Now what is this?" Niwa asked Lucy. "You were on the sea bridge. Why?" The gold cuffs around her wrists gleamed as she crossed her arms.

Pete spoke up. "That's our business." He stood close to Lucy; he was protecting her, she realized . . . which was sweet of him, but unnecessary.

"We can talk to her, Pete," Lucy said. "She's the girl I was telling you about. The one I met on the train."

The leader of the raven men—perhaps sensing that he was about to lose control of his prisoners—barked, "We take them to Arekwoy." He pulled roughly on Lucy's arm and his henchmen grasped Pete.

"No, you do not," Niwa said haughtily. "I can do that myself." She followed this with something quick and dismissive in Lupine. With angry looks the raven men turned and walked away.

They were free. Lucy heaved a deep breath. "Thank you." Niwa would get them out of here. "I don't know what we would have done if we hadn't seen you." There was so much to tell her. And so much she wanted to ask. "I don't know why those men stopped us. We were just—"

Niwa quickly raised a hand. "Don't speak here," she said in a rasping whisper. She looked up and down the corridor. "Follow me."

The Lupine girl swept ahead down the leather-paneled corridor . . . Presumably she was leading them to the exit? Lucy felt the first twinge of doubt.

Pete muttered, "Don't think we've got a choice." He fell in line behind Lucy and they followed Niwa through the maze of hallways.

They came to an opening in the skin wall. Niwa stopped with her hand on the flap as if compelled to make some explanation for her behavior. "The red sickness has spread so far the clan leaders have come together to decide what to do," she said. "That you are here and coming from the sea bridge at this time . . . Some will see a meaning in that and try to use it." Her eyes lowered. Then, as if not trusting herself to say more, Niwa lifted the edge for them.

There was an instant before they ducked beneath the skin curtain that Lucy and Pete looked at each other. *How could their presence on the sea bridge mean anything to the Lupines?*

There was no chance to talk. They entered a room so large and packed with curiosities, Lucy had the oddest sense they'd entered a Lupine museum.

But no. In the center a man sat at a desk, writing. Lucy was aware of several things at once. He was in a wheelchair and was old—gray braids came nearly to his elbows—and yet, despite that, she had the impression that he was the most important person in this lodge.

Around him the room was cluttered with shiny, obviously precious things scattered carelessly about: crystal goblets jumbled on a shelf and silver platters stacked like newspapers. But here and there were a few old and rather used-looking objects. A ratty feathered headdress hung on one wall next to a dusty mask. And Lucy, who had seen ceremonial artifacts before, guessed that these were the room's real treasures.

As they came in, the man looked up. "What's this? Who are these children?" He had piercing eyes, so dark they appeared black, which shone from under the brim of his homburg hat. Around his neck he wore an elaborate necklace of polished wood and shell.

Niwa answered. "This is Lucy, from the train. And . . ." She frowned at Pete.

"And I'm Pete Knightly," Pete said, planting his feet apart and crossing his arms, "from Pentland." He had taken in the room in big, wary sweeps.

The old man regarded them without surprise . . . but without any detectable welcome, either. "I am Governor Arekwoy, leader of the Lupine Nation," he said with stiff formality. "Are you the reason my daughter has not yet changed clothes for dinner tonight?"

Daughter! Lucy looked at Niwa, the Lupine girl standing so straight and poised, her long dark hair with its woven charms framing her face. Lucy had thought the girl held herself like a queen—she wasn't that far off.

"Greetings, Governor," Lucy said with a curtsy, although she felt ridiculous executing such a movement in her thick dungarees and soggy shirt. Her thoughts were racing—*be polite, diplomatic, flattering, but not overtly fawning . . . help!* Was there a certain protocol for talking to First Peoples heads of state? Probably, although she didn't know it. She would have to hope for the best. "We didn't mean to delay your daughter, sir, but our business can't wait."

"You were on our land without permission," the governor said, studying them as if they presented a particularly vexing puzzle. "What's more you were caught trying to go to a place that has been forbidden to our people for generations."

Lucy felt a weight settle on her as she realized what his words meant. The governor already knew where they'd been trying to go and the raven men were *his* men. Now she understood why Niwa had looked so troubled.

Governor Arekwoy clasped his hands together. "Traditionally the penalty for trying to cross the sea bridge has been death."

Death.

"Just for crossing that little bit of rock?" Lucy burst out before she could stop herself. She paced to the edge of the governor's desk. It was covered in neat stacks of paper, and a carved stone fetish of a bear stood at one corner. "Yes," the governor said coldly. Even the deep wrinkles in his cheeks seemed to contract with disapproval. "Death. That is how serious an offense you have committed. But we are in the modern world and no longer punish trespassers in that manner." He sighed, perhaps regretting this. "You will spend the night in my lodge. In the morning I will send you home to your families."

He bent once again to the document he'd been reading,

picked up his pen, and gave his signature with a flourish. The nib scratched violently against the paper—the only indication he gave of being annoyed.

"Excuse me," Lucy said, feeling her cheeks grow hot. "But you have to let us cross that bridge, sir." She twisted her hands together as if they could hold back the outburst that was building.

Niwa stepped forward on silent feet and put a warning hand on Lucy's shoulder.

"Have to?" he asked icily. "Why is that?" He looked down his nose at Lucy and she felt herself quail under his gaze.

Lucy swallowed. "My father went there, sir. William Darrington, the inventor."

Governor Arekwoy shook his head. "The bridge is guarded. You must look for him somewhere else."

"No, he's there all right," Lucy said stubbornly. Here she went, contradicting the head of the Lupine Nation, but Lucy felt more sure of herself now that she was talking about her father. "He's resourceful. Once, we were trying to get to a haunted fort in Florida—only it was surrounded by swampland just crawling with alligators. And you know what? He talked a carnival into lending us a hot-air balloon and we *flew* to the fort. So I know he's on the Thumb, sir, sea bridge or not."

But the governor was not moved by stories of hot-air balloons. "It does not matter. There are other ways there, but they all bring death." For the first time the governor looked at her with a measure of compassion.

It lasted only a second, however. He turned to his daughter. "Take them away."

Niwa pressed her lips together and shot an agonized look at Lucy. Then the same girl who had tossed her head and told Lucy she would live her own way nodded obediently. "Yes, Father."

"No, wait." Lucy had to think of something. She remembered what Niwa had said: *The red sickness has spread to the trees down the coast.* She blurted out, "There's dreamwood on the Thumb and it's the cure for Rust."

Niwa startled. Governor Arekwoy said something under his breath that sounded like a curse. If Lucy didn't know dreamwood was so valuable she would have thought he was frightened.

Maybe they didn't believe her. "I'll prove it to you," Lucy said, feeling desperate.

Lucy dug through her pack and produced the vitometer. She held the brass disc on the palm of her hand, and felt its mysterious whir, as if a bird were trapped inside. Solemnly, Lucy raised the lid revealing an ivory face, like a clock's, inscribed with spidery black markings. A thin brass needle hovered above the surface, then began a tentative dance, ticking over the compass points.

Niwa and Pete huddled around her, and even the governor—although at first reluctant—leaned forward in his seat to see.

"This is an instrument my father made to measure changes in life energy," she told them. "According to his notes, dreamwood carries a very high charge, more than anything he's ever seen."

After a moment, the needle settled, although the disc continued to vibrate.

"Which direction is this?" Lucy asked.

"The direction of the setting sun," Niwa said, shooting a significant glance toward her father.

"You see!" Lucy exclaimed. "West, the direction of the Thumb. The closer we get, the more it will vibrate. It will lead us to dreamwood *and* my father."

The two Lupines were silent. Seeing their expressions, Lucy closed the disc. What was wrong?

"Don't you want there to be dreamwood?" she asked, slumping inside her shapeless clothes.

"Dreamwood." Governor Arekwoy rubbed his hands together in a gesture that made him suddenly look old. "You should call it nightmare. We believe—we fear—that one tree remains. But such a tree is more dangerous than you can imagine."

Lucy didn't understand. Dreamwood—she still remembered her first sip of Ulfric's tea, the glistening web that made his toys move—was wonderful.

"But dreamwood heals," she said, turning to look between Niwa and her father.

"Yes," Niwa said, her slender neck glowing in the lamplight. "His-sey-ak could help us."

"His-sey-ak destroys." Governor Arekwoy looked at them from under the brim of his hat. His eyes fell upon Niwa, and Lucy had the impression this conversation was something he long dreaded. "That is dreamwood's name in our language.

The name of the dreamwood spirit. *He* is the Devil of Devil's Thumb."

Lucy could feel her mouth hang open stupidly. This made no sense. And just as it made no sense, at the same time it brought up old memories of the Maran Boulder—the ancient hunger she'd felt coming from the rock, a sense of something alien and dangerous. But dreamwood wasn't like that at all. She was going to tell the governor so, when the flap to the room opened and a man came in, bowing his head and saying something in Lupine.

The Governor listened, then nodded. "I must go," he told them. He wheeled himself from around his desk, his broad upper body dwarfing two thin and childlike legs.

As he left he turned around one last time. He spoke to his daughter. "Send them home."

9

The creak of the governor's wheelchair faded away. The three of them were left in the room with its strange, half-shadowed treasures and lamplight as rich as gold.

Lucy looked quickly at Pete. They could not get sent back. He nodded at her. So they were decided, then.

"We're leaving," she told Niwa. "But we're not going back to Pentland."

"And don't try to stop us," Pete said. He stepped behind a wooden music stand, as if that would defend him.

Niwa looked between the two of them, tilting her sleek dark head to the side. "Do not think you have to fight me, settlers." She gave the faintest hint of a smile. "I am coming with you."

In her relief Lucy almost knocked over the carved stone bear on the governor's desk. "You are?" Lucy broke into a grin.

"You are?" Pete furrowed his brow.

"Yes—"

Voices sounded outside the passageway, and for a moment the three of them froze. But whoever was talking passed them by.

Niwa continued more softly, drawing closer to them; she smelled of wild sage and soft leather. "Do you know what is happening here? They are meeting in council to decide whether to cut all our trees. Nobody knows what to do. My father wants to wait. Maybe the red sickness will slow down and kill not so many trees. But others say it is already too late. I will go with you and stop it."

Lucy was pleased—if a bit taken aback by Niwa's certainty. After all, Pete had laughed at her the first time she'd told him of her theory. But the Lupine girl seemed perfectly convinced.

"Your father seemed like he didn't want to believe me," Lucy remarked, hoping Niwa would offer an explanation for the governor's behavior. She could understand that a nature spirit lived in dreamwood—that was like the Maran Boulder. But she didn't understand why the governor had called the dreamwood spirit a devil.

"Yes," Niwa said brusquely. "Many people are afraid of His-sey-ak. He used to allow people to live with him. But now my father thinks he wants them to die."

Lucy shot a quick glance at Pete, who now looked as if he needed the music stand to steady himself. "That seems like a good reason to be afraid . . ." Lucy began hesitantly. She stopped when she saw what Niwa was doing.

The Lupine girl had unslung from her shoulder the leather bag that she wore, and to Lucy's surprise began to fill it with precious objects. "Help me," she said, looking up at Lucy.

Pete went right to the skin door, clearly not liking this new development. If they were already in trouble for trying to cross the sea bridge, how would the governor react if they were caught stealing from his office? He raised his eyebrows significantly at Lucy.

"Niwa, what are you doing?" Lucy asked, taking a cautious step toward her.

"We must have offerings," Niwa replied as if this were obvious. She stepped lightly around the room like a cat burglar, quickly sweeping up whatever valuables she could find. Eagle feathers, a carved stone whale, a small dagger with a jewel-encrusted hilt. She stood for a moment in front of a glass-fronted cabinet and scrutinized its contents.

"Offerings for what?" Lucy asked uneasily. Ulfric had said nothing about making offerings.

Niwa ignored her. Reaching into the cabinet she brought out a small porcelain figurine. It was a laughing shepherdess in a froth of pastel petticoats and ribbons.

"Is this precious?" she demanded of Lucy, waving the little shepherdess in the air. "Does it have power? A duke sent it from France so I hope it has something. It is pointless otherwise."

Lucy felt woefully unprepared to comment on the figurine's power—or lack thereof. She crinkled her nose and tried to think of the correct response. What was one to make of such a dainty, delicate thing except that whoever made it had no idea what a shepherdess actually looked like? "I don't know. But it's probably worth a lot."

"Hm." After a moment's consideration, Niwa put it back on

the shelf and examined some silver cutlery. She swept the larger pieces into her sack and then took it all to her father's desk, where she began to go through it, looking at the same time both girlish and fierce—like a teenage pirate chief.

Lucy's anxiety grew and she tugged at the buttons on her flannel shirt. "Niwa, we should go."

"Yes. Yes." Niwa hooked one gleaming lock of hair behind her ear. "Don't you have anything?" She looked pointedly at Lucy and Pete.

Pete squirmed like someone with fleas. "Erm, to offer? We still have some money, I guess." He looked at Lucy and shrugged. He stood by the door, ready to make a quick exit if necessary.

"And I've got some of my father's instruments," Lucy said, even though she did not want to contribute them.

To her relief, Niwa frowned in a way that told Lucy these offerings would not be acceptable.

"Perhaps what I bring will be enough." Her glossy brows flexed like bird wings. Then, making a quick decision, she wrenched off one of her gold wrist cuffs and added it to her plunder.

"But *why* do we need offerings?" Lucy asked in frustration.

Niwa's dark eyes widened in surprise at the note of protest in Lucy's voice. "How much do you know about dreamwood?"

"It's better than gold," Pete said from the door.

"It gives you strength and hope," Lucy said quickly; she didn't want Pete to appear crass. "And it's a carrier for spirit energy."

"Those things are true, but there is much more than that."

Niwa stood up and again a slightly mischievous smile flickered across her face. "I'll show you."

Reluctantly Pete left his station by the exit, and he and Lucy followed Niwa to a corner of the room dominated by a large armoire, inlaid with chevrons of ivory and a polished black wood. Stealthily the Lupine girl bent to its lower half, unlatching the door. A squat metal safe lay behind it.

With the air of a magician about to perform a dazzling trick, Niwa produced a key from a cord around her neck and fitted it into the lock.

Inside were stacked trays of black velvet. The first contained an oblong wooden mask with a severe expression. The face was vaguely human, with empty black eyes. The wood was soft and creamy looking and shone like gold.

Only it wasn't gold. Lucy could feel that from two feet away. She swallowed, feeling a slight buzzing in her ears as if the sound of the blood rushing through her body had been amplified a hundred times.

Pete crouched down, his mouth agape. "That's a fortune right there," he said with a gulp.

"Several times a fortune," Niwa said matter-of-factly. "And it is just one of many things our people used to have. The shamans of our people would wear this and heal the sick. My father was born with legs too weak to carry him, but he would have been dead without this mask. The wood is magic."

"Why don't you bring that as an offering?" Pete suggested. "That's got to be the best thing here. You could buy the whole territory with that." Unable to help himself, he reached out and touched the mask.

Niwa whisked it out of his reach. "Would you offer someone the body of their own child?" She acted as if she'd never heard of anything so barbaric.

Pete's face went bright red. "No, of course not."

"That is what I would do if I gave this to His-sey-ak." Niwa flashed in outrage. "He is the oldest tree, the first tree, and the other dreamwoods were his children."

Pete got interested in the floor. "How would I know that?" he protested quietly to Lucy. "Pancake Walapush never said anything about any of this."

Niwa put the mask aside impatiently. "This is not what I am showing you, settler. Look!"

On the tray beneath the mask was a book—a very old book from the looks of it. The cover was of thick tooled leather. Niwa brought it out and sat down cross-legged. Lucy sat beside her, close enough to brush the soft fringe of the Lupine girl's tunic with her hand. Pete, hesitating a moment, folded his legs underneath him. Niwa held the book on her lap and opened it reverently, revealing parchment pages with finely detailed illustrations and writing in a gothic script Lucy associated with illuminated manuscripts she'd seen in museums. Lucy squinted and puzzled over the words, but couldn't read them.

"*This* is what I want to show," Niwa said. "This is the *Codex Saarthensis*—the oldest book in the territories. The sailor who came here made these pictures."

"Denis Saarthe drew these?" Lucy stared mesmerized as Niwa turned the pages of the centuries-old book. Fantastic pictures paraded across the yellowed parchment: giant wolves with long curving fangs, trees with faces.

"And what language is this?" Lucy asked Niwa, creeping closer.

"A settler language I cannot read." The Lupine girl turned another page. In the dim lamplight the colors seemed to glow with the intensity of stained glass. "I thought maybe you could."

That was certainly a flattering hope. Lucy yearned to read obscure languages. A family friend studied Etruscan inscriptions on sarcophagi thousands of years old. But Lucy was too impatient for such things; as yet, her language abilities were limited to saying it was a fine day in French. She hiked her shoulders, admitting she could make no sense of it.

And then with a sly look Niwa turned the page—something in her movement suggesting she knew that what she was about to show them would get their attention.

Pete leaned forward, his mouth open.

"Wait a minute." Lucy felt dizzy. The double-face illustration showed a beautiful tree, the bottom half of the spread taken up by its roots. And among its roots were clearly, unmistakably, body parts—legs, hands, feet . . . faces.

"How do you call things that eat meat?" Niwa asked Lucy coolly, as if the question were of purely academic interest.

"*Carnivorous,*" Lucy replied automatically. At least she could give the right answer.

"Yes." Niwa nodded, satisfied to have the correct word for the horror they stared at in the shimmering picture. Denis Saarthe had painted the tree's skin with an ink that made it shine like old gold. "Dreamwood is *carnivorous*. In older times the people may have sacrificed to His-sey-ak. I think this is what this page says. My father will not tell me. He wants me to be by his side and take on his duties, but then fathers will keep secrets."

Or they'll make sure you're NOT by their side, and still keep secrets. Lucy tugged so hard at the buttons of her flannel shirt that one popped off and plinked to the floor. Her father might have thought to make a mention of this detail in his notes. Which was worse? That he knew dreamwood was dangerous and kept it hidden? Or that he went to the Thumb in ignorance of dreamwood's true nature?

"It ate people," Pete said weakly. He looked around the room as if hoping to find someone as alarmed by this as he was. "Jumping bullfrogs, it ate people."

"She just told us she doesn't know if that's what it actually says." Fear made Lucy irritable.

"Well, that's sure what it looks like." Pete stood up and paced with his hands on his hips. "Whoo boy."

"This is why we need offerings." Niwa raised an eyebrow. "*In case.*"

"Whoo boy," Pete repeated. He stood in front of one of the display cabinets and looked bleakly at the treasures inside. "That's all I'll say."

"Good," Niwa concluded, studying him as if she found him

an intriguing but ultimately unsatisfactory specimen. "I do not wish you to say more." She shut the book and carefully returned it to its tray.

Lucy put her face in her hands. *Dreamwood was wonderful,* she told herself. *It could never be like the tree in the picture. That was a monster. Her tree—the tree her father had gone to find—was going to heal the forests and save everyone.*

There were noises outside the passageway. They heard voices and the creak of a wicker wheelchair. With her eyes wide, Niwa hurriedly replaced the mask, shut the safe, and locked the cabinet. She darted soundlessly to her father's desk and retrieved her bag. There was an exit on the other side of the room. She motioned for them to follow her and they had just enough time to slip out before the governor returned.

Niwa led Lucy and Pete through the bewildering skin passageways of the governor's lodge. The three of them were silent, and Lucy was sunk deep in thought, the brilliant, monstrous pictures never far out of mind. Governor Arekwoy's words echoed in her head: *You should call it nightmare.*

But you always knew going to the Thumb would be dangerous, she told herself. *Why does some picture in an old book make it worse?* Except that it did. She wondered if the pictures made Pete nervous, too.

She didn't even notice that Niwa had stopped. They were in a dark, narrow corridor away from the bustling center of the lodge. "Here," Niwa said, her hand on a gap in the leather.

They passed through a flap in the wall and into a small room. A bed piled high with furs and blankets was in one corner; in another was a bookshelf with a handful of leather-bound volumes along with scrolls of thin bark. A bow and quiver were propped against the bed. Lucy assumed this was Niwa's room. At another time, she would have explored it eagerly. Now she felt too demoralized to do more than stand in the center and await her next instruction.

"You may sit." The Lupine girl indicated the furs.

Pete sat down warily as if expecting a trap; Lucy flopped down, not caring how she appeared. She was exhausted.

Niwa crossed her arms over her huntress's tunic. For the first time she appeared uncertain. Maybe she realized now how much she had shocked and unsettled them with her revelations. Her proud features softened and an expression that was almost apologetic came over her face. "I will get you some food," she said after a moment and left them, bowing her head ever so slightly.

"I really wish I hadn't seen that," Pete confessed. He looked hollowed out.

Lucy took a deep breath and turned on her elbow among the furs. She had to know at once how Pete felt. "You're not thinking of turning back, are you?"

"What?" he gave her a look that said *are you crazy?* "Of course not. What about you?"

Lucy was more relieved than she'd expected. She tugged her hair back into a braid and sat up. "Well, I'm going on. I've dealt with nature spirits before. If His-sey-ak is the spirit in the last dreamwood, he's no different from the Maran Boulder." She thrust her nose into the air, trying to disguise her unease with bravado.

"Wasn't that the rock that almost swallowed you?" Pete asked with narrow eyes.

"*No.* I slipped and got stuck. I was never in any danger."

Pete pressed his mouth into a line. Lucy didn't think he was convinced.

"You can't go putting stock in *legends*," Lucy said, trying to dismiss Saarthe's book as nothing more than folklore.

"Who knows if it's even true." Pete hit his knee a couple of times as if to bang away his doubts.

"Exactly." Lucy leaned back on the furs.

"And Denis Saarthe had to be crazy anyway," Pete said. "The story they always tell about him is how he fell off his ship because he was drunk. Course he was pretty good at painting. I sure didn't expect that much, er, detail."

His shoulders sank and he stared at his feet.

"Hey," Lucy said, peering closely at Pete's cheek. His rosy skin was dappled with golden-brown freckles. "Is this the side where you got hit?"

He looked startled to have her so close, but didn't move away. Instead he brought up one brown hand and stroked his cheek wonderingly. "Yes," he said slowly, "but now it's like it didn't even happen."

A look passed between them, both of them slightly awed. "It was that mask," Lucy said with certainty. "It healed you."

"Do you think?" Pete kneaded his cheek, harder this time just to make sure. "All I did was touch it once."

"Absolutely." Lucy sat back watching Pete—he was going to hurt his cheek all over again if he didn't look out. Her fears about the pictures in the *Codex Saarthensis* retreated. If dreamwood could heal Pete like that, surely it wouldn't harm them.

At that moment, Niwa returned carrying bowls of a thin charbroiled meat, berries mashed into a paste with nuts, and bunches of leafy greens.

"We eat," she told them.

Here was one order they were both happy to follow.

Lucy didn't realize how famished she was until she licked the last bit of berry paste from her fingers. She put down her bowl, feeling steadier now that she'd eaten, only to find Niwa eyeing her critically.

"I must find you traveling clothes," the Lupine girl concluded. "Our way will be difficult and what you wear is not sufficient."

Lucy could not agree more. Although she rarely got to indulge in them, she loved clothes, and she especially admired Niwa's, which were beautifully made but also functional and comfortable looking. Here at least was one benefit of having been captured by Lupines.

Niwa went to a handsome kodok wood trunk at the foot of her bed. She opened it and began a violent rummage through its contents, tossing out bits of rope, some leather pouches, and several small weapons.

"We cannot go by the sea bridge," Niwa said, continuing her

search. "It is guarded. Doubly guarded after what you told my father. Many people fear the place, fear what lives there. They keep watch on it always."

Lucy did not want to encounter the raven men again. "So how do we get there?"

"We go by boat," Niwa said simply. This seemed reasonable to Lucy, so she was surprised when Pete dropped his bowl on the floor.

Pete had gone very still. "No," he said. "Wait a minute." He turned to Lucy. "Five years ago a Russian schooner got lost in the fog and sailed too close to shore. Now there's a place they call Bone Beach because of all the bits of those poor fellows that washed up."

Niwa shrugged as if to say those Russian sailors merely got what they deserved. "That was in the month you call September. The spith are hungry then."

"Oh, they're always hungry," Pete said. He got up from the furs, shaking his head. "Snakes," he clarified for Lucy. "Sea serpents. They use the beaches for their spawning grounds. That's why we need the railroad. You can't do anything by sea." He turned to Niwa. "Going by boat's a good way to get us killed."

Sea serpents? Really? But then Lucy remembered Ulfric's story about Denis Saarthe, *the only one to have survived the wreck of his ship by sea serpents.*

"There are strange, backward people who live on the coast," Niwa explained, pausing from her search of the trunk. "The Ss'til. Cheaters, thieves, gamblers. Lupines let them have their territory, but they have no gratitude and no manners. They do not like us."

"Can't imagine why not," said Pete under his breath.

"They make a little business selling oil from the snakes. We use it for light," Niwa continued, pretending not to have heard him. She pointed out the lamp that cast a genie's glow over the room. "But there are no better sailors. If you can find them—and if you can persuade them to take you—they will bring you across the bay."

"And they can really do this?" Lucy asked, lying on her stomach with her elbows plunged deep into furs.

"Of course," Niwa said as if it wasn't worth a second thought. She'd finally found what she was looking for in the trunk. "Here." She tossed Lucy a pale chamois tunic, leggings, and soft-soled chestnut-colored moccasins. "These are mine from many seasons ago. They are yours now."

Her own Lupine clothes. Here was something she much preferred to hearing Pete gripe about sea serpents. Lucy took them gratefully and slipped behind a leather curtain to change. There was no mirror, but the tunic was beautiful. She loved its soft fringed edges, and she was thrilled to be out of the ill-fitting clothes she'd bought in Pentland. Niwa even gave her a deerskin pouch for her vitometer, so she could wear it around her neck like a pendant.

Lucy emerged from behind the curtain, feeling that she'd become someone the world had to reckon with. Not a schoolgirl any longer.

"How do I look?" she asked Pete.

"Hm." Pete shrugged indifferently.

"What?" Lucy asked, running her hand over the smooth leather. "They fit perfectly."

"No, it's just . . ." Pete shifted. His eyes flicked up and down. "You look like you're trying to be someone else."

Lucy sagged. Just who did Pete think she was? Did he suppose she looked more like herself in boys' clothes two sizes too big for her? "Don't be jealous because I get to dress up and you don't."

Niwa frowned as if realizing she'd been a poor hostess. "I can find something for you, too," she told Pete.

"No, no," Pete said quickly. "I'm all right as I am. I like my settler clothes." He put his hands on his chest, protecting his ratty old cotton shirt. He could suit himself, Lucy thought, still feeling strangely let down.

They slept little that night and left Governor Arekwoy's lodge when it was still dark.

Lucy tried not to feel awkward beside Niwa, who moved through the forest with a cat's silent, slinky grace. But at least she didn't make as much racket as Pete, who went crashing along the trail, walking as if he might still be half asleep.

It wasn't until they had crossed the wolf bridge over the river that Lucy began to relax.

They stopped briefly for lunch: smoked salmon Niwa had brought with her from her father's lodge. But it was late in the day when they reached a small cup-shaped grove, protected on several sides by steep rock faces, off which plunged hundreds of waterfalls as delicate as lace.

A secretive mist veiled the trees, giants even by the standards of Saarthe.

The grove was still and quiet, yet not at all sleepy. There was something intensely alive about the place. Lucy looked up into the dizzying heights.

"This is *Gunasho shaleh*," Niwa said, coming to stand next to her. "The grove of the wolf woman."

So this was where Niwa had been coming from the day they'd met on the train. "It's even more beautiful than I imagined," Lucy said.

"Yes, and this is where I would stay," Niwa said with a sigh. The wind stirred her black hair and made the charms woven into it shine like bright jewels. She pointed to a rock with a large crooked crack in it. "In our stories this is where Gunasho the wolf woman first emerged into this world. But I am afraid the red sickness is here, even in this sacred place."

Lucy would not have noticed it if Niwa hadn't mentioned it, but there was a faint smell of decay in the air: the rotten scent of Rust.

"They will cut this place away with all the rest," Niwa said. Her beautiful face looked older as she turned to face the towering kodoks.

Lucy thought of her first glimpse of Niwa: She'd been so proud and wild, with her bow and arrows, her hunter's tunic, and her dislike for school. If a place could ever be a part of a person, the forest was part of Niwa.

"I thought the Lupines didn't have Rust," Pete admitted. His mouth gave a sideways lurch of embarrassment. "Sorry."

Niwa faced Pete. The fierceness in her eyes softened. "We are suffering just like you. I've told my father before we should ask His-sey-ak for help," she continued in her raspy Lupine voice. "His-sey-ak is the reason we survived the settler diseases while the other peoples of the coast sickened and died. The golden wood healed us. We traded his wood with other nations and became rich. He gave us power so our warriors turned into wolves that no bullets could hit. Always he has protected us. So now when the red sickness is in our forests, His-sey-ak will stop it."

Pete had been listening with an uncomfortable expression on his face. But at that moment he looked up. "Is that a raven?"

A black bird flew across the sky.

Please keep flying, Lucy thought. The three of them were absolutely still, waiting for it to pass.

And then it turned around, heading back for them.

Silently they watched it come closer.

When it was overhead, Niwa grimaced and let out a strange, croaking cry. The bird circled around, cawing to her in reply. And then it flew east, hurrying back to its master.

Niwa's posture—always so straight and controlled—seemed to crumple. "His men are coming," she said with an expression of defeat. "There will be too many to fight. They will be too fast to outrun."

Lucy bent her head, studying her new moccasins. She worried that she particularly played a part in Niwa's assessment of their chances against the raven men.

"What can we do?" Lucy asked. It seemed unfair to have come so far only to be stopped again.

Niwa straightened herself up again. "They will bring me back. I will tell them . . . I will tell them you ran from me," Niwa said, "and I couldn't find you. I don't know where you are."

Lucy thought it unlikely anyone would believe this. But she nodded her head. She supposed Niwa was the one they wanted anyway—Governor Arekwoy's daughter. *Niwa's* father would send raven men after her rather than be parted from her.

Niwa gestured toward a cut in the western hills. "Go through that gap; there is a canyon, follow it. Find the Ss'til in their sea caves on the coast." Her dark eyes were full of emotion, glistening like stones in the rain.

They couldn't give up so easily. They should try to run—together. But even as Lucy thought this, she could see movement along the eastern edge of the forest. Men were emerging from the trees, their black capes fluttering. Five, ten . . . more than ten. And something else was with them, breaking from the shadows with a low-slung stride: dogs . . . though from their long muzzles she thought they might have wolf in them, too.

She watched as the animals jogged ahead, ears up, snouts low and sniffing, tongues lolling out of their mouths in eagerness. Lucy's heart galloped in alarm.

Pete's knuckles on the straps of his pack were white.

Niwa cursed in Lupine, then turned to Lucy and Pete. "You must go. *Now.*"

Lucy stepped toward her, close enough once more to smell her perfume of sage and wilderness. "We'll bring back the cure," she said, embracing Niwa quickly. She hoped the Lupine girl believed her.

"Good-bye. Good luck," Niwa said in a voice that had gone especially rough and raspy. She pressed her palm against Lucy's as they had done once before on the train. And then she walked out to meet her father's men.

10

It was nearly dark when Lucy and Pete reached the coast. Gulls screeched overhead and little plovers darted back and forth across the sand, outrunning the waves. In the fading light, the wet sand near the waterline looked as smooth and glassy as a dark mirror. Here and there, the beach was strewn with long garlands of tobacco-colored kelp. Out bobbing in the crashing surf were the sleek dark heads of seals.

It got colder as the sun dropped. Lucy shivered. They'd made it safely to the coast, but they had no idea where to go next.

There was a boiling hiss in the surf just offshore. Out of the churning froth rose a scaly head as big as a bull's.

A snake's head.

The serpent opened its mouth and one of the seals sloshed into it, disappearing down its black gullet along with a flood of water. There was a booming crash as the snake submerged again.

Beside her Pete shuddered. "And we're supposed to find a boat to take us across that water? There's no way we'll survive."

"Stop it," Lucy snapped. She shared this assessment, of course. But she would stamp out her fears the way one did coals from a fire. "There's a way across and we'll find it."

Pete gave a victimized shrug. His chestnut hair was damp with sea spray. The wind was driving it right to them. "All right, I suppose there is."

"We just have to find the Ss'til." She looked to her left, south: The beach stretched into a vast blackness. The Thumb was that way . . . somewhere. But the other way, north, she could see cliffs rising gray as a shadow kingdom. Niwa said to find the Ss'til in their sea caves.

"That looks like the only place there might be caves." She pointed north. Of course when it came to direction-finding Pete had to have the last word. He stroked his chin and looked up and down the beach several times before finally agreeing that north it was.

They turned right along the beach and began walking toward the cliffs. A freezing wind came off the ocean, and soon Lucy's teeth were chattering. Snake track was everywhere—in wide curving trails through the sand. A couple of times they saw a scaly heap coiled in the surf like a giant mound of glistening beach rubble. After trudging for what felt like several hours, Pete tugged on her arm. "Do you hear that?"

Over the growling sea came the faint strains of music. It was a witchy, dancing tune that made Lucy think of bonfires and tinkers' wagons and the long smoky nights of harvest time back home.

"And look." Lucy pointed just ahead where enormous driftwood logs and large boulders had been dragged up onto the beach to make a series of barriers. The bare driftwood branches looked like the drowned remnants of some vast, silvery forest.

They clambered over the logs and rocks, among the spiky wood, following the sound. When they were on the other side of the barrier they made their way to the nearest cave, from which came a flickering glow and the sound of a fiddle.

Lucy had counted on Niwa being here to deal with the Ss'til, and so, uncharacteristically for her, had asked few questions about the people who lived on the beach. Now she worried that her lack of curiosity was a grave error. *If you can find them and if you can persuade them*, Niwa had said. It looked like they had found them, but it was the second *if* that Lucy worried about.

A strange, translucent curtain covered the cave entrance, blocking the cold wind that came off the ocean. It was snakeskin, twitching and shivering on the night breeze.

They ducked underneath it. The shimmering scales floated closed behind them. They were in a large, sandy grotto that stretched far back into the rocky cliff, in a cave crowded with people who were busily playing music, playing dice, eating, talking, carrying children, and throwing darts. Some, bewilderingly, did all at once. Lantern light cast a rich golden glow across them all. Unlike the Lupines, the Ss'til men kept their hair short, and many had tattoos inked into their dark skin.

A boy who'd been sitting by the entrance saw them and got to his feet. In one hand he carried a long staff of polished driftwood. He had a dagger at his belt as well as another small knife with which he'd been carving.

He was lean and straight with a shock of dark hair. The ragged cape draped over his naked chest was fastened with a gleaming brooch made of abalone shell.

"Well met in this life," he said, approaching them. His teeth were stained a midnight blue, and Lucy tried not to stare at this fantastic adornment. Then he stopped and looked at them quizzically. "Where's your skin?"

"Skin?" Pete blanched.

"For oil," Lucy said, remembering Able Dodd's oilskins the day the Knightlys turned off their electricity.

The boy began to clean his nails with his knife. "Unless you mean to carry oil in your pockets, girl, you need a skin."

A draft came through the snakeskin curtain, and Lucy shivered. She wished Niwa were here; she didn't think this boy would be so disdainful then. "We don't want oil, we're looking for someone to take us across the bay," Lucy said.

"You two, go across the bay? Don't know anything, do you?" The boy had a good laugh. Then he peered at them more closely. "Are you beach haunts, then?" he asked. He raised a lantern up so he could examine them. "You have the look of shipwreck about you. And you're pale like old bones."

"That's because we're cold," Pete said irritably. The snakeskin curtain kept slapping him on the shoulder as it was pushed about by the sea breeze. "We've been out on the beach in the wind."

"Just like a ghost, eh," the boy said. "I hear them out there, complaining of the cold and their seaweed hair. "

Lucy was losing patience with this blue-toothed boy, especially if he thought he could scare her with his silly ghost stories.

"Well, I make ghosts disappear," Lucy said, snapping her fingers. "So they'll make themselves scarce while I'm around."

The boy looked unhappy; she was spoiling his fun. "Fetch your skin, pale," he said rather sullenly, "and I'll get you your oil."

Lucy drew herself up. "I told you, we're not here to buy oil. We've come to hire a boat."

He cocked his head at her. "Ah. But we have no boats for hire." Behind him some of the other Ss'til in the grotto were turning their attention to Lucy and Pete. Their frank stares were making Lucy uncomfortable.

She took a different tack. "I thought the Ss'til were great sailors. Do you mean to tell me that's not true?"

"The best sailors in the world. But it's bad luck to bring *karabeho* on water. The snakes like the taste of their pale meat." He grinned blue.

Pete had been watching this exchange, a look of dull dislike on his face. He must have been as cold and tired as she was. "Come on, Lucy," he said. "I doubt these fellows could pilot a boat across a puddle."

"Get out of here, then, ghost," the boy said. "You are nothing but foul vapors." He flicked his fingers in Pete's face.

Pete reared away but then quickly recovered, clenching his

fist. "I'll show you a ghost," he said. "I bet you never had one give you a black eye before."

"Pete, stop." Lucy clutched his arm, then turned to the boy. "Let us at least talk to someone about it. We have money."

Money—that was the word she should have said from the beginning. Hearing this, the boy shrugged. "If you like." He motioned for them to follow.

Lucy and Pete drew curious glances from the Ss'til as they made their way deeper into the grotto. The musicians and the card players, the mothers and the crones all turned their faces to gaze at them. Lucy couldn't help staring back. Both men and women wore jewelry: necklaces, bracelets in particular, but also piercings through the nose and earlobes. Their clothes were long, dark, iridescent garments, scaled and shimmery. Underneath their ethereal capes, many wore vests of purple mussel shells, which glittered and tinkled as they moved.

The boy led them past several branching passages until they came to a small cavern where they found a tall, heavyset man whose plump rolls of flesh put Lucy in mind of an upright seal. Numerous bone earrings pulled at his earlobes. He wore a necklace of polished shells that shone over the frayed snakeskin collar of his robe.

This man peered at them from heavy-lidded eyes, and Lucy felt it would be dangerous to assume he was as sleepy as he looked.

The boy said something to him in the sibilant language of the Ss'til, and Lucy was almost certain she detected mockery in his tone.

"Sit," the man said. He indicated a nest of sealskins piled on the ground. They all sat down. Next to the man was a carved driftwood platter on which lay strips of a dark and reeking meat. He took a piece of the meat and chewed it slowly, licking his fingers and smacking his lips. His mouth and chin were slick with oil.

Lucy settled cross-legged onto a sealskin beside Pete. Tired as she was she kept her back straight and tried to stay alert. This was the man she needed to convince.

"Pale strangers, you are far from home," he said, making a vague gesture of distance with his hand.

She supposed the thing to do would be to speak in equally flowery language. But she was never good at dancing around what she meant. "We need passage on a boat."

The man raised his eyebrow at this direct approach. "Where would you go?"

A snake oil lantern at the back of the cavern cast dark shadows on the rock walls. Lucy looked him full in the face. "To Devil's Thumb."

The man laughed, and his shells and bones clicked together with a sound like a wind chime in a gentle breeze. "We do not take pale strangers to the cursed place."

The boy grinned as if to say *I told you so*, then scooted close to the plate and thieved a piece of meat, which he stuffed into his cheek.

"You took a man there. Maybe a month ago," she said, gambling that this was the way her father had come.

The man fingered his bone necklace with greasy fingers. "Perhaps," he said. The expression in his heavy-lidded eyes was guarded. "A man who went away in a boat would have paid us well."

Lucy swallowed. So he wouldn't reveal if her father received passage. Still, the important thing to focus on was *paid*.

"We have ten dollars," Pete said. It was all Lucy could do not to groan. Ten dollars was all they had left of Angus Murrain's money. And now they had no bargaining power.

"Ten dollars." The man wiped an eye as if the thought of so mean a payment made him laugh. "You must pay us twenty-five."

"Twenty-five? That's crazy!" Pete sat up in the sealskin; even his freckles seemed to blaze with outrage.

What did Pete expect, having started at ten?

"Ten dollars to take us across," Lucy said firmly. She'd seen her father bargain at many trading posts. He always acted as if he was prepared to walk away if they didn't meet his price. She elbowed Pete. "I'm sure we can find someone else who will take us for less."

The big man didn't like this so well. "But it is very dangerous to cross the sea of snakes." He held out his hands as if *she* were the unreasonable one.

"I told them, the snakes like the meat of settlers most of all," the boy chimed in. His quick fingers darted to the platter again.

Lucy really was beginning to dislike him.

"We can pay you more on the way back," Pete said. He leaned forward earnestly on the sealskin.

This made them laugh.

"The way back?" The boy's eyes sparkled maliciously.

"You think anyone comes back?" The man held the rolling folds of his gut with laughter. Then he belched.

"*We* will," Lucy said, clutching the pouch that held her vitometer. She looked at Pete and he nodded.

"You bet we will," Pete said. "You take us for ten and we'll pay you twenty-five when we return."

Don't get carried away, she wanted to tell Pete.

"If you aren't ghosts now, you soon will be," the boy said with satisfaction. "With spiderwebs for hair and tatters for clothes. Maybe some night I'll see you out on the sands, moaning your laments."

That did it.

"Wait," she said. "I have something to trade for the fare." She reached into her pack and drew out a long cylinder, wrapped in worn blue velvet. Made of brass with ivory inlay, the device inside resembled a spyglass—or it would have, if not for the series of strange interlocking rings about its barrel, engraved with arcane symbols that her father once told her corresponded to the location of certain stars.

"It's an archevisual spectrometer," she explained as she handed it to the big man. "Worth *fifty* dollars. At least."

He studied it without much interest, then handed it back. "No."

"It sees fifteen minutes into the past," she continued. "Like a telescope, but for time." It was another of her father's many inventions, built for the purpose of determining whether household disturbances had been caused by poltergeists. It used to see an hour into the past, but then she had dropped it from her rooftop lookout in Wickham. Her father was always saying he would repair it but never had—presumably to teach her a lesson about spying on the neighbors. Fifteen minutes, however, should be enough.

"Look," she told him, and somehow she put enough steel in her voice that he raised it to his eye.

The man squinted into the eyepiece.

She knew what he would see.

He frowned, glaring at the driftwood platter. The boy had been careful not to take all the meat. Without the spectrometer the man might never have noticed.

The big man's expression changed. First she could see his wonder, then his anger. When he finally put it down he looked like a man who'd made a decision.

"Pale strangers, you have a boat," he said.

Pete's jaw dropped. Then he turned to Lucy with the biggest grin she'd ever seen. For a moment she almost thought he was going to hug her.

"Hm," the big man nodded. "I'll take you now."

As they walked out, he gave the boy a good kick.

"What was that for?" the boy cried.

"Now *he's* moaning *his* laments," Pete noted as they passed out of the cavern.

◆　◆　◆

They were given space in a rocky alcove and told to sleep for a few hours. Even with a pile of sealskins underneath her, Lucy felt the hard-packed sand of the grotto floor, and it seemed like she had barely closed her eyes before they were awakened. It was very late by the time Lucy and Pete followed the Ss'til man out of the grottoes and onto the beach. The surf pounded violently against nearby rocks and the air was freezing. A high, distant moon shone down on them like a cold spotlight.

Ahead of them they could see a black boat pulled onto the sand. A lone boatman in a long black robe was waiting beside it. In one hand he held a tall, hooked pole.

Pete whispered to her, "He looks cheerful."

She eyed the ominous boatman. "As long as he gets us there."

"This is Obwe," said the fat man nervously; he seemed eager to get back to his warm cave. "He will bring you where you want to go."

The two men exchanged quick words in Ss'til. Obwe nodded.

Then, sensing something Lucy could not, both men tensed.

Without a word, Obwe reached over and picked Lucy up under the armpits, heaving her into the boat. She struggled to get her balance, only to fall to the bottom again when Pete was flung in beside her. They were in a hopeless tangle. Obwe pushed the boat into the water, running and picking up speed. The other man was already loping over the sand, surprisingly fast for someone his size, headed for the protective barriers of driftwood.

Lucy disentangled herself from Pete (who seemed to have

many more elbows and knees than a normal person), and raised herself up to sitting. The sea and beach were dark. Her senses firing, she peered into the blackness.

Moving on the beach they had just left was something she'd first thought was a dune. Only, as the dune slid toward them it became the midsection of a gigantic snake, almost as high as a man's waist. The head went gliding smoothly along the sand, searching.

She stared at it transfixed, and only after a moment realized Pete was beside her, staring, too.

"Do you think it's . . . coming for us?" she asked Pete.

"I hope not," Pete groaned.

The snake had submerged, and they could no longer see it. Lucy watched the surface of the waves with increasing dread. Where was it?

Obwe strained at the oars, struggling to get the boat farther out.

And then the head raised up. Close. Moving closer. Moving *fast*.

"That thing is really coming after us," Pete said in a tight voice as if he didn't want to alarm anyone but he *really* hoped Obwe had noticed.

Lucy watched the dark hump of the snake close in on them.

In one movement, Obwe left his paddles and stood up. He grabbed hold of the long pole he'd stowed in the boat and stood motionless, waiting. Lucy held her breath.

A huge head—easily the size of an orca's—rose beside them,

surfacing with a groaning hiss that sounded as if it came from the depths of the ocean. It hovered there like a cobra about to strike. In that moment Lucy didn't care what Pete thought of her; she grasped Pete's arm and clung to him. The head came swooping toward them. Lucy screamed.

Obwe jabbed at the snake with his pole. The serpent hissed and turned its attention to the boatman, seemingly mesmerized by the pole's movement. Obwe shifted his balance—the boat rocked, Lucy was sure they'd be overturned—and then somehow Obwe caught the snake in the gills with the hooked end of his pole. Quickly with his other hand he cast a heavy braided harness over its head, just as if he were bridling a horse. Grappling hooks caught hold of it. The snake shook and thrashed— the sea boiled—but Obwe held the reins with one hand and with the other used his hook to draw the snake into line. In an amazingly short time, the snake settled down and began to pull them through the waves. Soon they were speeding away from the mainland, moving faster than any boat.

And then, for the first time that evening, Lucy allowed herself to relax. She let go her death grip on Pete's arm and looked about, marveling at the unexpected beauty of the night sea. Even the serpent was magnificent, with its shimmering scales and its wonderful speed. She found herself grinning helplessly and turned to Pete.

He was leaning forward, a look of pure joy on his face.

"We're flying!"

She laughed. It was wonderful, and crazy, and it was useless to talk; there weren't words for the exhilaration she felt. The ocean streamed by, and the moon seemed to race across the water to keep up.

She looked at Obwe, standing upright at the prow. His head shone hairless in the moonlight, shadowed here and there by a net of tattoos. His gloomy vestments flapped about him like sails. Her heart swelled as she thought of his bravery and skill.

Obwe caught Lucy's stare, and unexpectedly, he smiled, showing his inky teeth. "First time traveling by snake?"

She nodded. Then laughed again.

The boatman leaned into the reins. "The Ss'til know it is the best way to travel."

"The only way to travel!" Pete whooped with glee. And to her surprise Obwe echoed him. She wouldn't be left out, she let out her own fierce whoop of joy. Their voices flew into the sky, for a moment hovering over them, like powerful ocean birds keeping pace with a boat.

Far too soon they reached the other side of the bay, where the Thumb loomed black and craggy against the lightening sky. Its forbidding outline bristled with spiky treetops, and its walls were sheer cliffs.

"Where can we land?" Lucy asked. From their small boat the Thumb seemed like an impregnable fortress.

"I know a place." Obwe released the harness and the serpent dove into the depths. Rowing, Obwe followed the contour of the Thumb.

The island's rocky sides were littered with broken trees. Bats flew above their heads, flapping and dipping home to their caves. Ominous birds croaked to the coming dawn. There was a long, chilling shriek that sounded like a large cat's. Lucy shivered and Pete stared nervously into the shadows.

At last they reached a cut in those grim cliffs, a bowl-shaped gash in the Thumb's side where Obwe could come ashore. The land was covered with a shiny gray stuff, and as they came closer, Lucy realized it was smashed timber, a giant river of deadfall emptying into the sea. There was something unspeakably eerie about the silvery dead wood, as if they'd come upon a vast graveyard.

Obwe pulled the black boat up onto the beach among the enormous logs. It was not quite dawn; the only sound was the quiet rolling of the waves.

Pete turned to her, his expression somber. "Well, this is it." He clambered out of the boat and held out his hands to help Lucy.

She jumped onto the sand, wincing at the crunch that sounded. Every noise was too loud, and she wished she had Niwa's gift of moving soundlessly. Never had she been in a place that felt so watchful.

Obwe stood with his pole, glancing up at the cliffs around the beach. "You should be careful here," he said, tilting his head as if he could hear a warning in the waves' soft murmur.

The trees on the surrounding cliffs loomed down like silent watchers. In the gray light before dawn all was still. Everything about their being there felt wrong.

Obwe started back to his boat. Then he stopped, standing with the pale gray surf around his ankles, and looked back at them one last time.

"Here," he told them, reaching into the boat and unwrapping a bundle. He handed them a length of wood with a pitchy bulb at one end. "A torch," he explained. His black eyes measured them. "You light it when you need a boat to come home."

Home. Lucy vowed to herself they'd make that return trip.

"Thank you." She pressed her lips together, took a deep breath, and raised a hand in farewell.

Obwe nodded and stepped into his black boat.

They stood on the beach and watched him go.

11

Lucy shivered while Obwe's boat faded into a distant speck. The dawn brought a chill ocean wind that seemed to blow right through her.

She turned to Pete and looked up the slope of fallen trees.

"So I guess we've got to climb this thing," Pete said, sniffing. His nose was pink from the chill.

The deadfall would be a challenge even if Lucy were feeling her best. But she'd barely slept in the Ss'til sea caves the night before, and cold and fear made her stiff and clumsy.

They couldn't stay on the beach, however. She'd noticed the slick black head of a serpent lurking just offshore, and she did not want to be its breakfast.

From somewhere above them came an ominous groan.

"What was that?" Pete ducked down. "That sure sounds like the devil's voice."

Lucy shook her head dismissively. Pete couldn't let himself get spooked so easily. "It's the log pile shifting," she said, pointing up at the deadfall. The whole mass was slowly moving toward the beach, like a glacier of wood grinding down everything in its path. She found a place where she could stand on a broken branch and clamber onto a nearby log. With a grunt she hoisted herself up and stood unsteadily. Its bark skinned away, the tree was slick; it was like standing on ice. She had to pull herself up to get to the next log. The cold made her hands weak and clumsy. *I'm not going to fall.*

But before she got very far, she slipped on the smooth wood and tumbled onto the freezing sand. She got up, wincing, and braced her hands against the log, searching for a handhold.

"Need some help?" Pete asked, before hoisting himself up onto the log. He squatted down to watch her, balancing on his toes the way the boys in Wickham used to crouch over their dice games.

"No . . . *hmpf* . . . I've got it . . ." Lucy jumped up and flung her arms forward, only to slide slowly to the ground again, her fingernails scraping uselessly against the wood; she felt like a cat trying to climb a curtain.

The best she could do was to hang on to a nubbin of a branch and try to swing her legs up. Each time, she scraped her moccasins against the bark before her feet crashed down. It was humiliating.

Pete looked down at her. He had to be thinking how strong and tall he was, with his sleeves rolled up and his skin tanned from the sun.

She could see in his eyes he was enjoying this.

"Would you like some help now?" he asked innocently.

Much as she'd like to refuse, she couldn't see a way around it. "Yes . . . please."

Pete bent down and extended his hand. She grasped his strong wrist and he pulled her up. She stood beside him, the salt breeze pilfering pale strands of hair from her untidy braid. She brushed them away from her face and took a deep breath.

"Thanks," she said lightly, shrugging a little so he wouldn't think she was *too* grateful. For the first time she wondered how she would have managed without Pete along.

"Well, then." Pete tugged on his bandanna as he looked up at the silvery jumble of logs above them. A soft mist shrouded the upper reaches of the deadfall. "Only about a million more of these to go."

The climb took ages. The timber was slippery—most of the bark was skinned off—and there were few branches to hold on to. And the wood was always shifting and rolling. Lucy had to jump to throw her arms over the top of the logs, then scrabble her feet sideways until she could pull herself up. After climbing a few logs like this she gave up and let Pete go first, then grasped his hand so he could help her. Silently she thanked Niwa for her Lupine clothes. She couldn't imagine doing any of this in her stiff dungarees and slick-soled boots. And when they returned, would it be so extraordinary if Niwa gave her more Lupine things? If out of gratitude for saving the forests Niwa treated her like a sister? Niwa might take her to the wolf woman grove again and teach her to talk to birds while the governor let her examine his rare books. And if she protested that they did too much for her, they might say, "But you saved us, Lucy."

These hazy fantasies occupied Lucy through the tedious climb. Though of course Pete *would* keep interrupting.

"So we can't even pick berries?" Pete quizzed her. Now that they were on the Thumb, Pete took new interest in Ulfric's rules.

"That's what the toymaker told me." *Governor Arekwoy would hold a dinner in her honor. She'd ask the raven men to fetch her things. They might grumble, but they'd have to—*

"What if a berry is lying on the ground? Nobody's actually picking it then." Pete stood still while a branch nearby cracked from the pressure of the log pile. It gave out a horrible groan as it splintered.

"You're welcome to test it out," she said in annoyance. Most of the morning fog had burned off, making their climb hot and sweaty. Lucy's hair, by now entirely escaped from her braid, clung in damp curls around her head.

Pete scrunched his face. There was a pink line of sunburn across his snub nose that made him look particularly boyish. "You don't need to bite my head off. I'm just asking."

At last they were at the top. Lucy slid off the final log and landed on a springy carpet of rotting bark and kodok needles. Trees stretched as far as she could see, between them ghostly strings of moss and jags of broken limbs were hung like rotted curtains.

The forest was as dense as a jungle. The pleasant visions

of triumph disappeared. Now her heart sank. Her father was somewhere in here, but where?

Pete, however, was concerned with more practical matters. "I'm starving," he announced, plopping down on the ground. "Somehow we went clear past breakfast."

Now that he'd mentioned food Lucy realized she hadn't eaten since lunch the previous day, when they'd stopped with Niwa in the wolf woman's grove. "And we skipped supper last night. Unless you managed to sneak some food from the Ss'til when I wasn't looking."

Pete held out his hands in protest. "What? No, if I had, I'd have shared. And I'm pretty sure what they were eating was snake. I, er, wasn't hungry."

"The first time I've heard that." Pete could be relied upon to eat under any circumstances.

Pete shrugged, conceding. "I admit, it's unusual."

Now that they were away from the beach, the air felt stifling and close: humid, as if they were inside a giant lung. The uncomfortable feeling of being watched—scrutinized, in fact—was even more intense than it had been on the beach. It was as if the trees themselves were staring at them.

Lucy rubbed her forearm over her eyes, wiping away perspiration. She was letting her imagination run wild. This was no different from any of the other hundreds of spooky places she'd been to.

"I'll get the food," she told Pete.

She delved into her pack without thinking. Something golden flashed and promptly kicked her hand.

"Ow."

Lucy put her stinging fingers in her mouth. She'd forgotten about her ghost sweeper. Its legs thrashed wildly.

"Do you have a stocking?" she asked.

"What for?"

"So I won't get my hand smashed by my ghost sweeper!"

All she wanted to do was tie up the sweeper and eat. But Pete—his eyes wide with alarm—crouched down and gingerly investigated her bulging pack.

"It's really moving," he warned her, immediately looking from side to side as if expecting ghosts to pop out at them from behind the fallen logs.

Lucy wiped her hands on her leggings. "I know. I think there are ghosts here *somewhere*." Hadn't Pete and Ulfric both mentioned something about a town disappearing? "But this whole place probably has residues of supernatural activity. I'll bet that's what it's reacting to." She squinted into the forest's green mist: It was certainly eerie, but she didn't think they were in any danger at the moment. "Now, would you please lend me a sock so we can eat?"

Rather grudgingly Pete pulled out a thin grayish sock.

"One of my last clean ones," he told her, holding on to it a bit longer than necessary. "And I'm giving you one without holes."

"I'll take good care of it," she promised, rolling her eyes.

After a struggle she managed to stuff the indignant egg head-first into Pete's sock and tie the end.

"There. That should stop the pummeling a bit," she said

cheerfully. This small achievement had already restored some of her confidence. "Now for some food."

She brought out biscuits and jerky, which they ate slowly, watching her pack bulge and wriggle as the ghost sweeper tried to escape.

After she'd eaten, Lucy leaned her head against the log and closed her eyes. The warmth of the day, along with the exhaustion of the climb, made her sleepy. What she'd like most right now was a good long nap.

But Pete was bustling about. The bit of dried meat they'd eaten seemed to have revived him. "I have an idea," Pete said. "Let's switch the food to my pack. I don't think your sweeper is going to calm down anytime soon."

"Are you sure it won't be too heavy?"

Pete snorted and then demonstrated how easily he could lift his pack. In case she missed it, he did it again. "I could carry both our packs and it wouldn't bother me a bit."

Lucy rather doubted that, but she helped him move the food anyway.

Pete bent over her, compulsively rearranging the way that she'd put things in. Flecks of perspiration shone on his face, and he smelled (not unpleasantly, she noticed) of kodok needles and sweat.

When that was done, they could no longer put off the question of where they would go.

"My father would use his vitometer to find the dreamwood," Lucy said. She did not add "if he made it this far." *Of course he made it here.*

She fished the soft leather pouch out from inside her tunic. The vitometer had been vibrating softly against her chest, almost like a purring cat.

Pete watched solemnly while she undid the clasp and lifted the lid. The needle shivered across the face of the instrument, ticking off points on its compass. Lucy held her breath as she watched it spin round. Numerals in the Odic force counter clicked steadily upward at the top of the disc. That had to mean dreamwood was still here. The idea of a tree that possessed such a quantity of life energy was interesting, in an abstract sort of way, as she had explained the concept in Governor Arekwoy's office. But now that they were on the Thumb, surrounded by a brooding forest, it struck her as threatening.

After a moment, fluttering like a moth toward the light, the needle stopped and pointed to a spot that would have corresponded to two o'clock on a watch.

"There it is." Lucy tried to sound pleased. But her mouth was dry and her hand quivered as she shut the vitometer's case. She did not tell Pete, but the reading had been so high she had to look at it several times before accepting it. Even at a distance, dreamwood was now showing fifteen times the amount of Odic force that could be measured from a full-grown man.

They walked for hours, stopping only to consult the vitometer. Pete tried to find their direction from his compass, but the needle just spun around crazily. After a few attempts he put it away and announced he could tell which way they were going from some combination of the angle of the sun, the moss on the trees, and his own innate orienteering genius. However, every time Lucy checked the vitometer, Pete was wrong—sometimes wildly so. The third time this happened he got upset before declaring the forest "unnatural," and he sulked until they stopped to eat again.

It was slow going. There were no paths, no tracks to follow, just an endless, painstaking struggle over fallen logs, through thickets of lichen-encrusted branches, under the spiraling fronds of mammoth ferns. Lucy got used to the dull thuds of her ghost sweeper, beating like a metronome against her back.

The jagged skeletons of dead trees poked through the green mist. They gave an uncomfortable impression of *lurching*, as if the minute she turned her back they'd move again.

Soon her knees were black and blue from falling. The roots were awful for shifting position under her feet, but it was hard to say if they were worse than the vines that were always tangling up her legs or the tree branches that had a way of whacking her on the head as she passed.

After one vine wrapped around her ankle she'd had enough. She took out her knife (the knife Pete had made her buy) and was about to saw through it.

Instantly the sense of being watched intensified. The sound of her own heartbeat pounded in her ears.

"Lucy, what are you doing?" The tense expression on Pete's face made her even more nervous. "Why'd everything get so quiet?"

"I was going to cut it." Slowly she put the knife away, realizing how close she'd come to making a stupid mistake. She bent down and wrestled with the vine until she could pull her foot free. Raucous bird chatter sounded from the trees above her.

But the next moment she forgot all about Pete. Shadows slunk among the trees. She heard the sound of animal breath, of growls.

"Something out there?" She searched the woods in fear.

Pete heard it, too.

Yellow eyes gleamed at her through the underbrush straight ahead. They belonged to something big and dark, with teeth.

She couldn't look away, grabbed blindly at the vine. It loosened just enough for her to get free. There was a low growl from one side, and an answer on the other. Three beasts crept forward, emerging from the shadows.

Wolves.

Saarthen wolves, which meant they were the size of oxen. Their jaws dripped with slaver, teeth like razors.

"Run!" Pete cried.

He waited precious seconds until she was level with him, then the two of them went tearing through the woods, leaping and crashing, running blindly.

But they weren't fast enough.

The wolves were gaining on them. In a second Lucy would feel the rip and gash of their teeth. She could see a shaggy black blur racing alongside her. *I'll never be able to outrun it.*

"This way," Pete yelled.

Ahead was a dense knot of trees where the kodoks grew close together, their branches drooping low and intertwined almost like a lattice. If they could get there in time they might be able to climb out of reach.

"Come on." Pete was just ahead, waiting for her.

Her lungs aching, Lucy put on one final burst and caught up to Pete. He lifted her about the waist and boosted her up so she could grab a branch just above her head. Then he leapt up, climbing easily. Lucy struggled to get higher into the tree.

The wolves gathered below them. They seemed to grin as they watched Pete and Lucy retreat.

She was still not high enough for safety. And the wolves were big enough to make the jump. Why didn't they?

"Why are you stopping?" Pete hissed. He was several feet above her in the branches. Tree sap and dirt streaked his arms, his throat shone with sweat.

But Lucy stared down into the wolves' yellow eyes, suddenly sure of herself. "They're not going to hurt us."

Without even a parting snarl the pack shifted and ran off.

"What was that about?" Pete asked, climbing down to her level. He stared after the wolves in confusion. "Are they really giving up that easy?"

Lucy had fled in panic, but she had no illusions about her running speed. "They could have caught us anytime they wanted. But they didn't." She felt for the knife on her belt. If she'd cut that vine, however . . .

Pete closed his eyes as if this was too much to take in. "So they were playing with us?" He rubbed his forehead, leaving behind dirty smudges on his skin.

Lucy's breathing slowly came back to normal. It felt safe and strangely nest-like up in the tree branches. She watched Pete with his eyes closed, his head thrown back. When he opened his eyes, she was looking straight at him. She saw him realize that. Blood surged into her cheeks—she hadn't meant to stare—and she began to climb down.

"There's a clearing on the other side," she said, fussing with the tree sap on her hands. "We might want to stay here for the night."

The ring of trees, their branches tightly woven, formed a circle.

Pete started to climb down after her.

It had been a strange day, and something made her feel it was about to get stranger yet.

Lucy stepped into the circle, surrounded by mournful kodoks. The last rays of afternoon sun came through the treetops, raking the grove with light and shadow.

A fallen log lay about ten feet away. Just visible under a coating of kodok needles was something that didn't belong. Something blue.

Her heart beat fast. With a small cry she ran forward.

It was a man's blue flannel shirt. Next to it lay a tin cup. And beside it was . . .

"A notebook." She held it with trembling hands. "My father's notebook. He was here!"

12

Lucy sat cross-legged on the ground, paging through her father's journal. His handwriting was small and secretive—he always said his wealth was in his ideas. They were locked up safely in his crabbed script. A few scraps of paper fell out as she studied the pages: newspaper clippings, pages torn from books.

Trees several territories over in Montana were dying from a disease that sounded suspiciously like Rust.

She found a printed page with many Latin words on it: "The dreamwood, which we shall call by its scientific name *Hypnogagous atrox*, is the largest flesh-eating plant in the world."

There was a note from her father: "It is my belief that, when feeding, it introduces a narcotic into the victim's bloodstream, producing the vivid dreams that give the tree its name."

Another scribbled note: "Saarthe's lost settlement . . . The key lies in uncovering the past . . . used to harvest dreamwood."

She put the journal with its patchwork of scraps back down and rubbed her eyes. She felt exhausted after their long day— which really had begun in the wee hours of the morning with

Obwe's boat. Their trip across the bay already seemed as if it had happened in the distant past.

"Lucy, take a look at this," Pete said. While she'd been reading he had been wandering nervously around the clearing. Now he stood in the middle, an unmistakably queasy expression on his face. He waved her over, then bent down, examining something on the ground—though whatever was there made him cover his nose.

Lucy walked over to see what he was looking at. This turned out to be a small patch of boggy ground covered with flabby-looking mushrooms the color of cooked liver. They were ugly, but unremarkable. She bent down to examine them and wrinkled her nose in disgust. There was a rotten, sinister feeling to the place, as if a terrible crime had been committed here and instead of disappearing with time, it had sunk in—spread through the ground and gotten stronger with age.

"What did you want me to see?" she asked.

"These, of course." Pete pointed to the mushrooms. "Did you ever smell such a stink?"

Lucy sniffed the air. They did give off an unpleasant smell, but she didn't think that warranted taking her away from her father's journal. Except, of course, boys often assigned an outsize importance to disgusting things.

"They're bad," she agreed. She stood up, wanting to get back to her reading.

Pete put his hands on his lower back and stretched. "Let's

go. I'd like to get some fresh air, sleep someplace that feels, um, healthier."

Lucy didn't think this was a good idea. "We should stay here tonight," she told Pete. "What if my father comes back for his things?"

The expression on Pete's face was almost pitying. "You know, by the looks of it, that stuff has been here awhile."

But Lucy didn't want to listen. Her father was absentminded, always leaving scraps of notes about. He might come looking for them. She wrapped her father's shirt around her shoulders, settled against the back of a broad kodok trunk, and picked up her father's notebook again.

Pete gave a loud sigh, in which she could detect boredom, impatience, and a desire to rile her up.

"What?" she asked.

He smiled. "I've just never seen anyone look at a book that way, like you're going to make it give up its secrets . . . or else."

"Oh," she said. For some reason the thought that he was noticing the way she read a book made her cheeks color. "I just . . . thought I should read these journal entries. Maybe I can, um, learn something."

Pete shrugged as if learning were a novel idea but one he was prepared to entertain. He settled down next to her. "Okay then. Let's get to it."

"Okay." She nodded back at him, but now it was hard to focus on the journal.

"Well," said Pete, sitting close to her. "Anything?"

She squinched her nose, not wanting to admit she couldn't concentrate. "I'm looking."

"Sounds good." Pete stretched his arms out and yawned.

She flipped through the diary and read a few bits here and there before deciding she would read from back to front. The last page was the easiest: It had only one line.

He killed them all.

Lucy felt her stomach take an uneasy dip. Beside her Pete had closed his eyes.

The sun had gone down, and with the twilight the sinister feeling of being watched returned. The moon was rising over the treetops. As the shadows entered the grove, Lucy kept glancing to the circle of trees. A few times she thought she'd seen *faces* in their trunks. She shook her head. It wouldn't help if she started seeing things.

She turned to Pete, but he'd already fallen asleep. His breath came lightly, rhythmically.

Lucy turned back to her father's journal. There was now barely enough light to read. She squinted to make out the words. "I believe that, like a spider that keeps its prey fresh by drugging its unfortunate victim, so, too, the dreamwood keeps its food in a state of suspended animation . . ."

Part of her wanted to put the diary down. The words reminded her too much of the pictures in the terrible *Codex Saarthensis*. But a horrified fascination compelled her to keep reading.

"According to legend . . . human food . . . months to digest . . ."

She swallowed on a dry mouth. Her chest was tight, as if she could not get enough air.

Beside her, Pete's breath grew shallow, his eyelids flickered with dream.

"Even if I survive his challenges, the forest turns deadly at night . . ."

Against her back she imagined—no, she felt—the tree trunk shift ever so slightly.

She didn't want to read any more. The diary fell to the ground.

I'm hungry, said a cold voice.

She jumped.

"Who said that?"

There was no one around except Pete. But she'd heard a voice as clearly as if it had been spoken by someone just over her shoulder.

"What?" A bleary-eyed Pete woke up; he was looking at her strangely. A tickle of panic ran up her spine.

The angles of his face were etched in the moonlight. Something about the light chilled her. The moon was dangerous, but she couldn't remember why.

Slowly, she got up and walked a few paces into the clearing where the moonlight was stronger. She held out her hand in front of her, watching the mottled shadows paint bruises on her skin. The sight was mesmerizing. It made her dizzy.

"Lucy?" Pete's voice was tight and thin. "Look at the trees."

She raised her eyes to the trees that ringed them. In the

stark moonlight she could see each tree had a face on its trunk: a twisted, evil, ancient face. She stared at the tree across the circle from her. The eyes—two fathomless holes—were overhung with a bristly ridge of bark. A crooked limb was a long and witchy nose. But worst of all was the mouth: open, ravenous, with stringy tendrils of moss strung across it like teeth.

And then she felt it, the vast *hunger* that surrounded them. The tree she'd been sitting under seemed to yawn open; its trunk was a dark mouth. The devil's face leered out at her. They'd been too foolish to see it before. The grasses swayed and twisted like they were all one being, and she saw with horror that each blade was barbed at the tip as if it bore a tiny tooth. In a second they would swoop upon her, biting her with hundreds of sharp teeth until she fell and bled out on the ground.

Run, said a voice in her head. *Run while you still can.*

She looked into the darkness beyond the clearing. If she ran she might be able to escape. She could outrun that hunger, leap into the sea, and swim away. That was the only hope. If there had been a cliff in front of her she would have jumped without hesitation.

The fear was overpowering. Like black smoke, it choked off her thoughts, all except one—*don't be food.*

"Pete!" she screamed. "Run."

"I can't!"

A web of branches trapped him. Roots came up from the ground, nosing blindly like worms.

From just behind her a branch reached out. She was going to be trapped, too. She had to save herself.

She started to run, dodging branches, twigs that poked up from the ground like spikes.

What about Pete? a voice inside her asked.

I don't want to be eaten! she screamed back.

But it was no use. She faltered to a stop. She couldn't leave him.

It took all her strength of will to turn back to Pete. He seemed to be fighting at shadows.

In the last sane corner of her mind she realized he *was* fighting shadows. Because this was a dream.

A nightmare.

Now she ran, but not from the clearing. She reached her pack, and grasped frantically for the small pocket where she kept the vial Arthur Lyman had given her.

Where were they? *Five drops before moonrise.* The warning rang in her head. Brocius Pile was driven mad. Brains turned to jelly.

She'd been so stupid. The one danger they'd prepared for and she'd completely forgotten about it—she'd been so addled by the journal, the lazy afternoon sunshine, and Pete.

She couldn't find them. She was too panicked. It took everything she had to slow down and search. And then there it was, a small glass bottle.

Her hand was shaking as she measured out five silvery drops

onto her tongue. The medicine was so bitter she squeezed her eyes shut.

But it worked at once, whisking through her head like a broom. When she opened her eyes the dream had cleared. The forest wasn't going to eat her.

The real danger was that they would run, leaving their supplies—and each other. Pete staggered to the edge of the circle, clawing his arms in front of him. He was almost past the barrier branches. If he ran she would never catch him. She threw herself around his legs, wrestling him to the ground.

"Pete, hold still."

"They're squeezing me." He twisted on the ground. "They're going to crack me open and suck the marrow from my bones."

He thrashed wildly. She held tight to the vial. If she spilled it while holding on to him they were lost.

"No one's going to crack your bones." Not if she could help it. But he was so much stronger. She swung a leg over him to hold him down, but he tried to throw her off. She dug in with both her legs.

This only frightened him more. "Aah!" he cried. "Aah!"

At least he opened his mouth.

There was no time to hesitate. She sent five drops in what she hoped was the direction of his tongue. She didn't know if they made it.

And then all at once the scream changed into something recalling a sick cat.

"Blechh."

Pete's muscles slackened, and he stopped fighting. Lucy went limp with relief. The struggle had been harder than she realized, and she fell back on the ground beside him. A few pinprick stars were just visible through the tree branches.

After a moment, Pete stood up. He peered into the shadows, then put a hand against the kodok bark, reassuring himself it would not come alive.

The grove was still.

"That rat Lyman might at least have put some sugar in it." Pete rubbed his mouth. "Now I understand why you wouldn't want to dream here. Though that's the first time I ever dreamed when I was awake."

She shuddered as she thought how close both of them had come to running blindly through the woods.

"Poor Brocius Pile," she said at last. "No wonder he went mad." She sat up and put her back against a kodok tree. It felt solid and not at all hungry.

Pete sat down beside her, leaning against the tree trunk.

"He didn't stand a chance," Pete agreed. "You kept your head, though . . ."

"Only because mine's so thick." She wasn't pleased with the way she'd almost run; she'd thought she was made of stronger stuff.

He gave her a sidelong glance. "Now you're making jokes. At your own expense, too. I think the forest has gotten to you."

"I'm actually very good at making jokes," she said, raising her chin. "My father always said I was the only one in the family who could make him laugh."

"That's more like it," Pete said, nodding appreciatively, like someone who'd managed to identify the call of a rare bird. "You sound like yourself now."

"I'm always myself," she said, frowning. Pete should know that by now. She picked irritably at some of the kodok bark between them.

"That you are," he said. He stretched out his legs and bent his head closer to hers. "No one else is like you."

This was what she wanted to hear—so much so she got flustered. She chanced a quick glance at his profile. Then she allowed herself a longer look. After all, she *had* saved his life.

Lucy Darrington saves the day. She grinned to herself as she looked out at the trees. The stark faces were still there, but now she saw them as a trick of light and shadow. Nothing to be frightened of.

13

Perhaps she should have been suspicious when the next day dawned gloriously.

Lucy woke up to see golden shafts of light breaking through the forest canopy. Butterflies the size of crows fluttered across the clearing. Curling tree orchids flashed in purple spirals from niches in the kodok bark.

That was when she remembered the faces in the trees. But in the morning light the trees appeared normal. She got to her feet and wandered over to the nearest kodok, studying it. There wasn't an actual face in its trunk. Just regular knots and bark and moss that happened to resemble faces, if you looked at them a certain way . . . if the shadows came at them just right.

The forest turns deadly at night, her father had written.

But was the forest deadly? Or was it simply scary, and fear was what made it dangerous? Was it a distinction that made any difference?

It was hard to think of it as dangerous at all right now; it was as if the forest was putting on a display just for her. Blue jays flitted among the branches, a dragonfly the size of her hand flew by, shimmering like a rainbow. The Thumb was *beautiful*.

Behind her, she could hear Pete wake up.

"Morning," he mumbled, brushing kodok needles out of his hair. He peered curiously around the grove. "How much of last night was a dream?"

"The faces in the trees were an illusion," she said. "I think they only appear when the light hits them a certain way."

But then Lucy looked down and saw the vial of *antimorpheus* solution on the ground where she'd let it fall. If the hungry forest was merely a trick of the light, why did they need anti-dreaming drops to see through it? The faces had been real until she'd taken the remedy.

"That's a relief." Pete started packing his things, not realizing his hair was mussed into peaks like meringue and he had kodok needles hanging in a fringe off his shirt. "I was afraid *all* the trees here ate people."

"Oh, ha," Lucy replied, still puzzling over how dreams worked on the Thumb.

She was staring absently in Pete's direction when he looked up. Staring at him *again*, she thought, and flushed—but then she saw his expression change.

His sea-glass eyes were huge, fixated on something in the shadows just ahead. Lucy blinked and felt her own eyes grow wide. A bull elk emerged from the opposite side of the glade, bigger than imagining, and on his head were antlers of a hundred tines or more, shining with velvet.

It was as if the elk carried his own forest upon his head. Light gleamed around him like a soft coating of gold.

The elk was the most beautiful thing Lucy had ever seen. A feeling of joy and wonder expanded inside her as she watched it go past.

Its soft wet eyes flicked to them fearlessly. And then the reef of antlers slowly receded into the forest's gloom.

She stared after it, trying to soak up the magic that seemed to float in its wake.

"Doesn't seem like the sort of thing an evil spirit would keep in his forest," Pete said. He got up from where he'd been kneeling.

"Nature spirit," she corrected him automatically. But inside, her thoughts churned in confusion. The elk had radiated nothing but good, the same as the dreamwood tea she'd had in Ulfric's cottage.

His-sey-ak saved us, Niwa had said. *Dreamwood heals,* she told herself.

It killed them all.

Which was true?

In the space of a few days, Lucy had adapted to the rigors of camping and hiking and become much hardier. She could lift her pack easily now and walk for several hours without complaint.

In the afternoon the landscape grew steep and hilly. The trees thinned out, giving way to great moon-faced boulders, jumbled precariously atop one another like giant sculptures. Scrub oak grew among the rocks, clinging with sinewy roots to the smallest fold or cranny. Without the forest's shelter, Lucy and Pete were soon hot and thirsty.

At last they came to a deep gorge that cut between two hillsides. Lucy brought out the vitometer and watched, disheartened, as its spidery needle danced across the ivory to point directly ahead. They had to go across.

The climb down was slow and treacherous. As they neared the bottom of the gorge, they heard a strange squorking cry.

A flight of birds came toward them, sailing lazily on thermals. Only they weren't *normal* birds. They were much too large.

Lucy watched in growing disbelief as they got closer, their wings casting gigantic shadows, like clouds blocking the sun.

"They look like vultures, but those wings must be twenty feet across," Pete said, scrunching his eyes against the sun.

Lucy sprang up on her toes. "I read that the First Peoples on the coast used to talk about something called a thunderbird. You can see them on totems from here to California. They're bigger than condors."

Pete didn't even have to think about this to dismiss it. "Naw, it can't be. Those are extinct."

"Just like dreamwood's supposed to be extinct?" She raised her eyebrows.

"Well, I don't think they're thunderbirds," he said, starting to walk again. "They're just some big, ugly buzzard."

Called a thunderbird, she thought in annoyance.

She was just about to start after him when she spotted a fat black feather on the dusty ground. It had drifted down the long corridor of air, into the gorge, to land before her. A thunderbird feather.

When she got back from the Thumb she'd take it to a natural history museum. In fact, she'd probably be famous for having discovered it. Lucy bent down and picked it up. Then she put it in her pack and ran after Pete.

They continued their descent until the walls of the gorge softened into pink bluffs bordering a wide dry riverbed. A muddy trickle of water threaded down the middle.

The sun angled down harshly, and they were sweating as they scrambled to the sandy bottom.

"Where's all the water?" Pete glared at the damp sand as if it had cheated him. "I could go for a swim about now."

If there'd been water in the river, the Lucy of just a few weeks ago would have stripped down to her underclothes and run straight into it. But now she stopped in her tracks, unsure whether she was glad or disappointed the river was dry.

She realized Pete was talking to her. "What?"

"I said, any reason you're still just standing there?" Without the prospect of a swim, he was ready to move on.

Lucy was startled out of her trance. "Nope." She ran after him, her boots kicking up little puffs of dust. Large skeins of tangled wood and briar—taller than a man's height—were scattered about the dry riverbed like abandoned balls of yarn.

Insects droned, the pink sand pulled at her boots. And

Lucy felt more tired and thirsty than she could bear. At last they reached the center where the little trickle of water shone brightly, reflecting gold in the sun. Just across the bank, the beach was lined with shattered timber.

"Huh." Pete stopped and stared at the damp ground. "Look at that."

Lucy wiped the sweat from her eyes. The sand glinted strangely. It couldn't be . . .

She bent down and brushed the sand with her fingertips. When she held them up to the light, she gasped.

"Gold," Pete said in a strangled voice. He fell to his knees and began rooting in the sand.

"Look," Lucy cried. She'd found a gold nugget the size of a pea. A moment later she tossed it aside; she'd found one the size of an almond.

There was a crazy grin on Pete's face. "We're rich!"

All weariness and thirst disappeared. Lucy poured sand through her hands, laughing. They could pick chunks of gold all day long and still not have it all. The entire beach was gold.

Pete was scooping big armfuls of sand to himself.

And then it was a game: She wanted only the most symmetrical bits, or only the largest. She sorted them like a child playing with marbles. There was a fortune here. More than a fortune!

She grasped handfuls of gold to her chest. A shadow passed above, darkening the sun for just a moment.

Lucy sat up, feeling lazy, warm, and content. Now she saw what had caused the shadow. A large black bird sat huddled on one of the driftwood tumbleweeds, its bald head crooked like the top of a cane.

That was an ugly bird for such a pleasant place, Lucy thought, as it regarded her with a black and beady eye. And why was it looking at her like that?

Uneasily she stared back. The bird had the bare, tonsured head of a vulture; its sharp yellow claws gripped the pale white driftwood tight.

There was something wrong about the wood.

And then she saw that the pale branches lining the river were not wood at all.

They were bones.

Her breath stopped. Gold spilled from her hands. What she'd thought was briar and driftwood was a weedy braid of bones: human bones, tangled among the branches.

Lucy's heart slithered to her feet. Her eyes traced the riverbank's horrid tapestry: skulls and femurs, tibiae and finger bones, all woven together.

She stood up. They were surrounded by the dead. She'd been too fixated on the gold to notice.

The gold. Her stomach realized the truth first, going heavy as a stone. *Take nothing that is not given*, Able Dodd had warned her the day they'd left Pentland. Now she understood. Somehow he'd known they were going to Devil's Thumb—and staying alive here was about more than not killing or eating anything. There was Pete kneeling in the damp sand, shoveling handfuls of it into his pack. He'd emptied his bags—his supplies were strewn about the bank—and he was filling his pack with as much river sand as it could hold.

A dull roar sounded in her head.

"Pete," she said. She tottered forward. He didn't hear her. The bird spread its wings, impatient.

The roar grew louder, and with a sickening turn she realized it wasn't inside her head at all. Now she understood the deep cuts on the bluffs, the smashed timber and skeletons, the growing rumble. A flash flood was coming, and they needed to get out of its path.

"Pete!" she cried.

He didn't look up. He was stretched out on his stomach, both arms full of the golden sand. His pack was full to bursting, and still he piled it with gold.

The rumbling got louder.

"Pete, stop!"

She reached him and tugged on his pack.

"What are you doing?" he snarled. His eyes were crazed, and for a horrible moment she thought he would strike her.

"Pete, it's a flash flood. You've got to dump this out. Now!"

He shook his head, still scooping and piling. "The river's dry. It'll never flood."

Could he even hear the water coming?

"You've got to leave it." She gestured wildly upriver. "Or you'll die."

They would both die, because she couldn't leave him here. The thought made her desperate.

"Just a little more," he said stubbornly.

"Look at the bones, Pete," she pleaded. She pointed to the tangled banks of branch and bone. "That's what will happen to us."

The skulls were watching, alive with anticipation.

But he couldn't see them. "You're just saying that because you want to keep it for yourself."

"The last thing I want is any of this cursed gold." She brushed off her hands and clothes to make sure none of it clung to her. "I'm trying to get you to see what's happening."

"You're *always* right," Pete said savagely, standing up at last. Golden sand poured from his pockets and filled his trouser cuffs. "You've always got the answer, you think you're *so* much better than me. You think I'm just some small-town know-nothing."

This was such a stupid thing to say—maybe she'd thought that way once, but now as the river smashed its way toward them none of that mattered. She grabbed his arm.

He wrenched away from her, but with such force that she fell back on the sand.

She hit the ground hard. Her eyes smarted with tears.

It's all over, she thought.

But then Pete was saying. "Lucy, Lucy. I'm so sorry. What's happening?"

When she looked up at him his gray-green eyes were frightened, like those of a person waking up in a strange place. Behind him was a wall of water, coming fast as galloping horses.

She got to her feet. "Run," she gasped. Pete hesitated. He

tugged the straps of his pack: overflowing with golden sand, too heavy to lift.

"Leave it!" she shouted over the onrushing flood.

He gave one last desperate look to the gold. Then he grasped her hand, squeezing it as they ran for higher ground.

Adrenaline propelled them up the sandy bluffs. They scrambled the last few feet just in time. The water burst through with the force of a dam breaking. Trees cracked and groaned, snapped like toothpicks, and the black buzzard circled overhead once before flying off, croaking its disappointment.

They'd survived.

But instead of exhilaration at being alive, Lucy felt empty and hollow.

"Lucy," Pete said. In his voice she could hear that he wanted to apologize. But she didn't feel like listening.

She didn't answer. Instead, she turned away and walked to the edge. She stared into the churning flood below, its destructive murk mirroring her thoughts.

There wasn't anything wrong with knowing things, she told herself. If she didn't know a lot, they'd be dead right now. But then she thought back guiltily to the many times she'd called Pete superstitious in her thoughts, and the gleeful way she'd corrected him when he was wrong. She *did* love knowing the answers; until now she'd never thought about how that made other people feel.

She glanced back at Pete, who was standing with his arms folded around himself as if he were cold. He looked miserable.

"Lucy," he said again, more pleadingly this time. She turned her back on him, not yet ready to talk.

She walked by herself along the edge of the bluff until she found a spot where she could sit and watch the water go by. The water was as brown as earth and full of things it had ripped apart on its way through the river channel: branches, small trees . . .

And then . . . an arm raised up suddenly from the muddy froth. It looked for a moment as if it were trying to grab hold of something. She jumped to her feet, watched its efforts with horror . . . There was a log right by it. Surely the person would feel the log and grab on?

She waited for the person to save himself. And then she realized it was only the water making the arm move.

She must have cried out loud.

"What is it?" Pete rushed to her side. "Are you hurt?"

At that moment she clearly saw a leg. All the clothing had been torn from it by the force of the flood.

Lucy felt she would be sick. She clapped her hands to her mouth. "Those are people down there." The broken, lifeless limbs had belonged to living bodies.

Those were people.

Could one of them be her father?

Her stomach folded into knots, Lucy barely breathed. She stared fixedly at the boiling brown water until the bodies were swept out of sight.

"Oh, those poor, poor people." She turned to Pete; the misery and shock were physical things inside her, and if she didn't get them out . . .

She reached for his hand—she wanted to clutch something—then remembered how he felt about her . . . how spoiled things were between them. Her hands dropped to her sides and she clenched her fists instead, digging her fingernails deep enough to hurt, all the while thinking, *those people are dead.*

Pete's brows drew together, darkening his face.

"You know what this means," he said, leaning over the edge of the bluff.

She thought of the many close calls they'd had since landing on the Thumb: the wolves, the nightmares, and now the flash flood. The dreamwood spirit caused them all.

"Maybe Governor Arekwoy was right." Lucy pulled on the fringe of her Lupine tunic. "Maybe His-sey-ak *is* evil."

"No," Pete said grimly. "It means we're not the only ones here."

14

Who were the bodies in the river? The question tortured Lucy through the rest of the afternoon. When she wasn't thinking about the bodies, she heard Pete's voice: *You're always right.*

But how shallow she was to keep thinking of herself when two people had just died.

And on her thoughts went, running and fluttering like silly chickens. She was so miserable that she didn't bother checking the vitometer, resulting in them wandering aimlessly over the course of several hours.

A sudden, violent conviction caused her to stop. "It couldn't have been my father," she said to Pete. "We saw two bodies."

Pete was walking like a person whose thoughts were elsewhere, stumbling over things, not caring where his feet went.

"So it wasn't your father." He sounded as if he were just agreeing with her out of habit.

This would not do. She needed Pete to put up more of a fight so she could argue with him. If they argued, she would win, and that would make her feel better. Frustrated, she carried on the best she could.

"He *was* traveling alone," she said, taking a big step to avoid a muddy patch of ground.

"All right," Pete said, walking right through the mud.

What had her father written? *Even if I survive his challenges.* A horrible sense expanded in her that they were up against something much bigger, more dangerous than she'd realized. The forest was full of booby traps and tests, and that diary entry had been written weeks ago. How could anyone survive weeks here?

"The gold was a trap," she said, working it out in her head. "Able Dodd told me something just before we left: *Take nothing that is not given.* But my father already knew His-sey-ak set challenges in the forest, so he wouldn't have been fooled by any gold."

"No, of course your father would have been too smart to fall for that." Pete's voice had an edge. He stopped walking, a bullish expression on his face.

But who else would be here? Lucy circled around him, unable to stay still.

"What if it was Niwa?" she said. "What if Niwa made it here after all and she found my father and now they're both dead?!"

"Don't be silly," Pete said. His reply was like a shove.

But Lucy's thoughts ran on in panic. For a moment she truly believed the bodies were those of Niwa and her father. This was more than reasonable, it was inevitable. "They're dead because of me." She turned to Pete, feeling her eyes brim with tears.

"They wouldn't be dead because of *you*," he shot back. There were hollows under Pete's cheeks she hadn't noticed before, and he stood with his chest collapsed, like someone who'd lost hope. "It was *my* fault the river flooded. Because I was greedy. Is that what you want to tell me? Do you want to make me feel even worse?"

"No." She shrank back, surprised and a little afraid. She didn't think of it like that at all. She watched him walking ahead: stoop-shouldered with guilt. With a sudden ache she thought of what he must be feeling.

She ran after him. "Let's stop," she said. "It's been an awful day. We should eat something and rest."

Pete didn't answer. He slid down the trunk of a tree and sat with his head thrown back.

"The river took my pack," he said hopelessly.

It took a moment until she understood; when she did it was like a punch in the gut. Pete had been carrying their food.

"We're surrounded by game. I could catch something easy." He spread out his hands. "But . . . I don't think it would be safe."

"So, there's an easy solution," Lucy said, determined to find a way out of their predicament. What they had was a set of conditions and constraints—a puzzle. All she had to do was figure out the answer. "We don't eat anything we didn't bring. What do we have left?"

Pete held out a frayed piece of dried meat, sandy with pocket lint. "This."

One piece of jerky.

An irritating voice in her head was saying they had failed and should go home now. They were doomed.

We are not doomed, Lucy told the voice sternly.

She took a deep breath. "Okay. I'll see what I have in my pack." She slung it to the ground and bent to look inside.

She already knew she had very little. But she felt like crying when all she discovered was one hard little biscuit.

Tightness gripped her chest. She looked up and saw two fat squirrels scamper up and down a kodok tree. They flicked their tails in her direction and one even threw a nut to the ground in front of her. She and Pete were going to starve in the middle of plenty.

She plunged her hand into her pack again, rooting past Obwe's flare and her ghost sweeper. And then her fingers closed over something rough and bristly.

The thunderbird feather.

Feeling drained out of her as if she'd sprung a leak. Turning her back so Pete couldn't see, she took the feather out, running her fingers over the stubby quill.

When she'd picked it up the only thing she'd thought about was how amazing it would be to bring back proof of what she'd seen. She'd thought of the interviews she might give and imagined meeting famous researchers: how grateful they'd be to her for this gift to science. All she'd wanted was a little attention.

And all Pete had wanted was gold to save his family.

She threw the hateful thing away from her, then covered her face.

"What's the matter?" Pete asked. He'd heard her gasp.

Lucy turned around and sat down beside him. A tiny part of her had been proud she hadn't succumbed to gold lust at the river. But she hadn't passed the test after all.

And now she had to admit it to Pete. "I picked up a thunderbird feather and put it in my pack to take back with me." She couldn't meet his eyes. "I made that river flood just as much as you."

Pete's face softened and he let out his breath.

His eyes lost their haunted look, and he gave her a soft, slow punch to the shoulder, something almost like a hug.

"Aw, you're just a little bit guilty," he said. "You really think a ratty old feather—even if it is from an extinct bird—counts as much as a pack of gold?"

"I don't know." It was funny, she'd never realized that it could feel good sometimes not to know the answer.

"That's right, you don't know." He grinned as if this were the best possible outcome. "So don't go blaming yourself."

She nodded gratefully. For some reason, she felt tears pricking in the corners of her eyes.

"We'll be all right," he said softly. Pete's long legs were stretched out beside her shorter ones. The sun-warmed bark of the tree at their backs felt reassuring.

Somehow, the feather made things right between them.

"Thanks." She sniffled just a bit and then recovered herself. "A person can go a long time without food," she told him. "I read it in a book somewhere."

Pete had found new energy. He no longer slumped like he'd been beaten. "Weeks, I think. That's what Pancake Walapush told me anyway. His granddad was some kind of medicine man who used to fast for a week and no harm done."

She looked at the biscuit she'd found. "Then this has got to last a while."

They ate the biscuit. At first Lucy intended to eat just a few crumbs and save the rest of her half. But one tiny morsel was torture. Two weren't much better. And soon she'd wolfed down the entire thing.

Pete had done the same with his.

So now they were down to one piece of jerky. Lucy wondered if stories she'd heard about pioneers eating their shoes were true. If so her moccasins would probably be a good deal tastier (and easier to chew) than Pete's boots.

Pete stood up and began to gather kodok needles together to make himself a bed; his bedroll had been swept away, too.

They took their anti-dreaming drops as soon as the sky darkened. Pete lay down on the ground and heaped needles over himself. He looked like he was disappearing into the forest floor. As the moon rose, Lucy fought a nagging fear she'd wake up in the morning to find he'd been swallowed up whole. She kept looking at him, checking to make sure his head was still uncovered.

Soon Pete's breathing was deep and regular. He was asleep.

But the moon kept Lucy awake. Something about its fat, self-satisfied face was infuriating. Why did it have to look so smug, just when things were going so wrong?

She sat up in her bedroll and shivered against the cool night air. As she stared out at the inky forest, a light flickered in the distance. She held her breath and stared. It was the orange light—the same one they'd seen their first night after leaving Pentland.

Her neck tingled. *What was it doing here?*

Someone was following them. For a moment she had a wild hope it was her father. But that didn't make sense—how could he be *behind* them?

Whoever it was, they'd passed through the forest's traps thus far. That meant they'd brought food. Lucy's stomach gurgled, reminding her of their most pressing problem.

Pete slept peacefully. In the moonlight his face was relaxed and innocent.

"Pete," she whispered.

He didn't wake up, though the nighttime stillness made her feel like she'd shouted.

"Pete. Wake up!"

His breath came in contented rumbles. Lucy crawled over and pushed his shoulder. It was like trying to push a log. She shoved; he heaved and flopped, then snuggled farther down into his bed of kodok needles.

This was getting annoying. She found Pete's ear, hidden

beneath a sheaf of hair. For a moment she felt strange touching him, but the feeling quickly passed and turned to satisfaction as she grabbed hold of his ear and twisted . . . hard.

"*Ow!*"

He sat up, rubbing the side of his head and looking hurt. "What'd you do that for?"

Lucy's knees were damp from kneeling on the forest floor. She stood up, brushing kodok needles from her legs. A few ragged patches of mist hung low to the ground like a trail of floating islands making a path between her and the mysterious orange glow.

"The orange light is here."

"What?" Pete said groggily. He lumbered to his feet in a way that suggested a sleepwalking bear.

Lucy took a few steps, stopping under a towering kodok. "The light we saw before. It's *here*."

He stood beside her, smelling of mulch. "Jiminy," he whispered.

"We've got to find out who it is."

"Oh no we don't."

"They could have food."

"Or they could take ours."

"Our one piece of jerky," she scoffed.

"That one piece is what's going to keep us alive." Pete was fully awake now; the sleepiness on his face had been replaced by suspicion.

"Well, I'm going." She knew Pete was probably right; they

should be more cautious. But she was tired of questioning herself, of being uncertain. She wanted to go back to being the old Lucy, before the Thumb. That girl simply did things, without worrying about the consequences.

"*Lucy . . .*" Pete pleaded.

She put on her moccasins, then started off into the woods in the direction of the twinkling orange light. The moon lit her way well enough, and she was careful to walk silently. Niwa would have been proud of her.

Behind her she heard a dramatic sigh and then Pete's footsteps, following her.

The orange light came from a phos globe. Lucy could see the glass orb—it was about the size of a grapefruit—as a man held it on his palm. Flames danced inside it.

Once in her life she'd seen such a thing, in the grand mansion of a St. Louis steel magnate. A maid had slapped her hand when she'd tried to touch it. Only a few hundred existed, and the inventor who created them died without passing on his secrets. The flame in a phos globe never went out, nor did it transmit heat. You could carry one in your pocket and never worry about it burning you. Or you could toss it in the air—as the man was doing now, as if this very rare and expensive thing were nothing more than a toy.

Pete crouched beside her, tense and wary. They had crept to the edge of a campsite. On the ground, sitting next to their bedrolls, were three more men.

They were settlers, burly men with short hair and beards and flannel shirts rolled up over meaty arms. Why would they be following her and Pete?

"It was the devil rigged that river to flood," one of them said suddenly, as if reviving an argument from before. He was boulder-size with a blocky head and seemingly no neck. "It was the devil what killed them."

"Anyone you ask says this forest is cursed, yessir." This man was anxious. In the faint light provided by the phos globe she could see someone small and wiry with a coxcomb of hair springing up from his scalp.

"*Bull pucky,*" said a cantankerous country voice, punctuated by the wet sound of spitting. "It was their own fault. If Rambles and Charley had left the gold alone and run they'd be alive right now."

So that was one mystery solved. It was Rambles and Charley—whoever those poor men were—whose bodies they'd seen. Lucy turned to Pete. He was listening so intently it was as if he'd forgotten she was there. But as she planted her knees on the ground to get comfortable, he gave her a quick nod. They should stay and listen and find out just who these men were. For the men hadn't figured out the river trap, but neither were they going mad from dreams—which meant they'd discovered at least some of the Thumb's secrets.

"No, it's the devil," the man without a neck said. He talked in a thick, stubborn way, and Lucy didn't have to see his face to know he was as big and dumb as an ox. "There wasn't a cloud in the sky and then it floods. That is the work of a Lupine devil. There's only one thing to do with devils and that is burn them out. Burn them out completely."

"Can't we have a fire?" said the anxious voice. "Your light is pretty enough but it doesn't warm a body, and I'm sick of cold food."

"A fire," said the cantankerous spitting man. "That's the first sensible thing I've heard. If we're burning things up, let's start right now, right here. I'd like a good bonfire myself."

"No fire," the man with the globe said, knifing through the men's grumbling. She'd heard that voice somewhere. Beside her, Pete stiffened—he knew the voice, too.

It was Angus Murrain, she was sure of it. She got to her feet, ready to rush forward. But Pete grabbed her hand and pulled her back down. He raised a finger to his lips.

Lucy didn't understand why they should listen instead of announcing themselves, but she humored Pete and settled back into a crouch.

"So you think there's truth to the old tales?" asked the man with the reedy, fearful voice. "The forest here hates fire."

Angus answered wearily, "This forest is like any other. It's just trees, Silas. And trees do not feel. I've cut down enough to know."

"But first Donner runs off mad in the night, then Rambles and Charley don't even notice the water coming. That's three men dead already," said the fearful Silas. "It wouldn't have happened in an ordinary forest."

"I'll tell you what's *not* ordinary—going without fire," said the spitter. His was a grumbly voice, and Lucy thought if they did have a fire he'd complain of smoke or too much heat.

"I won't have a fire, Cranbull, and that's that." The timber baron was losing patience.

"Because of what the girl told him," Cranbull said in an aside, hocking spit again. "*She* told him about the hoodoo here, and part of it was no fire. So guess what, fellas, we're taking orders from a girl."

"Her advice has kept us alive so far," Angus said coolly. "I only hope we can find her in time."

Lucy held her breath. *The girl.* They had to be talking about her. And he was trying to find her . . . save her.

She scrambled to her feet, no longer caring what Pete thought.

The men startled at the sound and the timber baron called out, "Who's there?"

"It's Lucy," she cried. "We're here!" She ran forward, stumbling into the circle of men, who looked at her in surprise.

And there stood Angus Murrain—his size and strength were comforting; he'd shelter her against this horrid forest.

"Thank goodness we found you," he said, crouching down to her level. Even in the dark, she felt reassured by his strong, handsome face. "You're not hurt? Are you hungry?"

She nodded emphatically. "I'm starving."

"What do you mean, '*we're here*,'" said Cranbull; the spitter was gruff and broad chested. "Who's we?"

That's when Lucy realized Pete was still hiding in the shadows. Why was he hanging back? Lucy pulled away from the timber baron. "Pete," she called. "Pete, come on."

She stared into the blackness of the woods, feeling a tickle of anxiety. Since the first night on the Thumb she could not escape the fear that the forest would swallow them.

But after a moment Pete did come, kicking the tree roots, a sullen, closed look on his face. Lucy stared at him in confusion.

For some reason he didn't want to be rescued.

In the morning Lucy was thrilled to find corn cakes with jam for breakfast.

She'd slept well and woke early. Pete was still not up; he lay in the abandon of heavy sleep. The blanket he'd been given last night was all bunched, one bare foot outstretched. A foot that was just asking to be tickled by a feather or leaf.

But since last night—when she'd stepped forward and Pete lagged behind—something changed between them. She wondered if he would laugh if she tickled him, or if he would just give her the betrayed look she'd seen in his eyes when he'd watched her take a blanket from Angus. Now she left him and went to join the men.

Anxious Silas had a weasely face that went with his sharp, nervous voice. He wore a greasy leather vest, and his rooster's crest of spiky red hair made him seem naturally combative. The man who'd talked of the devil was Jank, broad and slow, small-eyed, with a deep black beard that covered his curious lack of neck. He wore a red-and-white-checked shirt that gave him the appearance of a giant picnic cloth. Both watched her eat as if they thought she might steal from them.

"No coffee," Cranbull griped to her as she reached for another corn cake. He had been the one in favor of fire last night. In daylight, gray showed in his fuzzy muttonchop whiskers, which clung to a jowly bulldog face. He was stout, and his suspenders curved around his chest like stays on a barrel. "Because *he* says we can't have a fire." He glanced darkly over to where Angus sat, eating his breakfast and studying a piece of paper.

When the timber baron saw them looking at him, he smiled at Lucy and waved her over. He cut a dashing figure, with his dark glossy curls spilling over the collar of his chambray shirt. He wore soft moleskin trousers and fine leather boots. A column of morning light fell on him just so, as if to underscore how lucky they were to have found him.

"I realized as soon as you were gone that I never should have let you go by yourself," he said, making room for her beside him. Lucy sat down, sitting cross-legged in her Lupine tunic and leggings. "I was beside myself. So I got a few men together to come find you."

Pete, who'd finally woken up, shambled over to them, still barefoot. "Did you tell my parents you were coming after us?" Pete asked without so much as a *good morning*. His face looked pinched and his eyes squinty; clumps of his hair flew up as if while he slept his head had grown scores of stubby brown wings, all trying to take flight.

Angus's eyes flickered over him. "No." He looked at Pete as if unimpressed by what he saw. "I heard some story about how you had volunteered to take Lucy down the coast toward San Francisco. And I decided to keep your secret safe."

So Pete was not in trouble for lying to his parents. That was good. Lucy looked encouragingly at Pete, hoping he would see it that way. She remembered how Pete had stood up to the raven men, and how he'd crossed his arms in Governor Arekwoy's office, almost daring the Lupines to mess with him. For someone who got spooked by any old ghost story he certainly was cocky around people. And now she tried to smooth things over.

"You found us just in the nick of time," she told the timber baron before he could draw the wrong conclusions about Pete. "We were in a real pickle."

"We were doing all right," Pete said. He did not sit down but continued to hover nearby, making vain attempts to control the chaos of his hair.

"For the moment perhaps." Angus turned from Pete, who he obviously found lacking in manners, and back to Lucy. He ran a hand rakishly through his dark hair. "But luckily we're here now. And we have plenty of food. Plus, we have other items of interest as well."

He indicated the paper he was studying, and Lucy leaned forward to get a better look.

"I was only able to find one map of the Thumb," he said, smoothing the paper out on a mossy tree stump. "I had to make this copy from the Pentland Historical Society. The map they have is one of the few surviving documents from the lost settlement."

Lucy loved maps, especially ones that had any hint of mystery to them, and she could think of no map more exciting than one from a lost settlement. She shivered deliciously as she bent over it, imagining that this crisply drawn copy was actually the stained and crumpled original, smuggled out from the doomed settlement with great effort and passed from hand to hand as secretly as a treasure map.

"And no one knows what happened to them?" she asked. She remembered the disquieting line from her father's notebook: *He killed them all.*

Angus stretched out his long legs. "Any number of things might have done them in. Disease. A bad winter. But people in Saarthe don't want such a boring explanation. It has to be curses or evil." He looked up to the sky, as if hoping somewhere to find the strength to deal with such idiocy. "The truth is, they were living on the edge of civilization, nearly cut off from the mainland. There doesn't need to be any mystical explanation for bad luck."

Such a simple truth, but Lucy was struck by this. Her father always looked to the spirit world to explain trouble—all the invisible currents of grievances and emotions that made houses unhealthy, crops wither, and factory equipment fail. But maybe sometimes bad luck was just that and no more. She looked at the timber baron's proud face. *He doesn't let the unseen world govern him,* she realized, *he simply does what he sets out to do.*

The thought was both thrilling and troubling—it felt disloyal to her father—and she bent her head to the map, trying to get her feelings back in order.

"The Lupines say the dreamwood spirit killed them," Pete countered, putting his back against a tree.

"*Some* of them think that," Lucy corrected.

Angus gave a tight smile. "Fortunately I don't put too much stock in stories like that," he said dismissively. "And what happened a hundred years ago matters little to our business today."

Pete shook his head. "I suppose that's what you think."

Lucy couldn't understand why Pete was being so disagreeable. She pointed to a squiggle on the map she thought was the river.

"Is this where we are?" she broke in.

Angus leaned forward. "My guess is here." He stabbed a finger at a spot two-thirds of the way to the tip of the Thumb. "And this should be the old settlement." He pointed to a triple line enclosing some triangles.

There were other strange marks on the map, and Lucy was determined to puzzle them out. "What are these little stars?" They were scattered about the Thumb.

"I've no idea," the timber baron said. "But my hope is they mark dreamwoods. The people who lived here used to harvest them. We should be closing in on one of these marks soon. But this map isn't drawn to scale. And so far, even with it, we've been wandering in the dark. Our compasses don't work, and even Silas, who could tell you which way was north after being spun around blindfolded, can't seem to get his bearings here."

He looked at her expectantly, and Lucy realized in a heady rush that he was hinting that he needed help. Of course, he wouldn't come right out and say he couldn't find his way—not in front of the others. Their nervousness and unhappiness with the expedition was thick as smoke. But she could help Angus lead them. Her hand reached for the leather cord around her neck.

"Dang it!" Pete exclaimed suddenly. He hopped about on one foot, wincing. Lucy leaned out of the way, trying not to get stepped on; but it was a bit like trying to avoid a deranged jack-in-the-box.

"What's the matter?" She snatched her foot away before he could smash into it.

"I stepped on something." Pete groaned and shut his eyes. He put one hand on Lucy's shoulder and leaned into her as if he'd fall over otherwise. "Can you help me back to my things?"

Lucy got to her feet, helping support him, while Pete made terrible huffing noises. She tried not to react to the sun-bronzed arm draped across her shoulders—an effort made easier by the fact that Pete continued to groan loudly in pain. "Come on, then."

Angus watched impatiently. "You should think about wearing some shoes," the timber baron pointed out.

"Good advice," Pete called over his shoulder as he hopped on one leg.

Pete's arm was heavy around Lucy's neck, but it grew lighter the farther away they got from Angus and his map. And Lucy did not think Pete was a very good actor—his emotions flashed across his face too easily.

They reached his blanket and Pete collapsed onto the ground.

"So what was that about?" she asked as Pete made a show of rubbing his injured foot before putting on his shoes.

"Nothing," Pete said innocently, looking up at her from where he sat, tying his shoelaces with excruciating slowness. But he had wanted to get her away from Angus. Why?

"What's the matter with you?" She put her hands on her hips. "Now we've got a real chance of finding my father—"

"We always had that," Pete interrupted. He cocked his head in Angus's direction and lowered his voice. "It's not like we need him for it. You're the one with the compass. All he's got is that lousy old map." He looked up at her and his face was suddenly earnest. "I think you should keep your compass to yourself."

Lucy rubbed her temples. She remembered their trip to Pentland and the reverent way Pete had mentioned Angus Murrain's name. She sat down beside Pete. "I don't understand. I thought you looked up to him."

Pete snorted. "That was before he wouldn't give Pa more time to pay him back. Instead he bought our house out from under us, and cheated us on the price."

She remembered the day Angus had come. *You've been more than fair,* Gordon had said.

"Your father didn't think he'd been cheated," she pointed out.

"My pa got ruined." Pete yanked hard at the laces on his boots. "Course he didn't want to admit that. I don't trust Angus Murrain farther than I can throw him."

"I'm sorry you feel that way," Lucy said primly. "But Angus

Murrain hasn't done anything to me. In fact, he invested in my expedition."

"Your expedition? What?" Pete forgot he was supposed to be injured as he jumped to his feet.

Straightaway Lucy wished she could take the words back. But there was no help for it. "You laughed at me, so I struck a deal with him."

"What kind of deal?" A heavy, angry look came into Pete's face.

Lucy pulled at the fringe on her tunic. She realized she should have told Pete—why hadn't she done that at the beginning? He'd surprised her by wanting to come. And then there'd been the excitement of getting started. She hadn't thought it would matter to Pete. Though now of course she saw that it did.

"He gave me fifty dollars for supplies," she admitted. "And I said he could have half the dreamwood I brought back."

Pete's jaw hardened. Then he laughed unpleasantly. "That's a good deal for him. He puts in fifty dollars and gets a fortune back."

Lucy bit her lip. Put this way it did sound like she'd made a poor deal—she just hadn't thought that way at the time. But she didn't want to admit this to Pete. And besides, if she hadn't gotten that money they wouldn't have gotten their *antimorpheus* drops. Pete had no idea how much the little vial in her pack cost. "Is that what you're sore about?" she asked. "When I talked to him I didn't know you were coming. If I'd known—and if I'd known how you felt about him—I wouldn't have done it. I know you need the money. I'd have let you have all the dreamwood."

Pete lifted his chin and his expression got stonier—she'd said the wrong thing. "That's not why I'm sore. I'm sore because I trusted you."

Lucy's stomach sank—she could tell from Pete's tone this was a much worse offense. "And I trust you," she began tentatively.

"No, you don't. Otherwise you'd have told me something this big." He snatched up his blanket from the ground and began angrily to fold it. Lucy looked up at him, feeling that if he would just listen she could explain everything.

"I didn't mean to keep it from you." She clasped her hands together, pleading with him. "It just happened."

"Maybe so," he said with a dark look. "But I guess it's easy to have all the answers if you don't tell anyone anything."

Lucy felt the blood rush to her cheeks. She thought for a second about apologizing again, then threw that thought away. Someone who made her feel so awful didn't deserve it. She stood up and faced him. "So you *do* think I'm a know-it-all. Those things you said at the river—that's how you actually feel."

His eyes flickered dangerously—the river still a fuse between them. "And you think I'm just some country boy who can't keep up with you."

She took in a breath, bouncing on her feet with anger. "That's not true."

"Lucy," Angus called. "Can you spare a moment?" He was

waiting expectantly with the map. Waiting for her thoughts and advice. She would much rather be with the timber baron right now. But if she went over there, Pete would think everything he'd said about her was true.

"Go on back to your *partner*," Pete said as if he knew what she was thinking. "Seeing as how they're getting half the dreamwood, the least they can do is feed me. I'm going to find some breakfast."

He stomped off. But by then everything was already packed up with the others waiting for them—and so they had to go on. Pete shot a knifelike glance at her. She had made him miss breakfast. If she'd wanted to make him angry at her, she couldn't have found a better way.

15

They walked for several hours, up and down a series of steep hillsides, as they tried to make their way to the Thumb's high point. Angus wanted a vantage point to look down from, hoping to see their way from his map. But the slopes were choked with fallen timber, and it was slow going.

Even though she was still upset with Pete, Lucy kept her vitometer inside its pouch. She should just bring it out and read the way forward. Several times she had almost done that. But at the last moment, she'd hesitated, grasping the cord around her neck. And as the day wore on, Lucy felt it would be awkward to suddenly reveal her secret compass, and so she kept it hidden inside her tunic.

Pete was not speaking to her. Instead of getting over his grievance, he was settling into it, testing it—she would say something and he would merely grunt a reply—like someone breaking in a new pair of boots. Gradually, he'd fallen to the back of the group, while Lucy walked on ahead with Angus.

Silas and Jank were in the middle, making an odd pair. Silas was compact and quick, with a suspicious face beneath his fiery crest of hair. His eyes darted at every noise, and he continually thrust his hands into the pockets of his dirty leather vest, bringing out a protection stone like Pete's, which he fingered obsessively.

As they walked, he kept up a running commentary: "Leaves of four, settle a score. That there's Widder's Nuckle. Make a tea of it and you'll be dead before you can take your boots off. Hear that? That's the call of the blue-breasted tolliver; if one of those crosses your path it's thrice bad luck. Throw salt over your right shoulder quick as you can or you'll be sorry. Wolf-face newts heal chilblains, but you have to catch the buggers first . . ."

And then there was his opposite, Jank, almost comically big and muscular, though it seemed all his muscles had squeezed out his vocal cords, for he was woefully inarticulate except on the one subject that excited and terrified him: the devil.

Periodically he would give them all a fright by stopping abruptly and crying out, "There it is. The devil in the woods! There!" Then he would unsling his massive ax and plant his feet while his small eyes glared tremblingly at his unseen foe. These were episodes—Lucy quickly learned—you simply had to wait out. For nothing devil-like would appear and Jank would eventually grunt, fasten up his ax again, and resume tramping through the forest with that dead-eyed gaze of his, saying nothing to Silas's constant chatter.

Not so Cranbull. He walked behind Silas and tried his best to ignore the little man, but it was an effort beyond his abilities.

About every five minutes Cranbull harrumphed and hocked spit, usually aiming in Silas's direction. Now and then he would simply stop and announce "bull pucky" to something Silas had said. Lucy was afraid the two would come to blows.

Angus paid them no attention. He helped Lucy over a series of logs, so the two of them were ahead of the others.

Gradually their lead increased. Lucy couldn't help turning around now and then to reassure herself that Pete was still following them. When last she looked back, Jank—impossible to miss in his red-and-white-checkered shirt—was having another spell of his, and as he stood there, twitching his ax, the others stood frozen in place lest he suddenly turn on them. But the timber baron saw no reason to wait. He kept walking, and Lucy, feeling important that she was by his side, walked with him as they climbed higher up the slope.

"Your father told me something of his research before he left," the timber baron said. "He said he was writing a book about the history of ghost hunting in the American States."

Her father had long spoken of wanting to write such a book, and Lucy always assumed she would help him research it. But since arriving in Saarthe she had seen how little he'd thought to tell her of his actual plans. She said rather grumpily, "I suppose that's why I was put in school in San Francisco. So I wouldn't interfere and he could write in peace."

Angus looked at her with amusement. "I think he worried that he would stand in your way and interfere with *you*."

That didn't make any sense. She stopped with one moccasin

braced against a fallen kodok branch and wiped the sweat from her forehead. "Stand in *my* way? How?"

The hillside was steep and even Angus's breathing was labored. He seemed glad to have a reason to stop.

"A ghost clearer?" he asked her, raising his eyebrows. "In this age of modern science and technology? Not exactly the sort of father one would wish for."

Lucy's cheeks burned. This was what the girls at Miss Bentley's had said, though in much crueler words. "He helped people." She scowled at him.

Angus rolled up the sleeves of his sweat-stained shirt. "Less and less. He told me electricity was putting him out of business. All the electric lights and currents we have around us are disrupting the spirit world. Ghosts are dying out, so to speak." He allowed himself a modest smile at this clever expression.

"Yes, but some ghosts persist," Lucy said, planting her feet.

"Perhaps. The only people bothered anymore by ghosts are the eccentric and weak-minded. Or the poor who light their homes by burning trash or snake oil." The timber baron rested a hand on a nearby kodok; Pete and the others still hadn't caught up to them. "But this is what I don't understand. Instead of turning to something current and modern—for instance he could have done great work in the study of energy and charges—your father decided to look back. He went further in the wrong direction, standing in the way of progress, almost as if he wanted to ensure he'd never be a success."

Lucy didn't answer, thinking of the Maran Boulder. Had her

father been standing in the way of progress then? He certainly had wanted to save the boulder from the railroad. *What would it mean, Lucy,* she remembered him saying, *if there are concentrations of the Od that were found in certain places? In rocks or rivers, perhaps trees. Things we don't usually think of as alive. What is that power source? How could we understand it?* But the railroad hadn't wanted to understand it, they'd simply dynamited it.

Angus smoothed back his dark hair. "I remember we were in the Climbing Rose, and he told me he'd left you in San Francisco. Even in a place as superstitious as Saarthe he had trouble finding work. He wanted the reward so he could afford to keep you in school."

"Keep me there?" Lucy was stunned. How many more knuckle raps and hours of being made to stand in a corner would she have accumulated in another year at Miss Bentley's? "So he never meant to send for me?"

The timber baron frowned. He'd caught his breath, but showed no signs of wanting to move on from where they stood on the steep slope. "Not that I know. He was worried about how he would pay the next year."

Lucy stared fixedly at the bracken on the ground. The letter she'd kept in her pocket, his promise to send for her—that was all a lie?

"He talked about you," Angus told her, while she grappled silently with her feelings. "Said you had a fine mind, were quick witted, and brave—all things I can see quite easily for myself."

These were exactly the things Lucy had always wanted to

hear about herself. But she didn't want to hear them with the rest of what Angus was saying.

"He also said you were getting to the age when a young lady's reputation mattered. How did he put it?" Angus searched the trees as if hoping they might remind him of the exact phrasing her father had used. "He wanted to protect you from the 'taint of his association.' He was sure that in time you would come to see that it was for the best."

Lucy didn't know what to say. He'd wanted her to stay at Miss Bentley's, a place she'd despised. That's what he'd wanted her to turn into? And he thought she'd think it was for the best? There was a lump in her throat as big as an egg, and her eyes stung with tears.

Angus sighed. "Of course he only did that because he cared for you."

That wasn't true at all, Lucy thought bitterly. If he'd cared for her he would have kept her with him. She thought of Governor Arekwoy sending his raven men after Niwa, unable to let her go. Niwa's father intended to have her take over for him one day. Whereas her own father had simply cast her away—caring more about spirits than his own flesh and blood.

She was biting the inside of her cheek so hard the copper salt on her tongue made her realize she was bleeding.

"I didn't mean to upset you," the timber baron said. He squatted down to be closer to her level. His deep brown eyes stared into hers with concern. She tried to turn her face away, but he *tsk'd* and cupped her face in his hand.

"There, there, Lucy." He brought out a fine cotton handkerchief, monogrammed with an *M*. "Maybe your father did you a favor. Have you thought of that?"

A favor helped somebody, so she shook her head. "What do you mean?"

"You're free to make new friends." He smiled gently at her. "Friends who care about you and see your qualities. Who appreciate you and think you're special."

If she spoke she would cry, and she wasn't going to blubber in front of Angus. She had thought her father did think of her that way. He'd praised her for knowing the answers to the questions he asked; he quizzed her about matter and physics and ghosts. And she'd misinterpreted it all, thinking that because she knew the right answers she was part of what he did. But, no, he simply wanted to pack her off somewhere out of sight while he continued his work—not *their* work, as she'd once thought. Just his.

How she wanted to go home. But she had no home. There was no place for her.

Angus stood watching her, waiting for her to speak. She sniffed once and handed back his handkerchief.

"Thank you," she said quietly, making sure her voice didn't tremble.

"Keep it," he told her as if he were made of pocket handkerchiefs. "I think you'll do better now. We're partners, aren't we, Lucy?"

She nodded. She remembered how excited she'd felt when

they'd shaken hands in Gordon's study. The memory seemed like something from a long-ago, uncomplicated time.

"And we'll find the dreamwood together, yes?"

"Yes," she said woodenly.

"I do need your help," he said. "You see how Cranbull and the others are practically useless. They don't have the head for this sort of thing. I can't imagine what your father was thinking not bringing you when you've got all the training, and you know how to use the tools."

Lucy scuffed the ground. "I guess he just wanted me to stay behind and be normal. Though I don't see how I would become a scientist if I stayed back there."

Angus put his hands in his back pockets. "There are other ways of being what you want to be," he said knowledgeably. "You can still be a scientist, for instance, but why muck around with ghosts? You're a smart girl. Why not be scientific and successful? You can *be* successful, you know—it does not mean you have to be dull. You could never be that."

She pressed her lips together; it was not a smile, but the grimace of someone trying to convince themselves they were not about to cry.

"Goodness, your eyes are so big, you look like a hungry kitten." Angus patted the pockets of his moleskin trousers. He bent down and confided to her, "I do have some toffees I've been keeping to myself. Here's one for you, but don't tell your surly friend. Can you keep it a secret from the others?"

Lucy nodded and clasped the candy in her hand. She supposed it was better to know the truth. And though she was not glad Angus had told her these things, the truth made her feel somehow older and more grown up. *For the best*, her father had said. *It's for the best.*

And this must be another part of growing up; for the first time in her life she did not feel like eating candy. But she popped the toffee into her mouth anyway and felt the sugar crackle against her teeth without tasting any sweetness.

They reached a lookout point, but Lucy didn't even notice the view. She felt like a sleepwalker, cut off from the world and trapped in some private despair. She raised her eyes only when she heard Angus swear.

"What are those idiots doing? I've told them, no fires."

Lucy felt her heart stumble as she saw what he was looking at: a thin plume of gray smoke rising into the sky. Without a word she started running back the way they'd come.

Please don't let it be Pete, she thought as she careened down the hillside. Any minute she expected to hear a tree fall or see a boulder smashing by.

But the woods were quiet—frighteningly so. A feeling of watchful menace grew so intense that by the time she'd made it back to where she'd last seen the others she was no longer running, but creeping stealthily.

And then she saw that things were much worse than a fire.

For there was Cranbull, squatting on his haunches by the small blaze, turning a small animal on a spit. He had *killed* something.

They were going to die—that was her thought as she flew in front of him screeching, "Put it out. Put it out now!"

"Hold on." Cranbull grabbed her hands, so she tried to kick dirt onto the flames. "What are you thinking?" he said angrily. "You're getting dirt on my supper!"

He caught her and lifted her off the ground, so she could only hammer at his shins with her moccasins. For the first time she wished she still had her boots on; maybe then he'd have let her go.

And where was Pete? Was he all right? She twisted against Cranbull's thick, crushing arms.

Angus came striding toward the fire. "What is the meaning of this?" he demanded. "Cranbull, put her down."

Cranbull dropped her as if she were a sack and Lucy struggled to her feet.

"He caught something." Lucy trembled as she pointed a finger at him. "You were cooking it."

"I got tired of the provisions," Cranbull said, narrowing his puffy eyes. "And the rabbits here will walk right up and put their head in the noose for you."

Lucy kicked dirt on the fire again. "You could get us all killed!"

"Now stop that," Cranbull said petulantly. "You're ruining a good rabbit."

"Go ahead, eat it," Lucy shot at him. "You'll be sorry."

The timber baron crossed his arms. "Where are the others?" he asked Cranbull.

Lucy scanned the forest, feeling she would burst out of her skin. "Where's Pete?"

"I don't know," Cranbull grumbled, pulling on his suspenders. "The kid said something about looking for higher ground while you two confabulated. They went that way. Should have been back by now, unless something happened to them." He sounded almost hopeful.

"Jank! Silas," Angus called. "Get back here!" His voice fell as if he'd tried to shout through a padded wall. To Lucy it felt like the whole forest were watching them.

Cranbull bent to his rabbit and tried to clean the dirt off it. Lucy watched him in amazement. Surely he felt it, too? Any minute now he was going to die.

"Quit staring at me," he growled at her. "Or I'll take a switch to you."

There was rustling in the undergrowth behind her and Lucy jumped.

But it was only Pete and the others coming back. "What's going on?" Pete asked as he and Silas and Jank came into view. "Everything's gone dead quiet and we smelled smoke." He saw Cranbull and the fire and he stiffened. "Now we're done for."

"Be quiet, boy," Cranbull said. "You and the girl are starting to get on my nerves."

But he didn't need to warn them to be quiet. No one felt like talking.

"We should move on," Angus said. He gazed around at the trees as if they displeased him. "I don't like the feel of this place."

Cranbull took a last, defiant mouthful of his meal and then fell in behind the others.

For Lucy, the next few hours were torture. Her conversation with Angus Murrain left her feeling broken. She did not want to walk with him; even the sight of him was enough to bring back every painful revelation about her father. Pete was still angry with her. And Cranbull was a dead man. She couldn't understand why he hadn't been punished yet—perhaps His-sey-ak was toying with him first. The forest had never felt so watchful or malevolent.

Lucy fell farther and farther behind until finally she was behind even Jank, who preferred being last so he could guard their backs from devils. She could see his picnic-cloth shirt through the trees.

They were moving through a stretch of forest thick with dreary hemlocks when it happened. The light had turned, evening was still hours away, but she felt it waiting in the wings. Her nerves were frayed to nothing, her shoulders tight around her neck like a cowl.

She heard a sudden burst of birdsong, loud and jeering, and she stopped abruptly, staring wildly into the bracken.

But nothing appeared. And after a moment she started

walking again, afraid of being left behind. Jank's broad back was already yards ahead.

They kept walking.

The sun, which had been hovering above the treetops, began to descend, urging on shadows. A nameless dread settled over Lucy.

Even Cranbull appeared to sense it. He took on the hunched, nervous look of a marked man, and he no longer had the confidence to spit.

Shadows reached out toward them like grasping fingers, and the feeling of being watched became excruciating. But no matter where she turned, she could see no sign that they were being followed. She felt it, though.

Angus had slowed his pace. They were barely walking, each of them trying to make as little noise as possible. The air had turned thick as molasses. It took effort to keep going forward and not simply stop and give herself over to fear.

They reached a streambed where the ground was soft and loamy. Even the water seemed to make no noise. The banks on the other side were a temple of wood and darkness. Angus crossed first, then the others in single file, disappearing through the trees.

Lucy had just leapt across the stream when the ferns ahead of her waved and shuddered.

She heard a soft rumble of breath. Lucy turned, feeling time slow down. A giant mountain lion emerged, padding on silent feet, its golden eyes glowing like a demon's in the gathering twilight. This was what had been hunting Cranbull all afternoon, the presence they'd felt but hadn't seen. It passed her by with a silent snarl of warning, long teeth shining like blades. Its whiskers bristled like wires.

And then suddenly time sped up. Lucy had a sense of fur, muscle, blinding speed.

She screamed to alert the others but it was too late. The beast was already in midair.

"Help!" Cranbull managed to say once, before he was seized in the big cat's jaws.

Lucy clapped her hands over her mouth in horror as she watched Cranbull being shaken like a rag doll. Then the cat bounded away, still carrying him.

They could hear Cranbull's screams echoing through the woods, and then, abruptly, they stopped.

16

That evening, after they'd made camp, Angus gave them what Lucy supposed was meant to be a cheering-up speech. Only no one was particularly cheered.

"We can't panic," Angus told them. "Yes, we've had some bad luck, but we knew that coming here would be risky. Let's all remain calm."

"Four men dead now," Silas said. He paced back and forth as if electricity ran through him. "Four men gone and we're supposed to remain calm. How can we do that when we're all wondering who's next?"

Lucy looked over at Pete. He'd laid out his blanket on the other side of the circle, as far away from her as possible. More than anything she wanted to bury her face in his shoulder, as if his rumpled shirt could muffle the screams she still heard in her head. But he'd made it clear he wanted nothing to do with her.

Jank, sunk into a slow-burning anger, leaned against a tree and watched the other two men without joining in. His dark beard spread like an ink blot over his face. He made Lucy think of the coals at the bottom of a fire. Every now and then he would send up some spark of outrage—"We're doomed!" he would announce, or, "There's evil in the forest. Can you feel it? *I can.*"—then sputter out, glowering silently by himself.

"The devil killed him," said Jank, sparking now. "Killed him for spitting that rabbit and making a fire."

"Oh, shut up," Silas said, running a hand through his rooster's hair. "That makes no sense. You saw it was a mountain lion."

"A devil," Jank insisted, crossing his arms. His red-and-white shirt bulged with muscles.

"If there was a devil here, why, he would have loved Cranbull's fire," argued Silas. "Joined in, in fact, and we would have had a good blaze."

"Not all devils love fire," said Jank sullenly, making it clear he had some insight into the matter.

"I suppose you've made a study of it," Silas retorted, bouncing near and away from Jank like a bantamweight boxer.

Jank, bull-like, turned slowly to face him. "That's right."

"Stop this!" Angus's voice was like a slap, and they fell silent. "Spirit, devil, lion—it doesn't matter. We take nothing, eat nothing, burn nothing. Is that clear?"

Jank glowered as if he'd had his knuckles rapped. "Yes," he said sullenly.

Silas nodded and with an angry glance at Jank started to walk away. His narrow eyes glinted in the moonlight. He'd never looked so much like a weasel.

"Let's all get some sleep," the timber baron said.

And that would have been it, but then Pete spoke up.

"That's fine, except why don't you tell them the kicker?" Pete said, his voice crackling with tension. He stood up and faced Angus.

Lucy stared at him with an open mouth. What was he going on about? She'd never seen him look so angry, like a spring wound tight. As if the day hadn't been bad enough already, now he was going to pick a fight?

"And what's that?" Angus asked, cool and composed.

"I guess I've got to spell it out." Next to the timber baron, Pete looked small and scrawny.

"Please do, Master Knightly." Angus waved his hand, extending Pete an invitation.

"Well, here it is." Pete's voice was loud in comparison. "How are we supposed to take dreamwood out of here if the forest won't let us have anything?"

Lucy felt like she'd gotten the air knocked out of her. *Of course.* She hadn't thought of this at all. If they couldn't take gold from the river, if they couldn't eat a rabbit when they were hungry, how could they expect to walk away with the Thumb's most precious treasure? *You think I'm just a dumb country boy,* she heard him saying. She felt like the dumb one now.

How stupid she'd been, pleased to know every little thing they should do or not do. But she'd missed the bigger puzzle, something she should have realized from the day they first set out when Able Dodd had made his cryptic warning.

A strange look of respect came over Angus's handsome face.

He bowed his head slightly to Pete. "You are right, Master Knightly. Bravo."

Pete, evidently not expecting this, looked over his shoulder as if to say, *who, me?*

"There better be a way around this," Silas said, nearly bursting out of his greasy vest with indignation. "I came here to get my fortune."

Jank's tiny eyes looked like two dark holes in his bulky head. "If we can't get the wood what are we doing here?"

"You'll get your fortune, don't worry." Angus flicked some invisible speck from his shirt. He sounded almost bored.

"But this forest *is* cursed," Pete said, turning to address Silas and Jank. "There's a spirit here"—he looked at Lucy— "a nature spirit. And it's not going to let us take anything."

"Nature spirit," the timber baron scoffed. "Let me tell you a story. When I first came to Pentland we couldn't float logs downriver half the year. Why? Because supposedly there was a spirit in the river that wouldn't let us. Do you think I got to be the richest man in the territory by letting that stop me?"

No one said anything. Of course Angus couldn't be stopped.

"We dammed part of the river for six months. After that we never had any trouble."

Silas hung his head and Jank nodded silently.

Lucy should not have been surprised by this story, but she didn't realize how conflicted it would make her feel. Her father would never have done something like that, not without trying to understand the river spirit first.

Angus continued, pacing in front of them. "It doesn't matter if I believe or not. All I need to do is disrupt it." He looked at Lucy. "That's something your father taught me. The people who lived here used to harvest dreamwood. If they could do it, we can, too. I did a little research of my own before coming here. They used a special ax blade." With a showman's flair he went to their supplies and brought out an ax. In the starlight the blade shone like black ice.

"It's obsidian," he said. "Sharper than steel. And this young lady's father told me something else. What else can obsidian do, Lucy?"

Lucy knew the answer, of course. "It can cut bonds on both the physical and etheric planes. It's one of the few substances that can. But—"

Angus cut her off with a thin smile before she could tell him that her father refused to use obsidian because it was so unreliable. "Thank you, Lucy. I think your father worried perhaps he'd told me too many of his secrets. But we're lucky he did. And when we find him, he'll be lucky, too. Because with this ax we'll cut dreamwood down when we find it *and* cut the bond that keeps the spirit here." His heavy brows furrowed in mock consternation. "I don't know if you can 'kill' a spirit, but it doesn't matter. This 'nature spirit' will be broken, we can take as much dreamwood as we like, and that will be the end of Rust. We shall have several birds with one stone as it were, eh?" He stroked the gleaming black edge of the blade before covering it and putting it away.

He made it sound very simple, but Lucy doubted it would be that easy.

In the morning, a weak sun broke through runny clouds. The feeling of distrust lingered so strongly around the campsite it might as well have been a bad smell.

Angus thought that they were near one of the star-shaped marks on his map that he believed indicated dreamwood, and so he urged them forward as soon as they had breakfasted. He led the silent and miserable group along a streambed, heading slightly northwest.

This was not the direction that her vitometer pointed. But Lucy, her thoughts in a jumble, didn't correct him. The vitometer, when she'd looked at it a few minutes ago, showed a reading of Odic force well into the thousands, an unimaginable amount of energy. No one could hope to stand up to something like that, obsidian ax or no.

It was a weary trek, and no one spoke for long hours. At last, when it was well into the afternoon, the timber baron began to slow his pace; he clearly expected to find something soon. And even Lucy, tired as she was, began to perk up with excitement.

They were traveling through a flat stretch of forest where the tall kodoks were spaced far enough apart to let in columns of sunlight. But ahead of them, up a gradual slope, was a dense grove of giant trees, their low-hanging limbs linked together in a way she'd seen once before.

Lucy ducked behind a tree, pretending she had to relieve

herself. But instead she squatted with her vitometer, frowning. The needle pointed away. Whatever this was on the map, it wasn't a dreamwood.

She quickly put the vitometer back into its pouch. Angus, at the head of their party, was waving them on. "This is the spot." Without waiting, he went striding up the slope.

Silas's eyes glittered. He'd been worrying his protection stone throughout the day, but now he thrust it back into a pocket of his greasy vest and began to jog ahead. Lucy could see his rooster's crest bobbing up and down.

Jank, who would never be called quick, followed like a slowly moving boulder.

"Wait," Pete called out. Silas and Jank both turned to look at him.

"There's nothing up ahead but a bunch of smelly old mushrooms," he explained. "And if you go in there, especially this time of day, you'll see faces in the trees."

It was near twilight, and Lucy remembered the way the tree faces had emerged from the wood their first night on the Thumb.

"He's right," Lucy said, coming to stand beside Pete so he would know she was on his side.

Jank's small dark eyes considered the clotted shadows in the trees. "Jank," Pete said seriously, "don't go. I've seen those faces, and they're really frightening."

Now Lucy understood: Pete was looking out for Jank. If the big man saw the devil in normal trees, what would he do inside the grove where the trees actually did have devil faces?

"Stay with us, Jank," Lucy urged.

Silas, who'd been watching them suspiciously, spoke up in his reedy voice. "Well, I'm going. If there's dreamwood, I'm getting my share." He started off.

"It's not that easy, Silas," Pete called after him. As Lucy expected, Silas ignored him.

Jank, meanwhile, was slowly rubbing his hands together. He sniffed the air warily. "The devil is strong here. I feel him."

Without any warning he took out his ax and began swinging it in menacing practice circles.

They jumped back.

"Listen, Jank," Pete said, speaking with extreme caution, "you really should put that ax away before you cut something."

But Jank merely twisted his head from side to side, black beard wagging. His tiny eyes seemed alight with eagerness—whether to find dreamwood or to face the devil he feared, Lucy couldn't tell. He grunted once and took off after Silas and Angus, who were now climbing through the latticed branches. She could see Silas in his weathered vest scampering past the branch barriers like a rat disappearing into a thicket.

"Oh no," Pete said. He turned to Lucy, his forehead creased with worry.

"What can we do?" She didn't dare get near Jank when he had that ax.

"I don't know." Pete began to run up the slope toward the knot of trees. "But I'm worried something bad will happen if we don't stop him."

Lucy followed after him, dread increasing with each step.

Then they heard a bellowing roar.

They ran for the edges of the tree circle and climbed into the branches, looking in. The linked trees shut out the late-afternoon light, and Lucy could see the terrible faces in their trunks starting to reveal themselves.

Angus stood with a stunned expression at the center of the grove. Silas was bent to the ground. "Mushrooms!" he cried in a cheated voice.

Jank spun in circles, his ax raised. The giant lumberjack was a red-and-white blur.

For a moment Lucy hoped Jank might simply spin himself dizzy but at last he seemed to focus and stop, standing square in front of one of the trees. He was panting, tiny eyes staring at the tree's leering face.

"DEVIL!" Jank cried.

He ran straight at the tree, ax raised high.

Lucy's breath stopped in her chest.

With a terrible *thunk!* the shining blade dug deep into the wood. The entire grove shuddered as if it were one being.

All at once the air exploded with *cracks* as a flurry of twigs, sticks, branches flew forward with tremendous force—like arrows being loosed at close range.

Lucy squeezed her eyes shut. She heard a gurgling cry. When she could bear to look she saw Jank lying on the ground. His red-and-white shirt was all red now, and he bristled with twigs and branches like a pincushion.

He spasmed once and was still.

17

They left Jank where he'd fallen. It hadn't felt right to Lucy to leave him without some kind of tribute. But what could they do? She didn't even dare pick a flower to lay beside him. They'd left the grove and walked a short distance farther when they stopped and took *antimorpheus* together. Lucy's bottle was nearly empty, but Angus had plenty in his—he would have, considering there were drops enough for five dead men in it.

Then Silas could no longer contain himself. "Each day we stay here another one of us dies," he told the timber baron angrily. His long, weasely face looked thinner than ever, and he'd chewed raw a spot on his lip. "Who will it be tomorrow?"

Angus ran his hand through his hair and sighed, facing Silas. "You're right," he said wearily. "The longer we stay in this forest, the more dangerous it is for all of us." He turned to face Lucy and Pete. "Our lives depend on getting to the dreamwood as quickly as we can. We're in a desperate situation." Angus looked pointedly at Lucy.

For a moment Lucy thought he was angry. But then he said more gently, "Your father is one of the greatest ghost clearers in history. Perhaps he gave you something that could help."

Pete cleared his throat. "Lucy has a machine that can clear ghosts," he announced to everyone's surprise, including Lucy's. "I'll show you."

He marched over to her pack and brought out the sweeper, which wriggled in Pete's stocking. It looked like a fat angry sausage.

As he held it up he shot her a warning glance. Now she understood. Pete still didn't want her to show them the vitometer, so he was going to parade the sweeper around instead.

"Don't, Pete." Lucy could already imagine how the men would react to the sweeper. There weren't any ghosts here; it would just march up and down looking silly.

But Silas thought she was trying to keep secrets from them. His eyes glittering, he held out his arm to stop her. "No, let the boy show us."

"All right," Pete said, "prepare to be amazed." He untied the knot in the stocking and shook the sweeper onto the ground.

The egg shook with excitement at being freed. As soon as he put it down, the sweeper marched forward issuing earsplitting blasts of steam. For a few moments it looked formidable. Even Angus seemed to regard it with respect.

But there was a downed log in its path, and instead of going around, the sweeper simply collided with it. This obstacle seemed to enrage the egg; it butted heads with the log again and again. Finally, it hit the log so hard it ricocheted backward and fell on the ground, legs waving in the air.

Silas let out a long hiss of breath and then spat.

Angus's face was a thundercloud.

Lucy knew what they were thinking—William Darrington was a crackpot, a failure. An image of the Wickham newspaper with the picture of her father wearing his thought interferometer rose before her eyes: *Ghost Clearer Gone Mad.*

"Maybe I put too much stock in William Darrington," the timber baron said, staring into the twilight. He put his knuckles to his mouth as if trying to temper his disappointment. "I certainly expected more than this."

"I told you the girl wouldn't be any help to us," Silas said to his master. "The ghost clearer was a fool and his daughter is no better."

Wounded pride built inside Lucy. Her father was a brilliant man. Angus, with his precious map, was leading them in circles. None of them would have gotten this far without her father's discoveries. She was tired of people making fun of him, she was tired of being underestimated. *You should show him some respect.*

Lucy stepped forward, her chin quivering. "I have something that will lead us straight to it," she said. She drew out the soft deerskin pouch she'd kept hidden inside Niwa's tunic. It was a relief not to have to keep it secret any longer. "This will save all our lives."

Pete sighed heavily and hung his head. "There you go," he said. "She's got the answers."

"What is this?" The timber baron's eyes were bright with interest. He and Silas crowded around her to see better. It was getting dark, and Angus brought out his phos globe. Their attention bolstered Lucy and made her confident once again.

"A compass of sorts. I wasn't sure it was working correctly," she lied. She needed to give some reason for not revealing it before now. "But I did some tests this morning and it's accurate. This needle points to dreamwood."

"Let me see," Angus demanded.

Lucy lifted the brass lid, revealing the needle and compass points inside.

Angus scrutinized it before saying under his breath, "So the ghost clearer was telling the truth about this, at least."

His shoulders relaxed in relief. Then he clapped Silas on the back. "This is the first good news we've had since we got here."

"Indeed," Silas replied sourly. "Lucky it came to light *now*." He squinted at Lucy, and his nose twitched. "I'm on to you, girl," he came close and whispered. Lucy jumped as if she'd been pinched.

But the timber baron was in a celebratory mood. "Extra food for everyone tonight."

"Course there's extra food," Silas muttered under his breath. "And the more of us that die, the more leftovers there's going to be."

Still, Lucy noticed, he took his extra portion when it was

time to eat. She took her meal of salmon jerky and oat cakes and went to sit by Pete, who had found a soft, mossy spot near a clump of wild rhododendrons. They sat cross-legged with the food on a tin plate between them.

"Looks like wood, goes down like wood, too," he observed, chewing the tough dried fish. At least Pete was speaking to her again.

After they'd eaten, Angus squatted down beside her. "Do you mind if I study your device?"

By this time it was black night. Lucy supposed he might look at it by the light of his phos globe. But he wouldn't be able to see much.

Pete stopped chewing, his cheeks full of jerky as he waited to see how she would answer. He'd been so suspicious, she couldn't help but feel guilty for letting the timber baron see it. *It's my vitometer*, she reminded herself. *Pete doesn't tell me what to do.* She took out the vitometer once more and held it out to Angus. But she felt bare without it; she'd grown used to its comforting purr against her chest, and almost immediately she reached out her hand to take it again.

"You can't see anything good now," she explained. "Better wait till it's light."

If Angus was disappointed, he covered it well. "Of course," he said genially. On a sudden impulse he reached out and tousled her hair. "I'll look at it in the morning."

"Sure," Lucy said, feeling honored by this new mark of his affection. She reached up and smoothed her unruly braid.

Pete had been watching the two of them with a funny look on his face. "Happy now?" he asked her once Angus left.

Even a day ago she might have stuck out her tongue at him. But Jank's death had taken away any wish she had to snap at Pete. Now she just wanted them to be friends.

"No," she said. She threw her bedroll to the ground and climbed inside, staring stonily at the tree branches above.

A fog came in that night, one of the thick coastal fogs that settles like a blanket, and come morning is so thick and veiling that the whole world is gray.

Lucy was asleep when a rough hand yanked at her neck. "Who's there?" she cried. "What are you doing?" The fog had closed off the stars; no light peeked through the darkness.

She fought like a wild thing and heard a gratifying *oof!* of pain as her heels connected with the man's shins. At least then she knew she was dealing with a person and not some beast of the Thumb.

But he wasn't trying to hurt her—merely snatch the deerskin pouch from around her neck. The slender cord broke and suddenly the vitometer's weight was gone.

Panic surged through her as she whirled about in the fog. Muffled footsteps ran away.

"Pete!" she cried. "Help!"

A dark shape loomed before her. This time she was ready.

"Ow!" came a boy's voice after her punch landed. "It's *me*, darn it."

She'd hit Pete.

"I'm sorry." She could see him now, doubled over and gasping.

"It's all right, who needs ribs?" He stood up and winced. Lucy's hand went to her throat, feeling again a burn where the cord had pulled against her skin. "Mr. Murrain," she cried. "Silas took my vitometer!" She turned this way and that—but the soft, protected glen where they'd stopped for the night was empty. Beyond it the night was a gray shadow.

Beside her, Pete was still bent with pain. A disturbing noise—it sounded like *snorgle*—came from him.

"Are you *laughing?*"

Lucy wheeled about. She faced Pete, who was holding out his hands to defend himself.

"Oh, Mr. Murrain!" he parroted, then snorgled again as he gasped for breath. "They're gone. *Both* of them."

She could hear the truth of it in the silence of the forest, broken only by Pete's rough breathing.

Pete eased himself to the ground, cradling his sore ribs. "Once he had your compass he didn't need us. We'd just slow him down. And you heard Silas last night. The longer we stay here, the more people die."

"But . . ." She still had the timber baron's handkerchief. *You're quick witted*, he'd told her, *brave*. How could he have said such things, then left her behind? She touched her hair—he'd patted her head last night, but perhaps even as he did that he'd had his plan in mind.

We'll find dreamwood together, he'd said.

Now she saw everything that had happened in the light of his betrayal. She slid to the ground beside Pete. "I was getting in his way." Just like she was with her father.

"Don't say that," Pete said, grimacing as he shifted position. "I think if anything, he was getting sick of *me*."

It was awfully nice of Pete to say that. She wished she could laugh. But everything inside her felt broken, as if she were filled with shards of glass.

"No, it was me. And I know. I've been left so many times I feel like a piece of old luggage." She turned to Pete, feeling her heart brim. "My father was never going to send for me at Miss Bentley's School," she said desperately. "He was going to leave me there until I grew up and he didn't have to bother about me anymore. He wanted me to become one of *them*."

She hadn't thought she would ever admit this to anyone. But there seemed little point in trying to hide the true reason she was separated from her father.

Pete didn't try to joke now. "You don't know that."

But Lucy knew it in her heart, which throbbed with pain. And now she couldn't help it—tears dripped down her cheeks. "No. He didn't want me around."

"Hey now! Don't say that." Pete rubbed her shoulder urgently, as if more afraid of her tears than anything else on the Thumb. His hand felt warm, sweet, and she wished she could simply let it be. "No matter what, it'll be all right," Pete told her firmly.

She shook her head. "I don't fit in anywhere. You're right, I *am* a know-it-all, I always have to have the answer, and nobody likes that."

"That's just plain wrong. Look, I know you're stubborn and bullheaded and you're always right. But you're not alone. Whatever happens, you've got friends . . . you've got *me*."

He grasped her hand.

She blinked back tears and looked at him. She had Pete.

Who she was now dripping tears and snot all over. Hurriedly she dragged her hand across her face.

Pete was good enough to pretend he didn't notice. "I know this isn't going to lick us," Pete said. "We've still got one piece of jerky." He brought out a deeply suspect piece of meat from his pack. "And we're closer than ever. So let's go find your father."

"We can't," she said, snuffling. "They took my vitometer." The wiry arm around her neck had to have been Silas. The man was an absolute *rodent*.

On a sudden thought she opened her pack and looked inside. There was her ghost sweeper. Sensing that the pack was open, it wriggled hopefully.

"They didn't even try to take the egg." She felt her cheeks flush. For some reason she couldn't quite work out, she felt insulted that Silas and Angus hadn't thought it valuable enough to steal.

"They're a bunch of fools," Pete concluded. "Now, how can you put any stock in what Angus said if he just went and proved himself *that* stupid?"

She laughed and wiped her eyes with the back of her hand.

"I guess I shouldn't put any stock in it at all." Easier said than done. But Pete was making such an effort she felt she ought to try.

"Darn right."

She pulled her knees up to her chest and leaned against the tree trunk. "What are we going to do?" It was nearly dawn—she could see the shaggy rhododendrons they'd slept near—but she didn't think daylight would help them much. They'd still be lost . . . on Devil's Thumb . . . with almost no food.

To her surprise, Pete grinned. It was light enough to see his freckles, sprinkled across his boyish face. He looked almost *happy*.

"Did I say something funny?"

He gave her a sidelong glance that—despite everything that had happened—made her tingle with excitement. "You just asked me what we should do. That's the first time."

Lucy tugged her hair, which she knew was a wild tangle. "I'm sure I've done it before."

"I don't think so." Pete stood up and held out his hand. "But it just so happens I have an idea."

18

"Your vitometer was shaking a lot, wasn't it?" Pete asked her. He readjusted the bandanna around his neck, examined the moss around some kodok roots, and looked discerningly at the sky. Lucy recognized these signs of direction-finding without much optimism.

"Like a pudding," Lucy said. As the day dawned the mist turned a pink mother-of-pearl. She and Pete were surrounded by its rosy glow. But Lucy was not in the mood to appreciate it. They packed up their things and Pete broke off two painfully small pieces of dried meat from the jerky stub he'd found. Lucy tried to eat hers slowly, but that had been very hard to do. Now she stood beside Pete, determined to be strong.

Pete found a stick he could use to make drawings on the ground. He made a line for the river and some waves for the ocean. His technique could be called *impressionistic* at best, and although Lucy yearned to take the stick herself, she did not. "So we must be close. And we were heading west the whole day yesterday."

"Southwest." Even low as she was, Lucy felt it was important to be precise.

"All right. Southwest." They stood under a kodok near a clump of huckleberry. "And you saw his map."

"It's not as if it had 'location of the last dreamwood' helpfully marked on it."

"No, I realize that." Pete scratched his chin. "Well. The old-timers say dreamwood grows in clearings—like the tree circles we've found. Now, I was looking at that map, too."

He hunkered down, cleared away some kodok needles and continued to sketch in the soft earth.

"So if the stars on the map are the devil tree groves . . . This one here, I think that's where Jank . . . um, died. And there were two more. I think here and here."

Lucy bent down beside him. She realized how lucky she was to have him here; when she thought of how she'd very nearly told him to stay home, she couldn't believe it.

"So should we head for one of those?" she asked, gesturing at the two remaining stars.

Pete's face had the look of fierce concentration she'd seen on him the day they'd first met, when he'd been whittling. "I don't think so, and here's why. The big guy—His-sey-ak—Niwa said he's different from the other trees. Every other dreamwood is chopped down, right? So what else was on the map?"

Lucy closed her eyes and tried to remember. She'd depended so much on her vitometer she hadn't paid that much attention to the map. "There were some squiggles like houses or walls and beyond that . . ." She opened her eyes. Pete was looking at her expectantly.

"Beyond that there was this thing that looked like a big black spider, right?" He finished for her.

Lucy nodded. "I thought it was an ink blotch." An ink blotch with legs.

"That's what I thought at first. But now I'm not so sure. Whoever made that map drew trees as stars, so why not another tree as a spider? We are kind of like flies in His-sey-ak's web."

Lucy licked her lips nervously. She remembered Niwa saying, *How do you call things that eat meat?* She cleared her throat. "It was near the tip."

"Right," Pete said. He gave her his hand and pulled her up. "So that's where we'll head."

She held on to his hand a second longer. "Pete," she began without knowing exactly what she was going to say. "If it weren't for you . . . I don't know what we'd do now."

She'd surprised him. And now he gave her a bashful smile. "Oh. Well. I'm not doing anything much . . . just keeping us going."

But his cheeks flushed beneath his freckles, and he whistled happily for a few moments—for a short time apparently forgetting where they were and whose woods they were traveling through.

They set off through the forest, hoping they were going in the right direction. Long rolls of fog hung like hammocks between the trees; condensed mist dripped down from the kodok needles, falling every now and then on their heads with a taunting pitter-pat.

Even as the sun moved higher, the light stayed gray and the day cool. The trees opened up, but the fog only grew thicker. Soon Lucy's moccasins and leggings were wet from dew.

And then, ahead of them loomed a dark blocky obstacle, not a forest thing at all.

Lucy's heart pounded. "It's a wall." She ran forward.

Large round stones had been fitted together, taller than she was. They were crusted over with lichen, and the cracks between the stones were frilled with plants. The ragged mist shrouded it in mystery.

"We've found the lost settlement." This was not where they'd hoped to go—again the Thumb's mysterious geography had turned them around. But it was a relief from the forest, and it felt strangely reassuring to encounter something made by humans. Lucy grasped the stones, feeling excitement build inside her. There were good handholds; it would be easy to climb.

"Wait a minute . . . what are you doing?" Pete looked at her suspiciously.

"I'm going to explore, of course." Lucy was already fitting her boots into toeholds between the stones and heaving herself up. "My father's journal said the key was in the past." It seemed obvious enough they should investigate.

And then she was over wall, jumping down the other side into a field of tall saw-toothed grass.

After a moment, Pete jumped down beside her.

"Look," she said in amazement. "People really did live here."
Visible over the rippled grass were the dark slants of roofs.

It was just an ordinary field and yet there was a strange atmosphere of menace to the view with its cluster of distant buildings. She'd thought the lost settlement would be a handful of shacks; she was surprised to see large houses—several of them.

"I don't know about this." Pete stayed by the wall, like a swimmer reluctant to leave for deeper water.

"What's the matter?" Perhaps if she had not spent so much of her life in abandoned spaces she, too, would have wanted to give the lost settlement a wide berth.

"Well . . ." He looked embarrassed. His freckles faded into his blazing cheeks and he scowled, not wanting to say what bothered him. But automatically, his hand went for his protection stone.

Lucy decided he was very handsome when he was nervous.

"We do have the ghost sweeper," she said. "That will protect us." She hoped Pete didn't think it was too ridiculous after its last performance.

"You're really not afraid of ghosts?" he blurted out, his pebble-green eyes staring out at the abandoned town. Lucy had the impression it was something he'd wanted to ask for a while—only was too afraid of what it might reveal about him.

"I used to be." It seemed funny to think she'd once wanted to keep this secret from Pete. "My father used to take me along with him when he went clearing. In one old house a ghost led me down the basement stairs and slammed the door shut. I was trapped there in the dark."

She did not tell Pete the rest of the story. How the ghost had come for her in the dark; he'd hanged himself in life, and the most frightening detail of his ghost—the thing that gave her shivers even now—was the way his ghostly legs jerked, as if dancing. In her mind, Lucy called him the Hanged Man, and he occupied a special place in her fears.

"But," she said brightly, figuring it did no good to dredge up details about the encounter, "my father found me, swept the ghost away, and then he decided that if I was going to come with him I should know as much about clearing ghosts as he did." She told Pete about how her father had taught her to read the signs of ghost presence, how to disrupt them, how to protect herself if she was ever caught alone again with one, and so on.

"He taught you all that?" Pete was looking at her with a curious smile, as if he were waiting for her to see something right in front of her nose. "You know, it seems to me like he was trying to pass on his secrets to you instead of leaving you behind."

No he wasn't, she was about to reply. But then, even though she didn't believe Pete's interpretation, she decided it wasn't worth arguing about.

"Maybe," she said, gazing at the field. She clutched the straps of her pack; in the last few days it had gotten so light—and maybe she had gotten stronger—that she hardly felt it.

They walked across the field through the wet grass. It was a gray and chilly day, but it seemed *especially* gray and chilly in the lost settlement. Lucy did not think much of Denis Saarthe's abilities to choose a location for his town.

The first house they came on they approached with caution, the way one might a dead animal. It sat there with dark, blank-eyed windows, waiting for them.

"Maybe we should try to go inside," Lucy said forcing herself closer to it.

Its eaves were thick and the roof steep with weathered wooden shingles like an old European cottage. But the front of the house was painted with a face, like the faces on the Lupine lodges.

"Funny mix of Lupine and settler things," Pete said, studying it. "Makes you think they lived together, maybe even in the same house."

Part of the roof was covered with a thick parasitic moss; Lucy had the disturbing impression that the carpet of moss was slowly consuming the house, and might digest it entirely in another hundred years.

Summoning her nerve, Lucy tried the door. But as soon as she put her hand on it, the door slammed shut with a noise like a shot, startling a sinister trio of crows that were watching them from the nearby trees.

The black birds rose into the sky with a noisy clamor, and Lucy's breath caught in her chest. She could have sworn the door had been swinging open just a moment earlier. In fact, it was open a crack right now.

"Maybe it's just stuck." Pete reached out, and the door

snapped closed on his fingers. "Ow!" he cried and scrambled away.

"A poltergeist," she told Pete, whose eyes were as round as coins. "I should have figured. It's nothing to worry about."

"Easy for you to say, I just had my fingers pinched." Pete held the tips of his sore fingers to his mouth.

Lucy pulled him away from the house. "What I mean is, they're not really dangerous. They were never people to begin with, like real ghosts, instead they're . . . bits and scraps of spirit. Nuisances." She did not add that poltergeists were attracted by the same energies ghosts were. Pete appeared unnerved enough as it was.

Pete looked in alarm at the squat, brooding house. "If that's just a nuisance, what can a real ghost do?"

Lucy knew the answer, of course. "There's electrical pulses all through your body," she explained. "They help your heart beat, and your brain work. And ghosts have a strange connection to electricity. So a powerful ghost—a dangerous ghost—can disrupt those signals in your body. And when that happens your heart can stop beating or your brain can stop working. People will say someone died of fright, but it's really a ghost messing with the electrical pulses of your heart."

"Oh, *great*." Pete looked aghast. "That clears *that* up."

Usually, Lucy thought information like this was fascinating. But there were times, like now, when she sometimes wondered if it were better not to know so much.

In silent agreement they turned away, and went on, passing

more buildings, flimsy and bent like paper left out in the rain. In a short while they found the center of the town. The street was overgrown with weeds and nettles, and on either side collapsing buildings leaned like stalks of rotten vegetables.

Lucy's neck prickled with the sense of being watched. At each building they tried to enter the same thing happened. Shutters came slicing down, narrowly missing their fingers. Doors slammed in their faces. Steps broke like eggshells under their feet. And occasionally Lucy thought she heard footsteps behind them, although each time she whirled around, the street was empty.

"A lot of ghosts here," Pete remarked with his shoulders up around his ears.

Lucy could feel their presence, but for a place so obviously haunted, something didn't feel right. "Yes," she said, frowning, "but I think they're just a few poltergeists. I wonder where all the *real* ghosts are."

"Hopefully far away from here," Pete said, giving her a look that said he would never be as comfortable with ghosts as she was.

While he went on ahead, Lucy looked in her pack. Her ghost sweeper was still trying to kick its way out of Pete's sock—but with no more urgency than usual. Lucy wrinkled her nose at it. Was it not paying attention? Or was her intuition right, and the ghost town strangely devoid of ghosts?

Pete looked in one window and whistled in appreciation. "Look at this."

Lucy stood on her tiptoes beside him. Hundreds—maybe thousands—of gold coins were spilled across the floor. She peered through another window and saw furs stacked like bales of hay.

She turned to Pete and saw him looking as puzzled as she was. "Angus said they might have had a bad winter, or gotten sick—but this doesn't look like the kind of place where that would make everyone disappear."

"Not with that much money," Pete agreed. "They could have bought all the food they wanted or shipped in doctors by the crate. Funny to think we've been looking all over for dreamwood when there's a fortune sitting in the lost settlement."

She elbowed him. "Pete."

"Don't worry," he said quickly. "I'm not taking anything. I learned my lesson." He gave the gold one last, regretful look and stepped away.

They turned a corner onto the main street and stopped short, both of them gazing up at the tree that blocked their way.

The most disturbing thing about this tree was not that it was plumb in the middle of the street, it was that the huge tree was *upside down*. Its root end stuck up in the sky, its top plunged deep beneath the earth. It leaned slantwise as if it had been stabbed into the ground.

Lucy's stomach twisted. The upside-down tree was so unnatural it disturbed her far more than anything else she'd seen in the settlement. "What could do that?"

"Look, another one," Pete whispered. A few yards away a tree had been sent straight through the window of a store. Its shaggy roots dangled outside the frame, black and sinister. There were other tree spears shot into the earth all up and down the main road. "It's like something used this place as a dartboard."

They wandered down the eerie street in silence. A ridiculous urge built inside her to run. But she looked at Pete; his face was tight but he was controlling himself. She took a deep breath instead.

They went on until they came to a large barnlike building. Through sagging open doors she could see the gleam of a saw blade. Many of the wall and roof boards had been peeled off or splintered, as if the structure itself had been flayed.

This is where it happened, she thought. She'd been in enough places tainted by murder, massacre, or crime to recognize the dark, brooding feeling that emanated from the barn.

"Lucy . . ." Pete said in a voice of quiet horror. He'd stepped up to the open doors and looked inside. "I found them."

Light spoked through the dark interior, crisscrossing the space in golden lines.

On the ground amid piles of rotten sawdust were tangled heaps of fabric and shoes and . . . sticks? It took Lucy a few disbelieving moments to realize they were skeletons. The people of the lost settlement were here, huddled together in death.

Fear and nausea rose up in her. She clapped her hands to her mouth while her heart hammered in her chest.

"Some of them have branches stuck in them," Pete whispered. "Like Jank." He stepped forward to investigate one of the frail skeletons, which lay curled in a fetal position. "And this one has an ax like Angus had. It's got a black blade."

With difficulty Lucy got her breathing under control enough so she could speak. "They must have come here to make a last stand," she said. It was impossible not to think of the fear and panic these people must have felt here, in their last moments, and she felt her own throat tighten in response. The trees attacked the town and drove everyone to take shelter. And then the wood from the walls turned on them. "They were trying to protect themselves."

"Didn't do them much good," Pete said. Lucy thought of the last time she'd checked the vitometer—the counter of Odic force spinning crazily into the thousands. She'd thought the device wasn't working properly because nothing could have that much energy. Looking at the destruction around her she realized she'd been wrong.

Add it to the list of things she'd been wrong about.

She bit her lip. "Now we know what happened to the lost settlement." She flicked a glance at Pete. For some reason she thought of the moment in Ulfric's cottage when she'd sat kicking her feet and drinking dreamwood tea. Ulfric had tried to warn her, she supposed. But even if he'd told her the dreamwood spirit was capable of destroying an entire settlement— killing men, women, children—she might not have believed him. The tea had caused hope and courage to surge inside her. Those feelings seemed foolhardy now.

"Whatever they did to get on His-sey-ak's bad side, I don't

want to make the same mistake." Pete had new gravity in his face; the hollows in his cheeks were stark slashes in the barn's dim light.

"We should go." Lucy had no idea what time it was, but intuition told her they had stayed here too long. Sinking into her was a kind of spreading hopelessness. The longer they stayed in this evil barn, the worse it would be.

She took his hand, pulling him along. They staggered out into the late afternoon light, shielding their eyes. Her legs felt rubbery, and she leaned against Pete; somehow, without her even realizing it, this had become something that felt natural.

In the tall grass across from the barn a shadow stirred.

Watching them, almost as if it had been waiting for them, was a wolf.

19

Lucy's first instinct when she saw the wolf was to turn and run
back through the ruined town.

But something stopped her. There was a strange intelligence in
the wolf's yellow eyes, and Lucy felt, as she looked at it, that it was
trying to communicate with her. And (she rapidly thought back)
they hadn't broken any of the Thumb's commandments—lately.

Like the other wolves they'd seen on the Thumb, this one was
massive: a gray-black boulder of muscle, sinew, and fur. It could
tear them both apart in an instant if it wanted to. But it wasn't
frightening like the others. It had a strange, almost melancholy
aspect to it that made Lucy feel they weren't in any danger. It
took a few steps and looked back over its shoulder at them.

Lucy dropped Pete's hand and went toward it cautiously.

"What are you doing?" Pete hissed. "Are you *crazy?*"

She'd sensed when the wolves had chased them to the tree
circle on their first day on the Thumb that she and Pete were
safe as long as they abided by the forest's mysterious rules. Now
she was certain of it. "I think it wants us to follow it."

The wolf went on ahead and then stopped again, waiting. Its tongue lolled out of its mouth in a doggish grin.

"See," Lucy said hopefully. "It's friendly."

"I think you're making a big leap to go from *not eating us immediately* to *friendly*." Pete watched it with obvious suspicion. But Lucy had already made up her mind to trust it.

"Come on. We don't know how else we're going to get there, do we? We'll be wandering in circles if we try to go on our own."

Pete brought out his compass anyway—she could tell it pained him to consider following the wolf. But she could see the needle spinning uselessly. "Still busted," he said, discouraged.

They had barely any food and they were running low on *antimorpheus*; they couldn't afford to waste time getting lost. Lucy put on her most convincing face as she turned to Pete. "We've got to try this."

"Because it couldn't possibly be dangerous," he muttered.

"I don't think so," Lucy said. It had been a while since she had felt this hopeful. After the horror of the lost settlement, something had shifted. They were getting help. *Who* was helping them and why . . . well, those were questions that could wait.

They followed the wolf as it passed in and out of the afternoon's shadows. It would stop every so often to make sure they hadn't fallen too far behind.

But after a few hours of marching at a brutal pace to keep up with it, the novelty of the situation had quite worn off.

"I don't like this," Pete said, stopping to catch his breath. He was bent down, elbows on his thighs, and there was a slick patch of sweat down the back of his shirt. "What if it's trying to get us somewhere where it can eat us?" The wolf, several yards away, watched them silently. Lucy knew if they stopped too long it would bare its teeth and growl at them until they moved again. That had happened a few times already; if they went too slowly for its liking it quickly became irritable—and this had been so terrifying they had run in panic, which only made them more exhausted in the end.

"Since when do wolves get their prey to chase after *them?*" Lucy was hot and tired. And the fact that they hadn't eaten in almost a day was beginning to affect her. She would have to rest soon, and not just for the minute here or there the wolf allowed. She groaned and put her hands on her hips. Sweat was trickling down her neck. Why was it in such a hurry?

The wolf's lips curled into a snarl. Even from several yards away Lucy could easily see the curved yellow points of its teeth— they were so long they were practically tusks. Fang tusks. She shook her head as she hoisted her pack onto her shoulders once more. Why did everything in Saarthe have to be so much bigger and badder than anywhere else?

"We're coming," she told it. Wearily she set off after it again. A moment later, Pete followed.

Sunset was no more than an hour away when they finally saw where the wolf was leading them. Lucy stopped in disappointment, exhaustion thrumming through her legs, and looked at the circle of kodoks ahead, their low-hanging branches knit together almost as if the trees were joining hands. Everything about the grove was familiar—it was even the same time of day, early evening, as when they'd encountered the other two devil groves. Inside the circle, Lucy knew the shadows would be lengthening, the tree faces emerging from the bark.

"But we already know about this," she protested to the wolf. "We've seen it, *twice*." Lucy had hoped so fervently that the wolf was bringing them someplace important; she'd expected it in fact to lead them straight to the dreamwood and her father. Now she felt near tears. And she couldn't look at Pete—she could feel the anger rising off him. They'd raced through the forest for *this*?

The great beast pawed the ground and its yellow eyes narrowed. Apparently, it wasn't happy with them, either. It tossed its head, waving them toward the grove. Then, as a last resort, it came forward and butted Lucy's arm. Her fingers touched the thick rough fur and she felt a spark of something wild and strange—a connection—pass between them.

"All right, if that's what you want," Lucy told it. Surreptitiously she examined her fingertips—perhaps she'd imagined the strange sensation. All she wanted was to sit down and rest her aching feet. But she forced herself to go on, ducking under the tightly woven branches and walking into the unnatural stillness of the devil grove. The wolf padded before her, silent and majestic, turning its head to watch her with its uncanny yellow eyes. She followed it to the center of the circle, where it stopped.

As she expected, the tree faces emerged from the wood. Even though by now she was almost used to them, she still hunched her shoulders, feeling small and helpless under their accusatory gaze.

"What is so important about this place?" She turned to the wolf, but its animal eyes were deep and impassive. It had brought her here, but she would have to figure things out for herself.

Lucy rubbed her arms. All right then. Where should she start? *Observe,* her father always said. *That is rule number one. Too many people simply act before observing what* is.

She stopped before the rubbery patch of mushrooms that grew at the center. For the first time, she really looked at them; previously she'd turned away in disgust. Lucy bent down. They were flaccid, slimy looking, and gave off a sickly odor that made her dizzy and nauseous. There was a slight hump in the middle of the mushroom cluster. She had a glimpse of wood. That must be what they were feeding on: an old stump.

But why did these mushrooms grow here, and only here?

And why did the mushrooms appear so sinister? What was so frightening about them? Lucy had encountered all manner of disgusting and revolting things in life. She had poked the swollen carcass of a dead dog to see the gases escape. She'd dissected a frog. She'd helped her father clean bones with maggots. What was she made of?

Lucy found a twig on the ground and with it gently touched the mushroom cluster. The oily caps quivered like jelly, and she caught a glimpse of orange-colored gills. With a startling puff, they released a rust-colored cloud, and Lucy fell back with the smell of decay in her nostrils.

Helplessly she watched the spores rise and be carried into the sky on the breeze. The air was full of the death-sweet smell of Rust—like a cake with a center of rotten meat. It came to Lucy in a sudden flash. *Rust is a fungus,* her father had written in his diary. She sat back on her heels, stunned.

"What was *that?*" Pete asked. He'd come into the clearing and stopped to stare at the cloud.

"This is what's causing it." She turned to Pete. "This is where Rust is coming from."

As they stood there, a flock of crows flew toward them, straight for the cloud. When they emerged on the other side, their wingtips were singed with orange.

Lucy shuddered as she understood what she'd just seen. "And the birds are carrying it with them to the other forests."

Pete's face was tight with distress. He watched the ochre cloud shift and disperse high in the sky where it disappeared in the sunset's burnished glow. "But if Angus's map is right, these tree circles are where dreamwood grew."

"Where dreamwood was *cut,*" she corrected, suddenly understanding. "Remember that house in the settlement with all the gold coins? They were rich from harvesting dreamwood."

"But . . ." Pete paced in thought. "But they'd harvested dreamwood for years."

"And what if they got greedy?" Lucy asked. "What if they took too many? The last dreamwood was supposed to have died out a hundred years ago—around the same time the people here disappeared. Niwa said the other dreamwoods were like his children. What if it's taken all this time, little by little, for Rust to spread and for His-sey-ak to have his revenge?"

He shook his head. When he looked at her his eyes were dark and wet. "You said dreamwood *cured* Rust." He picked up the stick she'd used to touch the mushrooms and threw it away in disgust.

The collar of his shirt was stained with sweat. Both of them were ragged and savage. They'd been pushed to the brink of their endurance—starved, without sleep, on edge for days. And now this.

Lucy flapped her hands in front of her, a gesture that was almost frantic. "*I don't know.*" She turned from him, looking at the tree circle as if she were trapped by it. The terrible faces seemed to laugh at her.

Why had she believed dreamwood cured Rust? Because that's what her father thought. But there'd been no proof. No evidence of it. And it turned out to be the very opposite.

Lucy felt a terrible plummet in her stomach as the world shifted.

"I think my father was wrong." She looked Pete full in the face.

The worst was letting people down. Pete was counting on her; she'd convinced him with her stories. She'd as good as promised Niwa that they'd find a cure and save the grove of the wolf woman. She felt sick as she thought of the spores she'd just released making their way to Saarthe's forests. Even Cranbull, Jank, and the others: They'd died because of her.

In despair she looked down at her moccasins, snagged and torn. "*I was wrong.*" It felt awful saying it, but it was also something of a relief to admit it—a first.

Pete took a deep breath and Lucy waited in horrible expectation of what he might say.

"I always knew coming here was a gamble," he said softly. There were streaks of grime on his cheeks; they covered his freckles and made him look older. His eyelashes were clumped together with sweat—or tears. He wiped one filthy hand across his sweaty cheek, adding a new smudge to his face. "I don't blame you for it."

Lucy closed her eyes, her whole body going limp with relief. She thought back to the day they'd set out, when he'd taught her how to make a fire and she'd been thinking only of how much she wanted to prove herself. "I'm sorry."

A few birds scolded them from the circle, reminding her of where they were.

Pete put his hands in his pockets; he looked slightly relieved that the moment for apologies was over. "I think our guide is anxious to get going."

She'd forgotten about the wolf. It was waiting for them now on the far side of the grove, flicking its tail as if brushing the forest with shadows.

At last when the light was truly fading, the wolf let them stop. They'd come to a patch of ground dotted with broken hollow stumps, fairy rings.

Lucy was so tired all she could think about was sleep, but

Pete insisted she eat a small piece of jerky, maintaining that it would cure her hunger if she chewed it more than fifty times (as he was doing). He was wrong.

She rolled over and rummaged in her pack for Arthur Lyman's vial of *antimorpheus* solution. But when she took it out she saw they were dangerously low.

"Here." She thrust the bottle toward Pete and let him take his five drops first. He shivered violently from the taste, as he always did.

"Brrr!" he exclaimed, shaking like a wet dog. "That's awful."

Lucy was studying the level in the dropper, trying to think how they could conserve what they had. Perhaps if she took two drops instead of five she would be safe. After all, she reasoned, she was smaller than Pete and probably needed less. She took two small drops and before she could change her mind, closed the bottle tightly and stowed it away. The wolf, who'd been watching over them, gradually faded into the shadows so that only its yellow eyes were visible. And then even those disappeared as it padded off into the forest, presumably to hunt. They heard the footfalls of its soft paws and its rumbling breath as it passed by them.

"That's a relief," Pete said. "I wasn't looking forward to sleeping with . . . " Before he could even finish his sentence he was asleep.

But for Lucy it was an awful night. First she thought she saw fireflies. Lights blinked on and off, floating through the air like giant soap bubbles. One drifted close to Lucy, allowing her to see a tiny winged creature inside it—a fairy! It snarled, and Lucy gasped. It wasn't a fairy but a creature with needle-like fangs.

Lucy recoiled and burrowed deeper into her bedroll. But even when she closed her eyes she saw faces in the forest, branches that reached out to grab her with freezing-cold hands. Around her the trees seemed to move and twist in a sinister ballet.

She dozed fitfully until early morning, and only when she heard the wolf come back was she finally able to sleep.

The day dawned, but Lucy woke up exhausted after her night of bad dreams. She and Pete barely spoke to each other before packing up and following the wolf onward again. Lucy retreated deep inside herself, hardly thinking. It was all she could do to keep moving. At some point she realized Pete had run ahead. She looked up to see him calling and waving to her.

"I see something," he said. The expression on his face told her it wasn't good.

She shuffled to catch up to him and saw what he was looking at: a pair of skinny shins sticking out from underneath a freshly fallen kodok.

"It's Silas," Lucy said, pressing a hand to her mouth. "I recognize his boots."

She wanted to do something for Silas. He'd annoyed and frightened her while he was alive, but she felt nothing but pity for him now. As with Jank, there was no memorial she could think to make that wouldn't also endanger herself.

"Maybe we could just say a few words," she suggested at last. Pete nodded and bowed his head.

"Here lies Silas," she said solemnly. She wished she had

something better to say, and she wished she could let Silas know she was sorry he'd gotten involved in this misguided adventure. But she couldn't think of the words she wanted, so in the end she cleared her throat and said, "Someone who deserved better than this."

Pete sniffed and kicked the ground. "He told me he just wanted to get enough to be able to buy a place of his own."

"He wasn't a bad person," Lucy said. She fingered a tear in the soft leather of her tunic, now covered with streaks of dirt and scratches. "Even if he did take my vitometer. I guess."

Pete's eyes were full of feeling. "You know, if someone offered me a whole log of dreamwood right now I wouldn't take it." He gestured to the forest around them. "I'd walk right on by, and consider myself lucky. Nothing is worth this."

Pete had come along for dreamwood. Finding her father was never his quest. Lucy wouldn't blame him at all if he decided to leave. In fact, she wouldn't have blamed him if he had wanted to leave days ago, after first realizing he couldn't bring dreamwood back.

And how were they to continue anyway? They had no more food. And their bottle of anti-dreaming drops was nearly empty. There were three, maybe four, drops left.

"You should leave," she said suddenly. "Get out of here while you still can." Now that she said it she couldn't imagine why it had taken her this long to figure it out.

Pete looked as surprised as if she'd slugged him. "I'm not going to leave. What are you talking about?"

"I never should have let you come." Lucy shook her head in distress. "It's all my fault. Silas and Cranbull and Jank. And you . . . I just wanted . . ." She stopped, her feelings getting bigger like snowballs. There was too much to say.

"What?" He moved closer to her, was looking at her so intently, she felt even more jumbled inside.

She had wanted him to come. She'd wanted his strength and his freckles and the way he laughed. And she'd wanted to prove herself to him. What had she wanted to hear? *Jiminy, if it hadn't been for you, Lucy, we would have been sunk.*

She looked up at him, cringing from embarrassment at the roil in her thoughts. "Nothing," she said and turned away.

The wolf snarled to warn them its patience at this delay was wearing thin, and for once Lucy was happy to have a reason to get moving again.

After leaving Silas they walked steadily west, toward the tip of the Thumb. They didn't speak. Pete even left off protesting that he was never going to leave and now he marched along in dull silence. Sometimes Lucy got a glimpse of the ocean through the trees, curving around the tip like a fingernail. It couldn't be far now, could it? From time to time she glanced at the wolf. Its presence had become familiar, comforting even. But it still hurried them along. The ground ran mostly downhill below them and the kodoks had thinned, giving way to hardy spruce, which could take the punishing wind and salt spray of the coast. At one rise they stood with the wind licking their sweaty faces and looked ahead. A dark gray stripe grew across the landscape, cutting off the very tip of the Thumb. From a distance, it looked like an enormous fuzzy caterpillar.

"What is *that?*" Pete asked, breaking the silence of several hours.

Lucy had no idea. She was running out of answers; it seemed she had only questions left. As they walked, scraps of thoughts, sentences from her father's diary entries, kept running through her head: *The key lies in uncovering the past.* And what had she found out about the past?

He killed them all.

She thought of standing next to Niwa in the grove of the wolf woman among the giant trees. *His-sey-ak saved us,* Niwa had said. *He'll save us again.*

I'm sorry, Niwa, she thought while she stumbled over the uneven ground. *His-sey-ak isn't going to save anyone. Jank was right, your father was right. He is the Devil of Devil's Thumb.*

"Are you crying?" Pete asked suddenly.

"No." Lucy hid her face from his scrutiny. She didn't think she was. But she was just so tired and discouraged she didn't know what she was doing anymore. She closed her eyes, but dizziness immediately overtook her.

Pete was watching her sway. "You can't keep going like this, you know," he said. He caught her by the forearms and steadied her. "You've got me worried."

"We have to keep going," she murmured. It was the only thing left to do—even when it was meaningless. *What was the Darrington motto? Onward.*

She laughed grimly to herself.

"No." Pete's chestnut hair hung in his eyes. He tried to brush it away, but it immediately sprang back. "I really think you should rest." He cocked his head over his shoulder. "Looks like we've got to stop now anyway."

Lucy blinked. She'd been walking in a daze, concentrating only on putting one foot in front of the other. She'd trailed behind Pete—her only goal was to keep him in sight—and so she'd lost track of their guide. To her surprise she saw the wolf had stopped, and she didn't think it was going anywhere.

It stood in front of a billowing wall of fog. Now she understood the fuzzy line across the Thumb that she'd seen earlier. It wasn't a hedge, it was a barrier of fog—about ten or twelve feet high, and so thick it looked solid. But it seethed like a living thing. Runners of it unspooled, and then rolled back in, the way curls of wave foam race up and down the sand with the tide. Only these tendrils of fog had a sinister air to them; even the wolf kept well away. And there was a chill, malevolent sense to the place. It was a feeling she'd had before—and for a moment her thoughts were back on those long-ago basement stairs, watching the dance of the Hanged Man's legs. This was far, far stronger.

It felt like a scarf of ice had settled around her neck as she realized what she was seeing.

"Pete," she said, "I think I know where all the ghosts went."

20

The ghost sweeper in Lucy's pack was shuddering so hard, Lucy worried it would damage itself. Lucy knew from long experience that ghosts, when they showed themselves, were often pale and misty. But she'd never seen ghosts like this: Somehow the spirits had become embodied in the fog—Lucy could sometimes make out faces and expressions—but they were trapped in it, too. An immense power held the fog in place, so that it tumbled and undulated, but never moved more than a few feet in any direction. And even with the sun climbing higher, it showed no sign of burning off.

Now that it had brought them to this final barrier, the wolf could no longer help them. After one last look from its yellow eyes, it bounded away into the forest, leaving them alone.

"Let's see if there's a way around it," Pete suggested. Even though the two of them were nearly dead on their feet, it was still preferable to walk beside the fog than to attempt to go through it.

Dejected, they followed it all the way to a sudden drop.

They'd reached the Thumb's northern edge, and the way before them ended in a cliff. A steep path led down to a narrow beach, but the ghostly barrier extended all the way to the water.

Pete followed the cliff-side path a ways to get a better view, but the ground crumbled beneath him and with a sudden shout, he lost his footing. He tumbled out of sight.

"Pete!" Lucy screamed. She scrambled after him, sliding on the loose rock and grasping at tree roots and scrub plants to steady herself on the steep slope.

He was about halfway down, sitting in the middle of the steep path. When she reached him she saw his face was shiny and worried as he held his left leg.

"I think my ankle's sprained or broken," he said, gritting his teeth. "I can't walk on it."

Lucy looked up the way they had come. She couldn't imagine how she could help him back to the top if he couldn't walk. Still, she bent down beside him so she could lift him up.

As if he knew what she was thinking he grasped her arm. "I can't go with you," he said. His eyes were green with pain.

"I can't leave you," she replied tearfully. She put her hands under his arms, but Pete shifted away, dislodging a few small rocks, which fell to the beach below them.

Pete shook his head and said forcefully, "I'll be all right. Look, I'm no use to you now. But you can still do it."

"I can't get through that fog." She hung her head.

A look of determination crossed his face, and he squirmed, reaching into his pocket to bring out the protection stone. "Take this," Pete said, pressing it into her hand. "Anya always said it was the best remedy against haunts. And you've got your ghost sweeper. So with the two of them together, you're set. I'll scoot my way down to the beach, and wait for you there."

Lucy closed her fingers around the black stone. It was warm from being in Pete's pocket. Perhaps because it was his, it felt strong, like him, and somehow friendly. She closed her eyes. Pete was making it easy on her. He knew she would never forgive herself if she didn't make every effort to find her father.

But she couldn't leave Pete without supplies. Lucy reached into her pack and found the precious vial of *antimorpheus*. There was a lump in her throat as she pressed it on Pete. "Here— there's just enough of this to get you through . . . in case, in case I'm not back by dark."

"I don't want it," Pete said. He looked at her with a grim expression that Lucy realized was a farewell. She ducked her head quickly before she cried.

"And here's the flare." She took the stick with its pitchy coating and gave it to Pete. "If anyone makes it off the Thumb, it should be you," she told him, her voice brimming with emotion. "If I'm not back by dark, use the flare, signal a boat."

Pete grunted with the effort of speaking. "I'll hang on to this," he said, "but I'm not leaving without you. So . . . just . . . hurry."

Lucy didn't trust herself to speak more. She gave Pete a quick embrace, and then, with tears running down her cheeks, she climbed back to the top of the cliff.

✦　✦　✦

The ghost fog was thick and gray. A chill came off it, so that even standing in the sunshine, Lucy felt cold. She had never heard of ghosts forming a wall before. She had never heard of ghosts acting together—here was another demonstration of His-seyak's power, she supposed.

The ghost sweeper, still in Pete's sock, kicked and struggled at her side. She knew she had to let it free so it could try to clear the fog, but she kept delaying the moment.

"It's almost pretty in its own way," a voice said behind her. She jumped and saw Angus Murrain emerging from the trees.

He sauntered toward her on his long legs. His blue chambray shirt was crisp and clean, his moleskin trousers still luxurious. Flecks of sunlight shone in his glossy hair. He looked impossibly triumphant.

"Though I wouldn't stare at it too long. You'll see faces in it after a while."

Lucy's heart felt raw on seeing him. People who hurt other people so badly ought to know about it and be sorry. But Angus did not look like a man with a troubled conscience. He was as straight and commanding a presence as ever, with windswept hair and piercing eyes. Only now he wore her vitometer around his neck. He didn't bother to try to cover it up.

"You're not surprised to see me?" she asked, hoping to shame him for the way he'd run. Darringtons had their faults, but she knew her father never would have done such a thing.

He came and stood beside her, studying the fog. "No," he

said evenly. "I've always known you were clever. I wouldn't have chosen you as my partner otherwise."

It galled Lucy to hear him call her partner—the word that had once made her feel so proud and special.

She gestured at the vitometer quivering like a frightened bird against his chest. "Why did you steal it?" she asked. "I would have led you here anyway."

"*Lucy*," he said, sounding like a fond parent whose child has asked an endearing but silly question. "I couldn't take the chance that you would turn against me. Your father, if he isn't already dead, hasn't cleared away whatever haunts this place. But I intend to do so. I will cut down that tree." He lifted a hand to the ax he carried on his back. "I told you he stood in the way of progress—once you realized he and I held opposite views, I expected you to try to stop me."

"You'll only make Rust worse," Lucy said, trying not to sound like she was pleading with him. "I was wrong. You can't cure it by bringing dreamwood back. Cutting dreamwood is what caused it in the first place."

Lucy saw surprise in his deep brown eyes. "Interesting," the timber baron said, sparing a look at the majestic trees around them. "I suppose that's why your father hasn't cut it down himself. Well, it matters little to me. You see, bringing back dreamwood may not cure Rust, but it will make *me* very, very rich."

He was forgetting one thing, though—and she hoped it would stop him just as it had stopped her. "How are you going to get through the ghosts?" She tightened her grip on the ghost sweeper, just in case he thought of stealing that, too.

"It's just fog, Lucy. Nothing more." He faced the seething ghost wall, his shoulders squared. "I shall walk through it."

Even though Lucy wanted nothing but revenge on Angus, she still couldn't let him think this was a simple fog. A lifetime of knowing the right answer made her blurt, "But these are the ghosts of the lost settlement. Don't you think you need to understand why they're here?"

"No, I don't." He paused and faced her, bending down slightly in the posture of someone about to impart a very valuable lesson. "I'm afraid, Lucy, that life comes down to two paths. You can choose the way of mystery or mastery. If you'd rather wonder *why* or *how*, by all means go ahead. Meanwhile, I will already have won. I think a more important question is how *you* intend to get through." He looked at the ghost sweeper, still fighting Pete's sock; his expression said *good luck*. "You don't trust yourself to make it through, even with that."

Lucy wished she had a biting retort, something that would make him realize that he was wrong. He was wrong about thinking it was useless to try to understand things. He was wrong about thinking the fog wasn't dangerous. But no words came; instead she watched helplessly as Angus took out his phos globe and held it aloft.

He walked toward the fog confidently, like someone without any care or fear. Just before he entered it, a thought apparently struck him and he turned to face her. "If you and Pete are still alive when I return we can get a boat together," he told her. "I'm afraid you won't get the reward—or any wood I bring back with me. Our agreement didn't say you'd get anything if *I* brought back dreamwood. No hard feelings, you understand—it's just business."

The fog parted and swirled behind Angus, swishing like a curtain over the black-bladed ax on his back. The phos globe's light was strong, however, and she could see it bobbing like a will-o'-the-wisp through the fog. It moved steadily farther away. *He's actually doing it*, she thought with a sinking heart. He would chop down the last dreamwood, severing His-sey-ak's connection to the physical world. Rust would spread to *all* the forests. And what of her father? He was there somewhere on the other side of that barrier, she was sure. Would he try to stop the timber baron just as he'd tried to stop the railroad from dynamiting the Maran Boulder?

Lucy's nails dug into her palms as she watched his progress through the fog. But then the light wavered. For a few moments it darted frantically back and forth. She heard shrieks; they were muffled and sounded very far away.

"Use the ax!" she cried, darting as close to the fog as she dared. Even though moments ago she'd been hoping for him to fail, she couldn't stand the thought of another death.

And then the light went out.

21

Lucy stood before the ghost wall and untied Pete's sock with trembling fingers.

She had to act now before she lost her nerve, or before the day grew too old and she faced a night on the Thumb without *antimorpheus* to protect her. Angus's disappearance left her thoroughly shaken. He'd been so cool and unruffled throughout the last few days, she'd begun to think of him as unstoppable.

But he hadn't believed ghosts posed any danger to him. And so even though he'd carefully threaded his way through Hissey-ak's challenges, he'd been undone at this last step. Perhaps at the last moment Angus used his ax to try to fight off the ghosts. But clearly it hadn't worked. Obsidian was unpredictable, her father always said.

Then again, these ghosts felt more powerful than any she'd ever encountered. She remembered the timber baron's scathing comment about the ghost sweeper. *You don't trust yourself to make it through, even with that.*

Lucy steeled herself. She was going to prove him wrong.

She held the stocking upside down and the ghost sweeper tumbled out. The egg was shivering—Lucy hoped it was from excitement.

"Come on," she told it, speaking to it as if it were a puppy. "Let's go! Let's sweep."

The egg walked flat-footed to the edge of the fog. Little eddies spun out and pooled around it. For a moment the sweeper didn't react, and Lucy had a terrible thought that it had injured itself in its collision with the log the last time she'd let it out. But she needn't have worried. The egg tilted forward as if into a head-wind and let out a mighty blast. The fog billowed back from it, and Lucy saw the egg had cleared a hollow in its midst.

She stepped forward, all around her feeling the icy mist, the ghosts' seething emotions. The egg blasted again, clearing another few feet ahead. They were going to have to tunnel through it, bit by bit. Lucy went forward a few more steps into the new space it had cleared. But behind her the ghost fog swirled to close up the way she'd come.

Immediately, claustrophobia descended. Ever since her encounter with the Maran Boulder, tight spaces had held particular horror for her. With nothing to see in any direction, surrounded by hostile spirits, Lucy's heart raced as she tried to control her fear.

The only way out is through.

Another few paces.

I won't give in to fear.

The ghost sweeper gave another blast and she stepped forward a few more feet.

I know these are ghosts, but I won't give in to fear.

But it was terribly hard not to give in to fear as she watched the churning fog struggle to reach her. And was it her imagination or was the little hollow she stood in shrinking? It felt smaller than it had a few moments ago. Lucy cast a worried glance at the egg. This was more sweeping than it had ever been called on to do. What if it was no match for the Thumb's ghosts? What if there were so many the fog stretched on and on? They'd never make it. The egg took a few more steps and blasted again.

This time the blast was tentative. Something was wrong. The ghost sweeper was hardly clearing any space at all. The ghosts were overpowering it.

Her pulse drummed in her ears, she felt like someone trapped in a flooded room, slowly watching the water rise. *Don't panic*, she told herself. But it was impossible not to. If only she could figure out a way to run, or knew how much farther she had to go, perhaps she could just barrel through. But she did not want to risk getting turned around, trapped in the fog, and running in blind panic as Angus had. That way was sure death.

Please keep going.

And then the sweeper blasted and only a few inches around it cleared: just a small circle, like a halo.

Lucy watched in horror as the mist slowly descended into the cleared space. The world was going gray. She dropped to her knees, getting close to the egg. It was shaking.

They were doomed.

She bent down and covered her head, knowing it would

make no difference—the ghosts would soon disrupt the electrical pulses in her brain. Next would come the hallucinations, then seizures.

She was plunged into childhood again, and the Hanged Man was coming for her on his dancing legs. Only this time there was no father to rescue her.

Pain in her chest made her gasp. Her heart was stumbling like a lame horse. She was going to have a heart attack at age twelve.

Her hand touched something metal. It was freezing cold: her sweeper, facedown, finished.

Spasms shook her body. She could feel her heart beat erratically, losing its rhythm. Sparks flew through her brain and then faded like fireworks.

Think, she desperately needed to think.

While she could still control her fingers, she brought out Pete's protection stone. It still retained a little warmth—from Pete, she thought, although she'd left him hours ago. She clutched it desperately, even though she had little hope it would do anything.

The black stone grew warmer in her fingers. She could feel something shift, a lessening of the attack. Her heart regained its beat. She gasped for breath, her eyes squeezed shut.

And then the fog slowly lifted and pulled back.

She was in a sunny green meadow. A few feet from her the ghost sweeper lay flat on its stomach. Slowly she got to her hands and knees, then for a few moments simply sat quietly and breathed, feeling the sun warm her. The black stone in her hand was actually *hot*.

There was the whirring drone of insect wings as a giant dragonfly flew past, shining with iridescent green, blue, and gold. Butterflies as big as birds took delicate sips from bright pink wildflowers. It was as if she'd emerged from the deathly gray fog into a world supersaturated with color, with life. Slowly she got to her feet. A lacy waterfall shimmered with rainbows in the distance.

And ahead of her was an ancient and gnarled golden tree.

Huge guardian spruce grew around it, protecting it from the fury of the Pacific Coast. Lucy felt an alert intelligence in the way its leaves shimmered in the air, turning toward her like antennae. It was a dreamwood—the last dreamwood—as big and broad as a mighty oak.

The mapmakers of the lost settlement were all wrong. It wasn't a spider. It was the most beautiful thing she'd ever seen.

A breeze from the sea made the tree's silvery green leaves sparkle like coins. Its bark was smooth like a skin and shone with a soft, pale gold: the precious gold of angels in old paintings. The tree glimmered softly in the sunlight, presiding over an enchanted clearing of soft mossy ground. Its branches were twisted and thick, growing out parallel to the ground for a long while, like arms that longed to embrace her. It would be a simply perfect tree for climbing, Lucy thought. The branches were so wide and gently sloping; there were so many of them. It was almost as if there were a network of dozens of secret pathways inside its canopy. She could climb inside and lose herself there, never having to come out, living off sunshine and dewdrops the dragonflies would bring her.

Lucy walked forward as if in a dream.

Rolling out from the dreamwood's trunk were huge white roots, as big as marble waves. They pushed up through emerald moss, and rose twisted and gnarled as a witch's finger, creating hidden niches and pockets. Lucy clambered among the root grottoes, wanting to get closer to that marvelous tree.

She felt faint from lack of food, and there was a curious scent to the air—lovely and dangerous, the way that some lilies smelled of death and funerals and women's perfume all at the same time. But she didn't feel in any danger. Instead she felt all the hope and certainty she remembered from drinking Ulfric's dreamwood tea. She inhaled deeply, breathing in the dreamwood's rich and strange scent. It made her slightly lightheaded and her legs a bit wobbly, but it was simply so delicious she had to keep going forward.

And then, as she made her way closer still, she saw him.

William Darrington was seated in an alcove created from interwoven roots, like a king on a throne of living wood. He was sleeping; his face was calm and peaceful. There was the slender Darrington nose, the high, intelligent forehead. His glasses were balanced nearly at the tip of his nose—how many times had she seen him asleep in his armchair back home and his glasses perched just like that? He was wearing his favorite traveling sweater—the one with multiple patches at the elbows, the one he swore the moths would have to eat entirely before he stopped wearing it. His quick, nimble hands were still; there was a book in his lap. His head, tilted gently to one side, drooped slightly as if he'd just fallen asleep while reading.

Lucy's heart felt as if it would burst. "Papa!" she cried and began to run.

He was here, it was really him. Tears streamed from her eyes, and she thought of all the horrors she'd passed through, all her anxieties and fears, how hard it had been to come through the ghost wall, how she'd been wrong, how Pete had been right, how worried she'd been and how much she needed him . . . And how he'd sent her away . . . how he hadn't told her . . . how he'd meant for them to separate.

She slowed to a walk, brimming over with emotion, until she finally stood before him.

"Papa," she said. "Wake up. It's me."

But her father continued to sleep peacefully.

Too peacefully.

"Papa," she gasped, as dread filled her like flooding water. Why didn't he answer?

Now she saw what she hadn't noticed before: There were twigs in his hair, his fingernails had grown long and ragged, dust and moss had collected in the creases of his dungarees.

No.

With her heart thudding in her ears she reached forward and touched his face.

He was cool, very cool, but he was alive: His chest still rose and fell softly, as if he needed very little air.

He slept. From his appearance he looked as if he hadn't moved in weeks.

Lucy fought down her panic. Maybe if she helped him move he might wake up. She tried to lift one of his arms, thinking she could help him stand. But he was stuck in place. She tried to move his other arm. It was as if he'd been cemented into his seat.

She bent down, alarm flaring through her, and peered at the place where one hand rested lightly on his throne of roots. Between his skin and the wood was a thin layer of something hard and clear, like glue.

He was stuck to the wood by a resinous membrane. Tiny suckers spread out from it, like those found on the back of ivy creepers.

She tugged at one of his hands. But the membrane pinned him in place. Fear took over. Now she tugged with all her strength. She *had* to get him free. Where she pulled she saw the skin turn pink. She pulled harder and managed to lift the tip of a finger. Then with horror she let it fall back—the suckers were part of him, they went *into* him.

He was being absorbed into the tree.

The dreamwood was feeding on him.

Lucy felt as if she were falling.

She was back in Governor Arekwoy's office, transfixed by Denis Saarthe's strange and frightening pictures, seeing their stained-glass beauty—and the horrors they contained: the roots with the faces and hands inside them.

Abruptly she turned and retched. But she hadn't eaten in so long, only bile came up. Her eyes smarted with tears and she turned back to her father.

"Why?" she cried. How had this happened? Her father, who figured out every mystery, who outsmarted every ghost, who'd made it his life's work to understand spirits, had finally been caught.

Her eyes streaming with tears, Lucy searched for some explanation. Her glance fell on the book in his lap, and she saw it wasn't a book he was reading, but another journal. She could see his pen now, fallen into the moss at his feet.

With renewed strength she tugged the journal from his hand.

She bent over it, so frantic it took her moments to steady herself enough to read what he'd written. The writing was nearly illegible, the letters formed as if by someone with barely any muscle control.

The cure for Rust is dreamwood.

Lucy shook her head, rubbing the tears from her eyes. She knew that wasn't true. Her father must have known it wasn't true. In despair she turned to the next page.

Already it is hard for me to write. I see into his mind, a mind that is spread into every molecule—every tree and bird and beast—on the Thumb. And now I've become one with him. I understand everything. But too high a cost.

Underneath this in a weak and struggling script he had written only one word:

LUCY

She was beyond tears now. She took the journal and, enraged, threw it at the dreamwood's golden trunk. It bounced off harmlessly and fluttered to the ground.

"You monster!" she screamed at it.

Nothing happened. The silvery green leaves continued to flash, the butterflies continued to soar. She turned back to her father. He looked so peaceful sitting on his white throne. The roots curved around him, like a giant seashell.

As she stared at him she saw a curious growth hanging from the topmost roots: a lumpy seed pod, about half a foot long. It was heavy-looking and golden, with a thick, resinous case that made it seem like something precious encased in amber. Lucy stood on her tiptoes and slowly reached out a hand to touch it.

It felt weighty and hard and somehow warm to the touch. The roots that fed it had a pinched look, as if the creation of the seed had sucked them dry.

It was a dreamwood seed.

And there was only one. Suddenly she understood. *The cure for Rust is dreamwood*, her father had written. But not in the way she'd thought.

The tree was taking her father's life energy in order to create this one precious seed.

It hung on by the thinnest of strands, almost ready to drop.

She gave the seed pod the slightest of tugs. It came free at once, falling into her hand with a faint rattle.

She looked at her father, sleeping peacefully in his strange dream. He was beyond her reach now. But there were others who needed her help. Pete, Niwa, the Lupines, even all the out-of-work lumberjacks on the Wanted posters in the Pentland train station.

She supposed even a dreamwood seed was like any other: It had to be planted. Lucy walked away from the grotto the roots had made until she found a place where the ground was soft and mossy. Lucy got down on her knees and dug a small hole. She put the seed inside and piled the dirt on top of it.

She thought of the pictures in the *Codex Saarthensis*. She knew what she had to do next, even if she didn't like it. The dreamwood seed didn't need water, it needed an offering. It needed blood.

Lucy's neck prickled, and she had the uncanny sense of being watched. She swallowed and took out her knife, the proper knife Pete had insisted she buy.

Its blade glittered in the late afternoon light, almost as strong as the light from the dreamwood's flashing, mirror-like leaves.

Then, before she could change her mind, she drew it across the inside of her forearm. It was a sharp blade, and she made as deep and long a cut as she could stand, gritting her teeth against the pain.

She watched the blood well up and gouts of it rush out, pulsing with the heartbeat inside her, and fall on the ground.

The blood sank into the dirt. She had the most disturbing impression that the ground was *thirsty*.

The surface rippled, as if a mole tunneled beneath it. Something down there was moving. It was coming up to meet her.

Lucy took a step back. Like a ship's prow crashing through a wave during a storm, something crested and burst forth from the ground. It was gold: a tiny seedling.

She was so surprised she cried out. And as she bent closer, another gout of blood fell. The little seedling shivered hungrily, absorbing it, and then rather alarmingly, it doubled in size.

It bent toward her, searching—like a kitten rooting for its mother. Lucy pressed Niwa's tunic against her arm to stop the bleeding—that was all she was able to give. One last drop fell down upon it.

She stepped back again and watched the seedling quiver. Like a peacock suddenly fanning its tail, the tree shook itself, and scores of tiny silver leaves burst out from its twiggy branches.

There it was, a miniature of the giant tree behind it.

With a tremble, the great tree shook itself from root to top. The mirror leaves flashed and from tiny pods a faint golden pollen rose into the air, shining like fairy dust. A group of birds swooped through, the edges of their wings coated in rich gold. They flew east, in the direction of the mainland.

The cure had begun.

She'd done it. And then Lucy covered her face with her hands and sobbed.

22

Lucy got to her feet. The breeze from the sea was colder now, and she shivered. It was time to go.

She went to her father where he sat on his dreamwood throne. She put her hand on his, stroking the hard, waxy skin.

"Good-bye, Papa," she said, leaning down and kissing his cheek softly.

It was like wrenching herself apart—the hardest thing she'd ever done, the hardest thing she could imagine doing. And then she turned to make the long walk back through the meadow. The ghost wall, still a heavy fog across the eastern horizon, didn't worry her now. Somehow she knew it would part for her. After all, she'd given His-sey-ak the one thing he needed. After a hundred years, he had another dreamwood, a child.

There was a faint sound behind her, a spluttering cough.

And then a *thud!*

She wheeled around to see her father getting to his feet. The roots he'd been sitting in flexed like the arms of an octopus— they'd thrown him to the ground.

He stood before her, wild-eyed, his glasses askew, clothes in tatters, his skin scraped raw, and a clear fluid like sap oozing from his sores.

But it was him.

"Lucy," he said hoarsely. His voice was breaking. "Lucy, is it really you?"

"Papa," she cried, running toward him.

With a cry he caught her up into his arms.

"Thank goodness," he said. He was stroking her hair, and clutching her, holding her hands as if he needed to assure himself that it was truly her. Lucy buried her face in his shoulder, feeling the scratchy wool of his lucky sweater.

"You were asleep," she scolded him. "I tried to get you to wake up but you wouldn't."

She looked over his shoulder and saw the root throne where he'd sat. A network of faint pink suckers ran across the roots where he'd detached himself; they waved blindly in disappointment.

"I know." His blue eyes stared into hers, and she saw him struggling to explain. His spectacles dipped crookedly on his nose. "I'm sorry. As soon as the roots attached to me, I tried to get free. But I couldn't . . . and then I fell asleep." He clutched her to him again. She breathed the smell of his pipe on his sweater, as well as the unsettling sweet smell of dreamwood. She hugged him, feeling great patches where his clothes were in rags. The dreamwood's creepers had chewed through his favorite sweater, she thought sadly.

The sparkly mist still hovered in the air, and through it she saw pod after pod in the giant tree shudder and release new, sweet-smelling pollen.

Her father looked at the mist in bewilderment. "And then somehow I woke up, and you're here . . ." He removed his crooked wire-rimmed glasses and polished them on the hem of his shirt. Putting them back on, he squinted into the shimmering air. "But do you see everything golden? Am I still asleep? I don't understand why he released me, when I begged and pleaded with him in the dream."

Lucy took her father's hand, being careful not to press his sores. "I think I have an idea," she said and led him to the patch of blood-damp earth where the little dreamwood grew. It was now about a foot high, shapeless and awkward, covered with downy silver leaves, like a baby bird. In the ground Lucy could see pencil-thin roots with tiny suckers on them, hunting for every last morsel of blood. She shivered, feeling that it was beautiful and terrible at the same time.

For a moment her father simply gaped.

"You planted it," he said. He turned to her with a look of wonder and smoothed her hair, tucking it behind her ear. "I saw you figure it out in my dream." He turned from the newborn tree to the glittering clouds of pollen still drifting in gauzy sheets across the meadow. In wonder he held up a hand then rubbed the glistening sheen on his fingertips. "You did it."

He looked at her in triumph as she turned away.

"Lucy," he said, dropping his hands to his sides. "What's wrong?"

Lucy hugged her forearm where the cut she'd made stung terribly. But why had he even been in the dream? Why had he sat on the root throne? Why had he left her? Tears welled in her eyes. She'd been through so much to get here and she thought she would be so happy—and she *was*—but she was crying, too.

"You weren't going to send for me," she blurted out, feeling childish. And yet, she was a child, she was *his* child. Her place was with him. Niwa's father seemed to understand that. Why didn't he?

What was wrong with the way they were before? She remembered the train tickets and he invented the instruments. They cleared ghosts together. They were a team. But then somehow they had diverged. She thought of the strange transformations they'd both narrowly escaped—she'd rescued her father from becoming part of a tree. She'd had to rescue herself from turning into a Miss Bentley's girl.

"Who told you that?" he asked, bending down to search her face.

"Angus Murrain."

"Did he tell you why?"

She shook her head: Her conversation with Angus was still too painful to talk about. But then she burst out, "He said you worried it would ruin my reputation. That I was better off without you as a father!"

She could feel her cheeks grow hot, and she dragged the heel of her hand across her eyes. All the hurt she'd carried until this moment came to the surface and now was as painful as a sunburn.

William Darrington sighed like someone facing a moment he'd long feared. "Of course that's not true," he said in a soft, sorrowful voice. "Although . . ." He readjusted his glasses. "Sometimes I *have* wondered if I was giving you the life you deserved."

"So I deserved being dumped at a school where the girls all made fun of me, and the teachers punished me, and I *hated* it?" Lucy's eyes were suddenly full and she felt the corners of her mouth sink.

She could tell she'd hurt him. She'd meant to.

"Lucy," he said. He pushed the ragged sleeves of his sweater up his arm—His-sey-ak's marks were all over him. Finally, Lucy thought, it was visible for everyone to see that spirits had sunk their claws into him and laid their claim.

"Lucy," he said with a sigh, "I've made a mess of things. I'm never going to be celebrated for the work I do. I'll never provide the type of life you should have. And as ghosts become scarcer, spirit work becomes more dangerous. I worried that I was putting you in harm's way by letting you come along with me. What sort of father puts his child in danger?"

Lucy said nothing, but stared stonily at the ground.

Her father ran a hand through his straw-colored hair and tried again.

"But . . . But now I know I was wrong," he said.

She looked up, hearing these unfamiliar words from him.

"Miss Bentley's isn't the right place for you. I should have seen that." He shook his head ruefully. "I'll give up spirit hunting. I can take up a trade. I do have some aptitude with electricity, after all. Perhaps I can find work at a power plant or transmission station. We'll live a normal life, stay in one place. You can tell people your father is an electrical engineer. That's a booming field. Electricity is the future. What do you say?" He held out his hand to her. "Onward?"

Lucy's throat was tight as she considered what her father was offering: a normal life, electricity, an end to being the "ghost girl." But then she looked at the dreamwood and saw its silver-dollar leaves flashing in the breeze, the shimmering dragonflies buzzing by, even its pale, wormlike roots. And she took a deep breath.

"I think there must be more like him," she said, raising her eyes to the towering dreamwood. "Maybe other trees or boulders. Maybe rivers or caves. But they're out there," she said. "And they've got so much power, if they're hurt or disturbed, who knows what harm they might do."

She raised her forearm to look at the place where she'd sliced the knife into her skin. It no longer hurt much, but she supposed it would leave a scar. "I don't think we should stop studying them."

Her father's eyes crinkled as he embraced her.

"You're a remarkable girl, Lucy."

That's what she always liked to hear.

They were walking hand in hand back toward the ghost wall. In front of them part of it was already dissipating, making a door for them to walk through.

"Speaking of remarkable," her father said, "how did you get through the wall?"

Lucy was surprised he had to ask. "I had my sweeper, of course."

The brass egg lay in the grass where it had fallen. Lucy picked it up, but nothing she did could make it move again.

"I'm afraid it's short-circuited," her father said, kneeling down to examine it. Her heart swelled with happiness to see him in such a familiar posture—frowning behind his glasses as he turned the egg over to see what was wrong with it.

He put it down and gave her a look that he often used when he suspected there was more to the story than what she'd told. "But I'm surprised this had the power to bring you through the fog. I barely made it myself, and I had a much more powerful sweeping engine. It's ruined as well."

"It did break down," she admitted. She felt bad for her poor egg, and a touch maudlin; after all, she had had it since childhood. "But Pete gave me a ghost stone." She produced the obsidian nugget.

"Let me see that." Her father drew back, scrutinizing it over the edge of his glasses.

"You always said the folkways were too dangerous." Lucy sidled close to him. "But this saved my life."

"I guess I was wrong," her father said wryly. He gave the stone a look of grudging respect as he handed it back to her. "What I've observed with protection stones is that your intentions matter when you use them. Your own energy interacts with them in ways that can be unpredictable. They're not mechanized like a sweeper. So, I always think my intentions are good . . . but I thought my intentions were good with Miss Bentley's and look how that turned out. No, obsidian is too unreliable for me. But I'm glad it served you. Very glad indeed. I need to thank Pete." He looked around. "I thought he came with you. Where is he?"

Lucy blinked in surprise. "He did come. But how did you know?"

William Darrington sat back on his heels. "Once the roots attached to me, I was part of His-sey-ak. At first it was like being in a wonderful dream. But then I could feel your presence here, and I was terribly worried about you." He pushed his glasses up and thought. "I had visions of you and a boy traveling through the forest, and I tried so hard to communicate with you. Sometimes I felt I was very close. One time I thought you touched me. Only I wasn't me—I was in a different body." He threw his hands down by his sides in frustration. "I can't really explain."

But to Lucy it was clear. "You were the wolf," she exclaimed. Now she knew why she had felt no fear from it, why she had followed it so unquestioningly. "After Silas and Angus stole my vitometer we were lost. But this wolf appeared—oh, Papa, you were beautiful, but very frightening. Pete said we shouldn't trust you, but I knew—"

"Wait a minute," he said, "Angus Murrain stole your vitometer? What on earth was he doing here?"

"Oh, I have so much to tell you," she said happily.

But at that moment there was a loud rumble and the earth shook violently under their feet. Lucy nearly fell over and clung to her father until the rocking stopped. It had lasted only a few seconds, yet it was terrifying.

"What's happening?" Lucy asked.

"Earthquake," her father said warily. "I think we should take it as a sign to leave."

They had started to make their way through the meadow when a thought occurred to her.

"Wait a minute," she told her father. Lucy grabbed her ghost sweeper and ran back toward the dreamwood. Carefully she placed it in one of the root grottoes and beside it she put her knife. She wished she had more to leave as an offering, but this would have to do.

The mist made way before them as they walked out of the meadow and closed up behind them again, hiding the dreamwood from view.

They came out near the place where she'd begged Pete to leave. And even though not long ago, it had been her fervent wish he'd taken her advice and left, now Lucy held out a secret hope that Pete was waiting for them. They began to walk north, toward the gap in the cliff side where they could climb down to the beach.

They were nearly there when a shadow sliced across the ground.

Lucy looked up, shading her eyes against the sun to see a giant winged shape wheeling out of the sky.

It was a thunderbird. And in its beak it carried a golden branch.

The creature landed in front of them. The great wings were cumbersome on the ground; folded, they gave the thing the look of a dinosaur having a rather awkward adolescence. Reptilian eyes studied them. The leathery red crest upon its head gleamed like a crown in the sun.

With a *squork* it dropped the branch on the ground in front of her.

Lucy swallowed. The wood gleamed like gold, the bark as smooth as skin. For a moment she simply stared at it.

"Go on, Lucy, take it," her father said quietly. "It's a gift."

She picked up the dreamwood branch in wonder, feeling again the strength and hope that had marked her first encounter with the golden wood in Ulfric's cottage.

The thunderbird nodded at her—apparently it had discharged its mission—and took to the air, climbing with great thrusts of its powerful wings.

The ground rocked again.

"We really *must* go," her father said, running a hand almost apologetically through his straw-colored hair.

They hurried to the cliff side and stumbled down a steep slope to a narrow beach beset by waves. Pete was crouched on a rocky promontory, his injured leg stretched out in front of him. He still had not lit the flare, and Lucy could see that he wasn't going to anytime soon. He was waiting. Silly tears welled up as she thought of Pete waiting for her, believing that she would come back.

"Pete!" she cried. "What are you doing? Hurry up. Get that flare lit."

"Lucy!" He hobbled to his feet, grinning wildly. "Mr. Darrington." He nearly lost his balance in his enthusiasm and winced as he came down on his sprained ankle. "You made it."

"We did," her father said as if he, too, couldn't quite believe it. "But now I think we must depart posthaste."

"Why? What's happening?" Pete asked. "I've felt the quakes."

They'd reached him by now and Lucy rushed to his side. He put his arm around Lucy's shoulders. Well, she supposed he needed help standing up, but she leaned close to him anyway.

William Darrington looked up the cliff, back the way they'd come. "I still see a little into his mind," he said thoughtfully. "He's leaving."

"Leaving? To go where?" Lucy asked.

Her father shook his head. "I don't know. But I feel he is done with humankind, at least for a while. Now that new dreamwood is growing, I think he will go someplace where he won't be found again."

They were silent for a moment, imagining Saarthe without its Thumb. Then her father clapped his hands and said, "Now let's get that flare lit."

Pete, for he was best at all things to do with fire, got it blazing quickly. The torch burned with a white hot light that was blinding even in the daylight. Her father took it from him and climbed halfway up the cliff, waving it in the direction of the mainland. With any luck one of the Ss'til boatmen would see it.

And yet Lucy felt it was an awfully slim chance. She tried not to think about what would happen to them if they could not get off the Thumb. All three of them were so weak, and Pete could hardly walk. She sat next to Pete and, as if he knew all her anxieties, he reached out his hand. They sat like that, hands entwined, silent, until sometime later when Pete craned his neck and got to his knees.

"Boat!" he cried. "A boat's coming."

There was a black speck on the water, driving steadily toward them.

They watched its approach together. As it got closer they could see a familiar boatman. It was Obwe, dressed in his snakeskin cerements and bones, and such a welcome sight her heart swelled as if he were an old friend.

If Obwe was surprised to see them again it was a shock he revealed only in the raising of one eyebrow. Lucy could see him try not to stare at the dreamwood branch she held.

"You need passage across the bay?" he asked. A small avalanche of rocks fell down and the waves surged dangerously.

"Yes," William Darrington said, clasping Lucy and Pete about the shoulders protectively. "We do indeed. You've come in the nick of time, my friend."

Another quake followed on his words like an exclamation point.

They scrambled into the boat as the rocks from the cliff side above them shook and fell. Obwe pushed them into the water and began to row. The waves grew stronger, wilder as the Thumb's shaking churned up the bay.

It was terrifying work getting them away from the Thumb. The sea was the worst Lucy had ever seen, and soon she was concentrating with all her might on not being sick or getting washed over the railing. Even the serpents seemed to have fled from His-sey-ak. But at last Obwe found a snake, harnessed it quickly, and then they were off, flying along the water, parallel to the Thumb, only this time heading back to shore.

Lucy watched its gray-green bulk go by with a strange lump in her throat. She felt as if she were watching a battleship go past—something mighty and terrible, a thing to fear and dread. At the same time she felt strangely proud of it, as if some part of it were hers, or she belonged to it.

When they were nearly to shore they felt one last quake. The water tipped up and then plunged them down again, so wildly her stomach flew weightlessly inside her. Lucy grasped the railing. *If I'm sick,* she thought, *please don't let it be all over Pete.*

"Look! The sea bridge is broken," Obwe said, his wonder audible even over the waves' roar.

The final tether holding His-sey-ak to the mainland had snapped. The water surged, pushing the Thumb out to sea.

Obwe released the snake from its harness and began to row. In a few minutes they would be on land.

"There goes one of the world's great nature spirits," her father said, staring after the Thumb. "I don't know if we shall ever see his like again."

She looked over at Pete, the wind yanking at his chestnut hair; he smiled at her briefly. A lump settled into Lucy's throat and she thought about how far they had come together.

Obwe's boat scraped against the sand and she felt the shock of being on solid ground again.

Then Pete was there, helping her stand up in the unsteady boat. During their journey, the dreamwood seemed to have helped his ankle, for he jumped out without any apparent pain.

"Come on, Lucy," he said, "we're back."

23

So why would a toymaker live way out in the woods?" Pete asked. "He can't get any business if no one can find him."

They were tired and sweaty from walking—*like the Thumb all over again*, Lucy thought—but they still couldn't find Ulfric's cottage. It was not for lack of trying. In the few weeks that they'd been back, she and Pete had gone into the forest several times to try to find the path she'd taken the day she had run away from the Knightlys' and ended up at the toymaker's.

"He did say he was retired." Lucy rubbed the back of her neck wearily. As she did whenever she and Pete went into the woods now, she wore the tunic and leggings Niwa had given her. For although they'd been back a couple times to visit Niwa in her father's lodge, Lucy had neglected to mention the clothes she had left there.

"I'll say. He's retired so much he doesn't exist." Pete had given up looking for different paths and was now throwing sticks into the ferns.

Lucy was terribly disappointed. She'd wanted so much to

find Ulfric and tell him that she'd been to the Thumb and returned. And she wanted to make a gift of dreamwood to him, for she would always remember his marvelous tea. Without it she doubted she would have had the courage to do any of what she had done.

Perhaps Ulfric was someone who could be found only when he was needed, she thought. And at the moment, Lucy had surprisingly little need of anything.

Her father was healthy and strong and newly energized after his ordeal on the Thumb. After a few days of Anya's cooking, William Darrington had regained most of the strength he'd lost in His-sey-ak's forest. He'd charmed and fascinated the Knightlys with stories of his adventures, to the point where Lucy heard Dot offering to let him store his papers with them however long he wanted. He'd introduced Gordon to contacts at the Climbing Rose who could help the lawyer untangle Angus Murrain's estate; for now that the timber baron had been lost on Devil's Thumb there was the question of who would manage the sawmill and who should be contacted about the sale of his properties. As he'd told Lucy, Angus was an orphan. Gordon searched, but he could find no relatives, even distant ones; Lucy even came to feel sorry for him.

Rust was disappearing from the forests. Niwa, who'd gone back to her father's lodge and argued that they should wait before cutting their forests, was hailed as a visionary leader; she had a seat on the Lupines' council now. And though when Lucy and Pete visited her she complained of paperwork, Lucy thought her friend seemed . . . well, content. Still, Niwa would always be happiest in the woods. She brought Lucy and Pete back to the grove of the wolf woman to see for themselves that the trees were regaining health. Lucy had been startled when a raven appeared overhead, but then watched in amazement as Niwa called it down. The raven men were hers now. And the bird was simply reporting to her on what it had seen in the forest that day: in this case nothing more exciting than two bull elk fighting near the wolf bridge.

As for herself, Lucy couldn't remember when she'd been happier. Her father talked to her of all the things they would do together—without any mention of Miss Bentley's.

"You know, you'd better write to me," Pete told her as they started on the path back to the Knightlys' home.

"Of course," Lucy said happily. She had assured Pete a hundred times that she would write from Kansas City, where they were going to visit her father's mentor, an elderly scholar of the ghost-clearing world who was in frail health. But she never tired of hearing him ask.

"We won't be gone that long, anyway." She reached out a hand to touch the sun-warmed ferns, feeling strangely closer to the forest now that she was just about to leave.

"Make sure you're back by September," Pete said. "Snow closes the passes after that and you know you can't come by sea."

"I know: *The spith are hungry in September,*" she said, quoting Niwa. It was surprisingly easy to look back on that night in Governor Arekwoy's lodge and laugh.

"You don't want to end up on Bone Beach," Pete said with mock gravity.

"Will you write me?" Lucy asked. She turned to look at him: His snub nose was brushed with gold from the afternoon light. He swept some auburn hair away from his eyes, and a second later it sprang into place again, just as she knew it would. Maybe stranger than her comfort with the forest was just how comfortable she'd grown around *him*.

"I don't know," he said, as if considering whether or not he would have the time. "Nibs and me have a lot of fishing to catch up on." He grinned at her angry expression. "Course I'll write you. I'll do you one better. I'll whittle you something. A keepsake so you can look at it and think of me and wonder, *Why haven't I bitten off anyone's head lately? Oh, right, it's because Pete isn't around.*"

This deserved a punch in the arm, which Pete happily accepted.

She thought back to the moment when they'd first met, his fierce concentration as he whittled. Even then she'd known she wanted him to pay attention to her.

Pete helped her jump over a downed log, but when they were on the far side of it, as if by some mutual agreement Lucy hadn't realized existed until this moment, they stood still holding hands, their faces close together.

Lucy's heart was thumping rapidly. The trees closed around them like a curtain, and there was a green mulch smell that Lucy would forever associate with Saarthe.

Pete took a deep breath, like someone about to jump into a lake.

She closed her eyes and felt his lips touch her cheek.

There was a tiny shock, like a soap bubble bursting on her skin.

After a second they broke apart, grinning.

That had been easy, like falling off a log. Maybe it was easier to like someone and be liked back than she'd realized. She'd always thought it must be terribly hard, almost impossible—at least for her.

But she was starting to get used to the idea that it might be nice sometimes to be proved wrong.

They started to walk again, shooting contented glances at each other all the way home.

The next day Lucy stood with her father outside the Pentland train station. It was uncharacteristically crowded at the station, and Old Wundt was busy selling tickets at the ticket window. Aside from being awake, the stationmaster looked exactly the same as he had on the day when Lucy first arrived. He wore the same ragged cardigan, and his pipe was clamped firmly in his mouth. But the rows of Wanted posters behind him had thinned significantly since her arrival. With Rust disappearing from the forest, there was more timber work to go around, and Saarthe was producing fewer outlaws.

Even though their train would be boarding soon, Lucy

lingered outside the station, wanting to soak in every last minute she could of Saarthe. Pete and her father had gone inside, and for a moment Lucy was alone with Able Dodd.

"Good-bye," she told Whitsun and Snickers, holding out sugar lumps on her palms. Looking up from the horses she noticed the handyman brooding near the wagon. He was dressed in his usual black duster and somber clothes. Lucy had barely spoken to Able Dodd since she'd returned from the Thumb. But she realized she did have unfinished business with him.

She took a deep breath—the Knightlys' handyman still intimidated her. "I wanted to thank you before I left," she said. "You gave me good advice."

Perhaps Able Dodd was unused to being thanked. He raised his shoulders as if some rare sensation tickled him. His good brown eye turned a melted butterscotch with warmth, while his wrathful dead eye was at peace for once. What's more, Lucy was shocked to see the beginnings of a bashful smile on his rough-hewn face.

But Lucy couldn't leave well enough alone. Tugging on her braid, she squinted up at him. "I just don't understand how you knew."

His smile—quite possibly the rarest thing she'd seen yet in Saarthe—faded, its place taken by something soft and yearning. He looked into the distance as if looking years into the past. "My grandmother was from there, you know."

Just behind them the station swarmed with people; wagons

and buggies passed by on the road leading into town. But Lucy felt for the moment that the world had shrunk to just the two of them.

"Your grandmother?" she asked, stunned. "She was from the lost settlement?"

Able Dodd bowed his massive head and sighed. "She grew up on the Thumb. When . . . *it* happened she was in Pentland, visiting relatives. She used to tell me stories about His-sey-ak. And the forest there." He trailed off.

Lucy put a hand on Snickers's bridle. "What happened to her?"

"She married someone in town," he said. His stern face softened at the memory. "But she missed the Thumb. She always wanted to go back. Said it was a magical place."

"It is," she said softly. On impulse she reached out and took hold of his hand.

And now he smiled for a second time: a kind, grandfatherly smile that made her wonder how she'd ever been afraid of him.

"What will you do with the wood?" he asked. He put his other hand on Whitsun's neck, somehow implying that the horses, too, were interested in her answer.

Once again, Lucy had to wonder how Able Dodd knew the things he did. "What do you mean?" she asked. Only a handful of people knew what she'd brought back from the Thumb.

Able Dodd chuckled: a gravelly sound that was actually pleasant . . . once Lucy realized he was laughing. "You wouldn't be here if you hadn't passed his tests and won his favor. Either you came back with dreamwood, or you didn't come back."

Lucy nodded: that made sense. "The truth is, I'm not sure what to do with it."

She'd given Pete half of the long branch that His-sey-ak had given her. He sold a tiny piece of that, using the proceeds to pay off the Knightlys' debts with enough left over to buy himself a new saddle and fishing rod.

But he'd shown little interest in acquiring a fortune with it. "I wish I didn't have it, honestly," he'd told Lucy before pleading with her to take his share back. She wouldn't have it. In the end, he'd bundled the wood into a bit of spare carpet and stuffed it behind a table in her old third-floor bedroom.

The Lupines wouldn't hear of taking any, because His-sey-ak had given it to *her*, and that gift was sacred.

She donated a small amount of the wood to the hospital in Pentland to help in healing patients. But the doctors in charge had begged her not to give any more, for they didn't want to attract the notice of thieves and robbers.

So she found herself the owner of a fortune's worth of dreamwood, but with no interest in trading it for money. Such a thing felt wrong.

"You'll find a use for it," Able Dodd said. He stroked the horses' forelocks as they whinnied softly in agreement. A few last-minute travelers scurried past them, hurrying to buy their tickets for the last train of the day.

Lucy touched the fine cotton voile dress she'd recently bought. Angus Murrain's estate paid her the reward for Rust's cure. She had plenty of money—more than she knew what to do with. "Maybe I'll return it to him someday."

Able Dodd took the reins and climbed up into the wagon. "Maybe you will. Though I'll wager it will be many years before you do."

Lucy never liked to be told by others what she was going to do. But in this case she had to admit the handyman was probably right.

Pete was hurrying toward her. "Come on, Lucy. They're getting ready to board, and Niwa's here."

Her heart hiccupped at the sight of him. For a moment—but just for a moment, Lucy wished she wasn't going with her father after all.

There on the platform stood Niwa in her Lupine huntress clothes. She grinned at Lucy and pointed to the sky, where a raven circled overhead. The bird cawed once.

"It says, *good journey*," Niwa translated for it. Lucy laughed.

"I'll take your word for it," she said. "Good-bye," she told the Lupine girl, holding up her palm to hers, and then quickly embracing her, smelling once again the perfume of wild sage that would forever mean *Niwa* to her.

"What about me?" Pete asked in mock alarm.

"Oh, I don't know . . ." She pretended to think about it, then flew into his arms, where she hugged him, trying to imagine that this moment wouldn't ever stop.

"Remember to write," he said softly in her ear. "I'll miss you."

They broke apart. Lucy swallowed and grinned and wiped her eyes; like everything in Saarthe, her feelings seemed to have become bigger and wilder than they were anyplace else.

"Ah, Lucy, there you are." Her father came striding down the platform, patting his pockets as if searching for something. He looked fresh and dapper once again: his straw-colored hair and beard neatly trimmed, his clothes pressed, his glasses, as usual, slipping dangerously low on his long Darrington nose.

Oh no. Had he mislaid the tickets?

She had been so busy making her good-byes, she'd forgotten to make her usual checks before a rail journey.

"Do you have the tickets?" She looked nervously at the train, which people had already begun to board.

"Tickets? Yes, in fact I have them right here." Her father produced them with a faint look of surprise, as if he didn't quite believe that he'd remembered them.

"Oh, well, that's good." She gave him a congratulatory smile. Usually any discussion of tickets was followed automatically by her father saying "I don't know what I would do without you."

She supposed a tiny part of her missed hearing that.

But now William Darrington appeared to have remembered what it was that had preoccupied him as he'd made his way across the platform to her.

"I was just thinking you should start keeping your own notebook," he said. "I don't think *A History of Ghost Clearing in the American States* would be complete without a chapter on how you managed to get through that ghost wall. I was doing some research, and I don't think there's ever been a documented encounter in which ghosts formed a kind of collective spiritual organism—"

"Sir," the porter interrupted, "we're leaving now. Please board the train."

"Yes, of course," her father said absentmindedly, as he went up the steps. "Anyway . . ."

She stepped onto the train, not quite listening as her father continued. She turned a moment to stand in the doorway. As it had on the evening of her arrival, the crowd on the platform had rapidly thinned, but with a few crucial differences: There were Niwa and Pete waving at her—she was leaving good friends behind. And she had her father beside her.

"So what do you say, Lucy?" he asked. "Do you think you'd like to try your hand at writing that?"

She'd answer in a moment. Right now she was waving to her friends.

The final whistle sounded and a cloud of steam streaked by. Viewed from a certain angle, one could almost imagine it as a ghost.

Acknowledgments

In a box of old papers of mine from grade school there is a story I wrote decades ago about a mysterious tree whose golden sap gives a girl the ability to fly. So perhaps I have been writing *Dreamwood* almost as long as I have known how to write. For my family, my friends, who watched me work on this book for years, I'm sure it feels that way—it's been a long haul. Thank you for sticking with me.

I am grateful to Tim Travaglini for seeing something in a random manuscript critique. And I'm grateful to the ninja duo of Tracey and Josh Adams, agents of warmth, acumen, and unflagging support. My extraordinary editor Arianne Lewin asked things of me I did not think I could do. Thank you for believing I could develop abilities I certainly did not have when I started. And thanks to everyone at Putnam for making this book so much better. Katherine Perkins and Paula Sadler, I'm especially grateful for your help.

To the people who have saved me on many occasions, whether with fish tacos or a well-timed phone call, thank you. Writer friends Cynthia Jaynes Omololu, who has been with me since this thing started, and Kim Liggett, who came in as it was ending, deserve special thanks. Nicky Ovitt, for the use of a key name, thank you. Juana Rodriguez, thank you for listening to reports of my often-slow progress. The largest debt is the hardest to express. To my parents, Eric, Kris, Grant, Jules, and Simone—there would be no reason to write without you. Nothing without you.

There is no Lupine Nation or Federation of First Peoples. And I would not want my poor inventions to be confused with any group of real people nor be seen as representing the customs, beliefs, or concerns of real people. But I have exercised the authorial power of "what if" to imagine an America where—in some places, perhaps—there was a different outcome to the wars and policies that have shaped the history of indigenous peoples on this continent.